CEMETERY SITTING

Cemetery Sitting

JOSEPHINE PLUMMER

GRAY STREET
PUBLISHING

Cemetery Sitting
Copyright © 2020 by Josephine Plummer.

ISBN-13: 978-1-970083-07-1
ISBN-10: 1-970083-07-7

This novel is dedicated to Perry and Stanley. My grandfathers, two men I have never met, born on different continents for different purposes.

20/2

Bob

June 2012

LOOKING BACK THIS ALL SEEMED LIKE A LOGICAL FIT. I JUST COULDN'T GET MY head together enough to run the company I had built from one piece of equipment and one job into a whole fleet of vehicles and heavy machinery, not after the loss of my Charlene. There had always been the state, county, federal and city contracts to bid on, places to haul the machinery and stir up some dust, then after completing a few it seemed the rest just flowed into cue Barton's Heavy Equipment was known in the business as reputable and dependable. Money was good, Charlene was a whiz at keeping up with the books. I never even thought about them, she always had everything in order. Sometimes I would get home and there would be a special meal with all my favorites. Other times we would go out but whenever it was something special, I knew a big check had come in. Keeping up with all the finances of Barton's Heavy Equipment was no easy task, checks rolled in with each project completed but expenses were great too. Charlene was always getting a delivery from the office supply store to keep everything rolling. We had to keep exact records with all the government contracts, each file had to be in perfect order and kept for a certain number of years, it was just a natural task for her. I am quite sure Charlene enjoyed being home and the flexibility of her part of our life together. Sometimes I would have to be out of town for a job doing part of a road creation, excavation of land for a new housing development or another project that we had been working on. It was always the best part of any contract to return home to Charlene. Oh ya, I am Bob Barton Charlene's husband and boss, haha maybe she is my boss, we work together well as a team.

I had been over the mountains for almost a week for some work on a prison that was being expanded and renovated. When I came home on Monday night the 14th of March Charlene said she didn't feel well, wasn't even sure what was wrong just knew she felt off and looked pale. In all the years we had been married she was never sick she just was not her usual bubbly self that night, not knitting which was unusual she always knitted for one charity or another, she didn't have dinner prepared and was laying on the big red leather sofa that we had recently purchased, by the next evening she had a fever and was coughing. Two days later she was on a ventilator in ICU and another day Charlene was gone, they said she had a rare virus, who would even know where she could have caught something like that. At the time I didn't even know what it was called, it didn't matter, nothing mattered at that point. People kept directing me on what to do, there was a whole slew of people from the church that I never paid much attention to before this they seemed to know the plan, I was asked a few series of questions on preference but really all I had to do was write checks and show up. I did know for sure that Charlene's favorite flowers were, all different colors of roses together in one bouquet. I suppose we weren't prepared for this, not at all, we were only in our early forties and in great health. One night right after Charlene's death I was going through the files to see what upcoming commitments I had even though I didn't care anymore and ran across a file labeled "Just in case", that would be Charlene to have everything in order. Included were the passwords, bank account numbers, contacts for repairs and anything else that you could ever think of. Then I saw the certificate, she had purchased a wall space in the mausoleum for us, this made no sense to me, but I needed to respect her wishes, I don't know how I didn't know about this, possibly she didn't want me to know and distress me when there was not a reason to worry before this, maybe she thought I would go first with my dangerous occupation I can't ask of her thinking now, she also wanted a butterfly-shaped wreath made of roses.

Charlene's funeral was exactly like she planned with the help of all those people, I couldn't believe she was gone, it was like life was on pause or mute and I was supposed to resume to normal scheduling. When would that be, after the funeral, a week from now, a month? They called one day after I had been home for who knows how long and told me her plaque was in, with her name. I went to the spot they had laid her; it had her name Charlene Burton June 1, 1969 – March 25, 2012, the second I saw it I knew my life would be turned around. I canceled all the contracts and bids, sold the company to Simon, my foreman who said he couldn't afford it, I made a contract and accepted payments from him, this was a done deal in my head, something had to change and this was it, I couldn't possibly resume my old life half of that picture was missing. Then I got a job at City Square Cemetery digging graves, setting up and tearing down after the funerals, it was the only way I knew how to heal and help others. I didn't need the money just something to do and to be close to the last place I had seen my wife. Before I came home to Charlene at night, now to spend time close to her I spend the day in this expanse of loss, this all seemed to be decided for me like written in a script, Charlene had a small glass vase mounted on the wall for me to add a couple of flowers, I never saw anyone add them, but it seemed every time I would go it was full.

Their equipment was miniature-sized compared to what I was used to but made more of a personal impact with people and in my community than anything I had ever done before now. Previously with my business I managed colossal projects with gigantic equipment, now it seemed just an emotional journey one site at a time, with each grave dug I knew there were family, friends connected and an entire life of the person they were attending the service for. Once someone passes everyone has a different healing process, I haven't been sure how to start mine except to help others with the inevitable, you never realize how often people pass until being at a cemetery. By placing the chairs and canopy at each graveside I began to slowly see and feel again when I became a gravedigger, I didn't have much contact with the public my duties were done before and after most people left, thinking back in my other occupation I rarely had human contact either, just the hum and vibration of machinery grinding up the earth. This was different, sometimes someone would stay and watch until the last dirt was put on top, ask to put the first dirt on or to do something like adding a rock or trinket. Generally, I waited until they were all gone which seemed strange to watch from afar and see them leave their loved one in the casket or urn alone. I would go by myself or with the rest of the grounds crew and finish up trying to put the soil and grass back in a respectful manner so if they came back anytime soon it would look peaceful, I never wanted anyone to think the area or their loved one had been disrespected.

Thinking back I believe my healing started with the flowers, once I started studying them and would wonder if the person had picked them out, their family or a stranger it seemed to open up something in me about the real definite individuality of everyone. Maybe when people are alive, we see them as people and nothing else, we are not as simple as I had suspected. There were so many kinds of flowers, it almost seemed like the arrangements were as individual as each person. I always wondered how some people could know so many others and in what way they had touched each life. Some of the funerals, memorials, celebrations of life were overflowing, creating traffic jams and all the people looked like from the same walk of life while at others the attendance was of people from all calibers of life. There was usually an individual or two who stood at the back of the service, that was the person I would watch, figured it was someone who was estranged from the family, a person who was greatly affected or sometimes an officer of the law would be there out of respect or looking for a suspect. You could always tell if it was someone who wasn't family by the way they stood back, on the expanse of lawn, listening in and not really feeling like part of the service or family, mourning the loss none the less, looking on scanning the people in attendance. Wishing they were closer or not there at all, you can learn a lot about people by the way they hold themselves up during a time like this. There is a whole other facet in this occupation compared to my last business, here I can make a difference.

Charlene

March 2012

HI, I AM CHARLENE BARTON. I HAD BEEN RAISED IN DOWNTOWN CINCINNATI AS Charley Simpson. When Grandma and Grandpa Coventry moved to Florida, I was about three years old, moving as a child is a big event. They let us buy their brick house, it was so big compared to where we lived before. My sister and I both had our own rooms; I especially loved the balcony and arched doorways. That is where our family resided until I was twenty-two and came out here to Seattle with a Suzanne my best friend from elementary school who was checking out a job, I instantly fell in love with this city. While Suzanne and I were at the airport getting ready to go home, I met Bob. He was the filthiest person, covered from head to toe with dirt, I couldn't even imagine what he was doing in an airport. It had been my first time traveling and it did seem odd, he told me he was part of the expansion team to add another parking garage and had been digging the foundation for a couple of weeks now. We heard the call for our flight, he said he hoped he wasn't too forward but handed me his dirty card, Barton's Heavy Equipment, Seattle, WA. I put it in my wallet and boarded the plane without another thought except getting back to Cincinnati which was home.

Suzanne got the job, I trailed along and found work too as a book-keeper in a Raspin Plumbing, we located a small loft apartment just north of the city center. One day not too long after Suzanne and I were living here I ran into Bob again. It seemed odd or possibly just fate, on a warm spring afternoon; the cherry blossoms were on the trees, earlier than in my prior experience, I could smell the saltwater which was different from Cincinnati's Ohio River smell and Lake Erie. After paying for my coffee, there was Bob's card in my wallet, I turned to look for an empty bench and he was right in front of me. We had coffee, lots of dinners, sightseeing, and marriage, it all went extremely fast. I was young, only twenty-three with no family close by to attend, we had a small wedding with just us two, Suzanne and Simon at the courthouse downtown on August 19th, 1992.

Before our marriage we bought a house, there was one thing I insisted on, that was to live in a brick house. Ever since we had the brick two-story on Pleasant Street, I always felt that families and relationships were built like bricks were laid. You had to lay them right, make them right or right them again. You couldn't just expect any relationship to work, it took conscience thought, consideration, and respect of each other, just like any contract spoken, written or silently agreed, I thought a brick house was the only way to go to build our future. We found a small three-bedroom in the north end of Seattle close to Bob's shop, it was only one story with a small yard and a circle drive, but it was all we needed, and we knew why we had a brick house, a large yard was not something we needed or wanted the house was the pillar. Marriages and couples have their own meanings to things, which is what solidifies their life, marriages are full of private meanings and jokes, everyone works on a different level.

I didn't know the extent of Bob's business until after we were married and I was still working at Raspin Plumbing, but we decided I could quit and manage the books, contracts and Bob would do the logistics and staff-ing; this went well for us. It was like we were together in the day even if we weren't because of our close relationship with the business, knowing the ins and outs of each project.

I had plans to live forever and retire in a hot place, not sure where but maybe somewhere like Mexico, summer was my favorite season, I loved the heat, flowers, and outside activities, our little garden always provided us with some sort of produce, for our first anniversary we bought two blueberry bushes and planted them out back. My job allowed me quite a bit of free time, I loved things just the way they were. Life was in balance. I had church, Bob, Bible study, knitting, potlucks, walking in the city, parks and on beaches. The climate here is perfect most of the year, unlike Cincinnati where I grew up. I don't miss the snow at all, there are plenty of memories of snowmen, shoveling and extreme cold, using our old mittens and scarves for the decorations. Seattle gets the perfect amount of snow here, just a day or two.

A few years back I saw an article about wall crypts, I thought whichever one of us went first we would never have to think of our grave being dug while we ran the business. So, after some research on prices, I went and purchased a couple that were being sold at a reasonable cost for a fast sale I even bought a wall vase for us to share. Never dreamed we would use them and didn't mention it to Bob, he would worry that I wasn't well or something catastrophic, he always tended to my needs and cared what I thought.

We had our favorite meals and restaurants, Bob especially liked burgers, we tried every new burger joint that opened or on the weekends travel to one he might pass in his work routes. We would travel around the city to different places that had recently opened for the perfect burger, he also liked my cooking and would grill often too, we would cook together on the weekend, I think food was one of our bonding spots. We didn't have many hobbies together, but we played games inside and out and boy could we talk. We had the same taste in music and even did quite a bit of dancing in our kitchen, neither one of us was much for nightclubs nor noise late at night. Someone gave us tickets to a play once but that wasn't our style either. We had quite a few friends but none remarkably close, we just enjoyed each other's company. After work, there wasn't that much left of the day. I had my social outlets during the week and just enjoyed our TV time and conversation, it was a comfortable life. I never dreamed I would get sick and die in a few days. Who knows how that even happened? I was well then suddenly not, literally not well. I was hot and cold, coughing and shaking Bob will have to tell you the rest because the last I remember I was thinking I am forty years old and they told me I would be sedated, I didn't even know what that precisely meant being as I have always been healthy. I think at the point of possible death if we are lucky enough or maybe it's not a good thing, we think of our secrets, should we reveal them or think we will be ok and say something when we wake up, I am sure now that I am faced with this moment that many people take their secrets to the grave, I am sure Bob has a secret or two also. There aren't any clues to verify that about Bob we just all have secrets.

I will have to mentally spill my secret, when I got to Seattle, I only knew Suzanne and a couple of people from work, the days were filled but the evenings and weekends were long, I continually missed my family in Ohio. I ran across a site for pen pals, after about a year or so writing I had a pal from almost every state. I even had one from Olympia, WA, we said someday we would meet but so far have not. When I started writing I got a post office box by my work and would check it on the way home from work, that is the box Bob and I used for business still. Since I checked the mail, I just never revealed that part of my life to anyone, all my incoming mail went into a file, the stationery and postage were all part of the job. It was not like I was trying to hide anything it was just in my world, my own circle of friendships, I had ladies that wrote novel length letters and others that wrote small notes, some on plain paper, others ladies' wrote in beautiful handmade cards or fancy paper typed and handwritten. Some recommended books and movies, others told me about their lives, children, weather, and seasons, some liked to trade recipes and poetry.

I had their names in a file with the date I wrote each of them. It was a cheap hobby for sure probably cost me about $30 per month with postage and stationery, I would get up each morning and start my day off writing one letter. It was like a challenge to me to write a letter Monday through Friday. The contracts and work paperwork were something to do but not something just for me, this gave me an outlet of friends and still allowed me to work. Our shedder always had various colored paper streams in it from the written pages of people's lives that they shared in ink. Letter writing seemed like a lost art; I would always imagine back in the day when that is how people of any distance communicated. Imagine the things they wrote and the surprise of someone who received a cherished letter, giving the postmaster a penny to mail a letter and how long it would take for it to be received. There were family stories, stories of men off to jobs, crops being harvested or destroyed, babies born, barn raising, land acquired, housed built, marriages taken place, joys, tragedies and peril all communicated with ink and pen, hoping the stagecoach or train wasn't robbed of its stories being transported. Being busy with this and the business helped pass my time otherwise the days would have been exceptionally long. It was a pleasure to retrieve my mail from a distance, a mini-vacation every day. I wasn't exactly a people person but loved being in a crowd, being anonymous, just another face, I always made up stories about the people I saw.

Bob and I have eaten recipes sent by pen-pals, watched recommended movies, and enjoyed television shows from pen pal suggestions. The local library has most shows on DVD so I would check them out and we would watch during the nights of reruns of our nightly line ups. I have learned a lot from my pen friends about each area, immensely enjoyed each letter and have had heartache when ones have passed away suddenly or from a long illness. As I lay here in the hospital not getting better, I wonder if Bob will notify my pen pals if I pass on, I also wonder what he will think of all the letters that arrive daily and he had no idea about them. Will he read them? I am not even sure he knows where the post office is as that was my part of the job. I am sure they will sit in a stack for a long time, but he will have to be curious, that is his nature. The various envelopes with ongoing stories, many of these ladies I have corresponded with for ten years or more. Their letters helped me get through some of my longest days. My friends will wonder what has happened to me, it was not like I had a long illness this suddenly hit me. Bob will have to straighten up the office someday to continue running the business, he will see my system of pen friends that ran smoothly right alongside Barton's Heavy Equipment.

I have more secrets what no one knew about me except those from the women's shelter, I had another side of my life, daddy always said if you can help someone please do. While checking the mail January 2, 2010, I saw an ad on the post office bulletin board, a board I stopped to read frequently, the ad stated there was a need for someone to volunteer, helping women write creative resumes, I wrote down the number and called the next day. After my first visit with Gloria at the shelter a couple of days later, she explained that some women there had never worked, and others have a criminal record creating a critical barrier to employment, but to obtain any employment through their system or any other avenue that was chosen, they needed a resume. This was to teach a life skill not to get a job since the shelter contracted with places to see if the specific woman fit into the position offered. They had places of employment from flaggers to receptionists, all the women needed to do was have a resume, pass the drug screen, complete the shelter program specific to their case, and interview, and show up every day to do a fixed set of tasks. For some that was an extremely pressing challenge as their time at the shelter was running out, others simply had never worked and needed to get into the groove of life to help themselves. This may seem natural for some but when you have been living in the fight or flight, get by day to day mode this is a change that is not easy to adapt to, even if it is being handed to you. Some of the women may think it's too hard, not see progress fast enough, run into an old friend that they allow to steer them wrong, get bad news, you never know what will break someone from the right path, this is not a natural order for many, maybe not ever experienced, taught or shown.

After leaving the shelter, on my drive home, ideas were floating in my head that would modify this program and help each woman have self-dignity. Upon returning the following week I met Gloria before the scheduled session, explained my proposal and showed her the supplies I had brought. Paper for the ladies to write their rough draft of their resume, stamps, envelopes, pens, thank you cards, notebooks to track their job search and special stationery sets for anyone who would like to correspond with me, a lost relative or friend. That first class went well, I am not sure this group of ladies knows their worth, they were created to help others, that is why they are at the shelter to learn how to help themselves and others, developing themselves will be the first thing to happen and the rewards will spill over onto others. As I stood and looked at these ten ladies that I had just met two hours ago Marsha, Kimber, Debbie, Fawn, Tanya, Renee, Landy, Jennifer, Mindy and Olivia I knew each had hurdles to overcome but their lives would be different within a year. Gloria was in the back standing under the exit sign with the light shining green in her white hair, smiling, and knowing this would make a difference, she loved these ladies, the ones who came prior and the ones that will come after these, each person makes a difference.

I agreed to meet once a week for the first month of the year-long program and every two weeks after that, also to keep the supply of postage, paper, envelopes, and pens. Everyone established that she wanted to get mail from me and would write back, it was ironic we were all in the same city but had different perspectives, barriers and challenges, some could spell others not, sometimes I received a hand-drawn picture but I slowly got to know each one individually and their everyday job search or if they had gained employment, some had families to reunite with after getting back on track, others family to stay away from, some were working to get their children returned to them and still a few didn't have anyone but they were all willing to keep writing. I think it provided a form of stability and accountability outside of the two hours I spent there, besides what was written to me unless the person wanted to share it in the group was never brought up so there was a bond of confidentiality that they may not have had anywhere else living in such a public place like the shelter, they probably felt their life was being monitored at every step, what a hard way to live but this is where they have landed. This was voluntary on their part, most things in their life weren't anything to be chosen so this was a special project. One that came right out of their mind and heart, all supplies were donated by me and whoever else Gloria could get to donate. I never asked who they wrote, they took turns passing out the mail, Gloria checked it and turned it over at lunchtime, the room was always quiet as each one read something private to themselves, now thinking of it their privacy had been taken away as well, maybe they never had any coming from who knows where they may have been living outside before the roof they occupy currently. I always felt uplifted when I left our meetings, sometimes they would have paper and stamps for me, this was starting to catch on as a give and take, what a privilege for me to let them give of themselves, a building of character.

Gloria

August 20/2

THE DISAPPEARANCE OF CHARLENE A FEW MONTHS PRIOR HAS DEEPLY AFFECTED ME, she had been coming to the women's shelter and teaching the art of writing, grammar, pen palling and decoration a couple of times a month for a couple of years now. Some of these women here didn't have anyone on this earth, they had burned all the bridges they were given, started with an uncaring family maybe even one that just didn't know what elements a family is put together with. I met a few ladies who had lost their children because of their choices, some could get them back others their children were gone forever. When you arrive at the women's shelter, I think you are deeply broken and in need of healing, you need to know someone cares, just to stand back up again, to decide you want to know where you will sleep or get a meal and onto providing your own roof, meals, transportation and clothing.

Charlene seemed to know just what to do, she didn't have training from us. One day she showed up with some supplies looking like a professional, asking if she could help and interact with the ladies. She taught them to write letters, even ones to her and each other, provided paper and stamps, taught others poetry and resume writing. She helped them fill out job applications, knew what kind of questions to ask and could see that they would be good at. She even helped them make appointments with clothing banks to have clothes for interviews all over the city. The shelter provided bus tokens and routing information to assure the clients would arrive at the interviews on time. It was as if Charlene had a degree in social service, the ladies all loved her.

I will never forget the last time I saw Charlene; it had been a cold long winter and spring was just getting started with the daffodils breaking free from the earth, fragrance in the air of warmer days and color springing forth on the trees. One of her letters had just gotten here for a client about the same time as she arrived loaded down with supplies. She was overly excited, the weather had turned warm, cherry blossoms were just starting to bloom, and she talked of the daffodils and purple tulips she had planted last autumn. She had a special surprise for everyone, a rubber stamp and markers to make some cards to mail to the family for fun, a birthday or holiday. In her example, she had colored her tulips a light dusty shade of purple, said she would mail it to her parents since those were her mom's favorite color tulips. After class, she packed up, just like every other time. Making sure everyone had enough supplies until she returned in two weeks. Then we never saw her again, we wrote her with no reply, didn't even realize I never had a phone number for her, she just disappeared like she had never been there. Charlene Barton's life was a secret to us, maybe she had a secret we didn't know about. We figured she had moved home or something, knew she wasn't from Seattle. You never really know what is happening in someone's life, something we realize quite well here. This was kind of like when you see someone at a stoplight, you know only what their car, music, or bumper sticker allows you to know and you see it through the lens of your past experiences. We could have only imagined life was good for Charlene, her style, excitement and willingness to share made us love her more.

About a year later, the next summer, it was uncomfortably hot, I remembered how much shade there was at my friend Rachelle's grave and took some flowers. It had been a couple of years since I had been there, time does heal deep wounds on some days. Rachelle had been my best friend for over thirty years and suddenly passed away one hot summer day, just fell over this shows how precious life is. That is probably why I thought of her today, as I was leaving, I looked over and saw the mausoleum, had never noticed it before. I was thinking of being young on humid days in Alabama so many years ago, the smell of wisteria and wondering where the time had gone. It was as if my life was on instant replay, I was a young girl, then married, had a child, husband, not sure what happened with my marriage, that was how I ended up working at the shelter. I think those ladies healed me as much as I helped with their process of healing. After walking through the arches and coming out the other side, a cool breeze kicked up, I noticed the name Charlene Barton the date of death was March 25th, 2012. It shocked me to see the name, as I had been there for Rachelle, I bet that is our Charlene, the special one we thought had disappeared, she didn't disappear she had died and we didn't know. How tragic, we have all missed her so, I walked back to my car with tears in my eyes and a heavy heart, grabbed my water bottle and a couple of purple tulips from Rachelle's grave for the dainty little vase on the spot for Charlene, I came back every couple of weeks to add flowers for both special ladies. They had touched my life at different times and when I needed them most, they were there for me.

Rachelle had added a variety of ideals to my life, she was there when Carl and I split up. I think she was the one who held me up by my boot-straps as they say if I started wallowing she was the one who told me to get back up, she had a way about her that always made me laugh no matter how down I was. That term was the only fitting one, I was a mess, didn't know what happened and still don't. One day we just didn't feel for each other according to him, he said he was moving out and needed space. We both had space then, Carl Jr was grown, after our split, we still attended all the same holiday functions together, like we were bonded for life on this cycle of the calendar and couldn't be anywhere else at those designated times. Neither of us remarried or seemed to have a social life, we just lived. I think I am happier now due to the help of Rachelle and Charlene along that hurtful journey, rejection is interesting when you don't know why you are being rejected, it could be a parent, friend or spouse that lost value to, it is traumatic no matter why. I need to go back and look at the date on that tulip card I framed in my office, I am sure it was right before the date on this headstone because spring had just arrived the last time, I had shared a session with Charlene present.

The light breeze, dampness of the lawn and shade of the overly powerful-looking white oak tree cooled the evening and gave off an aroma of earth as I walked to my car parked just over the hill. I noticed there is an entire other level of this cemetery and a groundskeeper that had been watching me from afar, that felt strange, I am sure many people stop all over these grounds here for various lengths of time. Why was he looking at me? Maybe he wasn't and was just looking in my direction.

That evening I decided to go to the main branch of Seattle Public Library on my lunch the next day to search the newspapers for crimes and obituaries for Charlene. I sure hope someone with such a big heart didn't suffer tragically. If I can't find anything maybe that groundskeeper knows something about her, I will get to the bottom of this tomorrow. There are still some ladies from the shelter that I keep in contact with, they would appreciate knowing what had happened to her, I feel since I know this much, I owe it to Charlene and the ladies to find out the truth. It will do me good to get out on my lunch, anyway, do something besides just working through it and eating an apple at my desk.

That night I slept well, better than I had in a long time. It had always been unsettling how Charlene had left, maybe it helped knowing she willingly didn't choose to leave us. Being young and in the times, we live in there were many possible ways for someone to pass on. I need to look at that frame that is hanging on the wall in my office and get to the library was my last thought before drifting off. The morning flew by, the date on my tulip picture was 3/10/2012, I walked a few blocks north on 4th Ave just as the day was heating up. After searching the papers for March of last year I only found a death notice, not even a proper obituary. I opened the exit door of the library more confused than when arriving, trying to remember anything about Charlene, I know she had a husband because she had talked about their fourteenth wedding anniversary. The smells of exhaust mixed with the saltwater churning comforted me as my mind turned over and over again facts I didn't have, without any more information or stories on Charlene my imagination didn't help. The more I think about it the groundskeeper was a bit eerie, I want to talk to him but don't want to ever see him again, at the same time. This is not something that is even my business, but I feel so strongly about her abrupt departure. I don't feel she would have just left like that without just cause being as she started this program.

It was time to purge the files of women that were here during that time so maybe I will find a clue in one of their letters that they like to keep. Most didn't have a place for safekeeping so they would hand the letters that were written to them to keep in their file. It seems that besides the writing skills and letters that was the only trace of Charlene. I am still glad I wrote to the Post Office Box shortly after her disappearance and the letter I sent wasn't returned, it is possible that the headstone is not hers and we were just too much of a responsibility on her life or schedule, but I don't think so.

Bob September 2012

Oh gee, here I am back to my old routine, work and home. It has been about six weeks of picking up mail and making new piles but no more sorting. When I get home from my new normal Saturday outing to the Post Office, I am going to open a few letters. I am enjoying the excursions to the new places and eateries, have even tried new foods, started the habit of taking some home in boxes for dinner the next day.

This is the only letter I have dared to open, the first letter addressed to my wife, dated just a couple months after her death. I chose this one because it was in a small envelope and kept falling out of the pile no matter which one, I put it in. Maybe it needed to be read, with no return address.

May 22, 2012

Dear Charlene,

Just a quick note to say we all hope that you are doing well and will be able to return soon. We deeply miss you and appreciate all that you do for us. Looking forward to seeing you again,

Call if you can,
Gloria, Marsha, Kimber, Debbie, Fawn, Tanya, Renee, Landy, Jennifer, Mindy and Olivia

This small card, from right here in the city where I live, had been sent less than two months after my wife's death, dated May 22, 2012. When I found it a few months later, I had no idea who these eleven ladies were. Chances are none of them were at her funeral otherwise they wouldn't have sent the missing you note. There wasn't a return address or phone number just a cute little card with a metallic butterfly on it, Charlene must have been close and have known how to contact this group of ladies who each signed the card. They weren't from the church; this was enough mystery for one day. I left the letter open and would come back for more another day. That evening I was still thinking about the note in the card, I had never received a handwritten card from one person in my whole life and for sure not a group of people.

After the one and only letter I opened, I was frightful that this mystery of my wife would be on a grander scale if I opened more. After thinking a few days on it, I knew I had to act on this somehow, that is how I will start to learn about the city as Charlene would. Again, I started with the zip code on the envelope 98121, the map says it is just north of the downtown core. I drove there the following Saturday morning, maybe too early to be out, most of the people that were out looked like they hadn't been home yet, some were already quite comfortably asleep on the sidewalk. I was surprised Charlene would even come here and by herself, maybe she was with the group of ladies from the card, she liked to read so maybe it was a book club. I walked a couple of miles around some blocks, saw some businesses that I wondered how they stayed open if people like me hadn't heard of them, most were still closed, there weren't any clues but strangely I felt closer to my wife, possibly walking the same sidewalk as her. I had been walking somewhere that she cared to go, it was nice to be out and see the city. In all my years I have never slowed down enough to look at the sights, I still can't believe she was down on these streets and I had no idea. Maybe I will have to go home after checking the mail, having lunch and look at more letters, I am starting to get the feel of observing the city and watching my back.

Bob

October 2012

BEFORE LOSING CHARLENE THE EBB AND FLOW OF SEASONS WERE NOT SOMETHING, I ever paid much attention to since I had to work no matter what the weather, a job needed to be done and I did it. I have since learned nature doesn't stop for death, maybe that is what keeps us going and gives us hope, there are many cycles of life here. This cemetery is like a park and there are over a hundred varieties of trees and a large array of flowers. They bloom from March until October, many just finished their final who rah for the year, some of the most beautiful roses I have ever seen, winding around the trellis in the crematory dedication garden, these are plants brought in by family from the garden of the person who has passed, previously tended to buy them, the deer like to frequent the rose garden in the mornings and late at night, when I come in early some of the blossoms are gone, I know the deer have had a late-night or early morning snack. The mallard ducks and Canadian and Lesser geese find this area a safe environment for their babies, you see them swimming across the pond in the spring. Of course, there are rodents, rabbits, and raccoons, so many species of birds I couldn't count. The sign says not to feed them, but I know some people come here and feed the birds for company, I see birdseed in different spots frequently, that may be the only interaction they see all day, the gracefulness and grate-fulness of a bird, it always gives me pleasure to see a sudden blue streak fly and try to distinguish between a Blue or Stellar jay. In the field next to us there is a gigantic flock of crows that nest, I find it ironic a murder of crows lives next to the graveyard. Contrary to what one would think this is a peaceful location, made for the comfort of the living, often picked out by the person who has passed.

My life and thoughts are making me uneasy with no real life, I need substance, some emotion, I am back to a new normal, home every night to an empty house, watching TV at night but never sure what the show was about, am not a big fan of reading, surely don't have any hobbies, I used to collect heavy equipment now it appears I collect dust. Maybe I should hire a housekeeper, get a hobby like possibly take a cooking class but they may use spices I am not fond of, I prefer simple cooking, I am not into looking for another spouse and prefer to live with my memories of Charlene. I could learn to blow glass, make furniture, something to stop what I do now I may even be able to talk to someone if I took part in any of those activities, during my day at work I am alone most of the time. There are a few other employee's, but my occupation is solo for the most part. All I do now is, have my morning routine, work, eat, lift weights, watch television, it is a cycle I need to add something to, I am thinking of starting a walking route and seeing different neighborhoods, will get a map to investigate that. I could also get a cat, but I feel bad leaving an animal home all day alone so maybe two cats, that may give me motivation or trouble, you can always learn something from an animal. I am not even sure I am of the right mind to take care of an animal at this point, it appears I am doing ok with the one house plant in the kitchen, maybe that is enough for now.

I would like to disassemble the office, put my weights in there and a fish tank, now I think I have a plan and something to look forward to. It's unbelievable I have been using my weights in the garage all these years, all through the cold winter and sweltering summer that have been endured while working out. We all seem to revert to what is normal for us, even in things we don't think about like the order of brushing our teeth and combing our hair, it is always done in the same order, I should attempt to mix that up too, for that to be changed we need to be intentional about it.

It is a good thing Charlene set up our utility payments on auto-pay years ago, I would have never found the bills in the amount of mail that is here. How did she sort through this? I suppose she saw it close to daily and I had never seen it, so it wasn't a build-up like this for her. There is a tremendous amount, I have had to wait in line at the post office to retrieve it a few times now. Our post office box across town and is closer to where she used to live and work from eons ago before I knew her, I do not believe I had ever been there to check the mail or in that neighborhood except maybe for work before her passing, the neighborhood is lively, people with purpose heading in all directions. After a month I realized that I had no idea where the mail came, we didn't get any at home, didn't even have a box, she had wanted to plant a flower garden where it had been, next year I should buy some of those purple flowers she liked so well. That is when I called to find out which one went with our zip code 98105. After seeing the post office, knowing Charlene, she picked this post office for its ornate lighting, special detail under the industrial looking windows and location. She loved the feel of the city and the movement, this place had that I always had to look for parking on my retrieval of mail, the parking lot was not sufficient for the traffic this building held. I know she enjoyed driving around and having to walk a few blocks, I can see her now with her tall rubber boots and special black umbrella with a large pink daisy inside. Maybe I never realized that she was bored at home being isolated, the days were stagnant while working solo, this was her outing, she probably had lunch or coffee at one of these places while watching people. I stopped at a small diner on a Saturday after getting the mail imagining I was Charlene all alone in the city during various seasons knowing then how she felt and how much she must have loved me to endure being by herself all day, every week on end with our business and welcome me with new foods while listening with empathy to my stories of traffic woes, weather related mishaps and employee issues. Every evening was the same for us whether we were in or our occasional going out, Charlene never complained, probably because she loved me and had gone on her adventure of the day. I don't think I knew her or what she was about, this hit me harder than I would have ever imagined since it was never a thought before my beginning trips of retrieving the mail, I just went to work and came home to my smiling wife, here I am in this diner that I never knew existed before this moment with this current revelation of my wife. How trivial was every moment of my life, my outside life was business then I brought it home and discussed it with Charlene? I didn't think there was anything more, but I bet she was lacking and made her way through the city I need to explore. This would be something else I could do to get to know Charlene Barton. I know she lived a full life but just never knew to what extent.

Well, my day was like every other normal one so far but after eating my turkey sandwich with extra cranberry, and sides of potato salad, pickle spear and chips I am not sitting down. My first task to tackle is the desk, since selling the business I don't even look at the mail, now there are towers in here falling all over, so many envelopes looking like a cityscape. That afternoon as I entered the office I saw the stockpile of mail, I wanted to close the door and go back to the monotonous rhythm that I had been in for the past few months but the pink envelope sticking out of one leaning pile drew me in. After looking there were many pink envelopes, what drew me to them was that pink was Charlene's favorite color, all shades. See I thought I knew her, but I only knew surface things, things like you could tell a stranger, like your favorite color or flower, I am suddenly happy I could answer the question correctly of Charlene's favorite color, that is possible happiness to cover my guilt of not knowing other things or creating the intimacy needed. Maybe whoever had sent them knew things about her that I had never paid attention to. How did I not see them before or even think of them, did I just wake up? I had been pulling them from the box and driving the letters across town to my home every week. It amazes me I didn't see them before, there are envelopes of every color, with stickers, different types, and a vast array of sizes. I didn't even know that envelopes came in so many shapes and sizes, some look handmade. Thinking back upon the last time I mailed something, it was an electric bill during the stay at my apartment before Charlene and I married or possibly the title to the Pontiac that dad left for me, both mailings were done with envelopes that had arrived with them. How different this was than my previous mailings, I am hoping I didn't miss any business mail either.

I started by sorting the never-ending stacks of correspondence, it seemed some were business related, others handwritten and junk mail, my best strategy would be to eliminate some of this mess, I tell myself I am not scared to open any of the letters. Once verified I recycled the advertisements, it's simply amazing how much junk mail a business receives, buy this, you need that, they think so they load down the mail system. You could go broke if you started buying even a quarter of what they recommend you buy. I have always had a theory that if I want something, it can usually be tracked down online and then you go purchase the item, buying from an advertisement was not my style and shopping at many stores is not my forte, I am not a browser.

While looking at the junk mail I noticed a few of those "have you seen me" flyers. It made me glad I didn't have children. I sat wondering about the children that are missing and their parents, many of these flyers could have arrived months ago so how long had they been missing and had they been found? I saved these to study the faces.

Time to explore the mystery of the office and get to know my wife. I sorted the colored enveloped stories by postmarked dates. They were from all over the United States and quite a few from Seattle. After all the sorting there wasn't much left in me, during my days there had never been office work, before Charlene I had an accountant, this is tedious, something I have learned about my wife already she has enduring patience. I would start with the Seattle postmarks, those could be work related, I knew somehow for sure the ones from other cities outside of Washington were not. These ladies all seemed to know Charlene like from in person, they said things like next time you are here and many from the same address.

It seemed that on Saturday I would get the mail and decided to have lunch somewhere I probably wouldn't have ever thought of going before, this week it was at a trendy little burger joint on NE 45th St., I wondered if Charlene had been there before suddenly wanting to share the news of my new found restaurant with her, isn't that the way death is, you have to get used to it and reprogram yourself to share ideas with someone but they may not understand. It seems as if we have certain things we share with select people and when that person is gone our whole being doesn't realize it until after we think I should call ... and then it sinks in a bit further, deeper into a greater depth of the loss and the value they added to our life.

There was the slow crawl of traffic heading towards the college and shopping center, I found a spot right on 45th, lucky me, as I pulled in it caught me off guard to realize the stacks of mail I had been picking up on Saturdays had recently become considerably smaller, I had been debating on canceling the box but not yet. Maybe I should wait until the stacks of mail waiting in the office have been gone through, this brought another thought, how do I keep this box going. I looked at the mail laying on the seat and decided to take it in with me, six letters the top one is from a Brenda Sullivan, Winterset, IA, also from a PO Box., who are these people and how did they know to contact my wife even months after her death. After eating I looked down and saw the stack of letters again, I see a long one that looks like a bill, it is from the post office, this is how I pay, must have been distracted with all the people strolling by in their autumn clothing, the boots always come out this time of year, as I think of Charlene's tall boots as she called them. That has always amazed me the vast number of styles, colors, length and materials in a boot, most don't even function for what a boot is made for they are just stylish. Some of these lady's wear boot shoes that are a bit elfish, skittering along, there are the hikers, and others wear boots that trail almost up to the top of their thigh. Where do they find so many styles, do they buy them as everyday wear or to go with each outfit, how do they walk in some of them? I have trouble walking along in the city with the jagged sidewalks in my regular lace-up work boots that stay with my feet as I walk. Some of these styles appear that maybe they would fall off or get caught in the ruts but there they go not missing a beat.

After spending an entire morning on one part of the city and an afternoon of lunch across town. I decide to go home and sort the mail, possibly get Charlene's clothes to somewhere that they could be used, it is only Saturday so maybe I will make progress this week.

I arrive home to our brick house that I love to live in, with what part of my life I have left if you can call what I do living. I love entering through the blue enameled, arch-shaped doorway with the extra-large satin chrome locks that Charlene picked out. She always knew what details would bring out the best in an object or person. Now I know where she got her ideas of style, from her time spent in the city, I am not even sure if she watched a whole other set of television shows while I was at work or away overnight on occasion, we appear to be us but there are many versions of each person, the real one, then you add marriage, friendship, occupation, hobbies and whatever else to the mix. I just wish I knew how to start on the office, I always wondered why Charlene left that old wood paneling in there. I would take it down if I had thought about it when we moved in, but it is there now and staying, she must have liked it or thought I did. I have for sure decided on a fish tank as a hobby and something to keep me company, the fish tank will look good with the appearance of wavy wood behind it.

I sort through the rest of the mail, the piles from are increasingly growing shorter. Each week I deposit the stack next to the last one. The piles from the beginning are towering compared to the current ones. After opening that first letter dated May 22, 2012, I was a bit scared to open more. Perhaps that had been the worst one to open with so many names attached and still no clues.

The first envelope had been pink, I am sure Charlene knew what shade it was and it was not called pink but something like Cherry Blossom, Bubble Gum or Flamingo, I was going to start with all the pink envelopes but now after a more extensive order of thought I have decided to open them in the order of postmark dates, this was either a stall technique or organization, I was onto my own procrastination and denial that I am repeating myself, actually getting nowhere with this.

The first one was a yellow envelope covered in tape and stickers, inside was a card covered in sparkling stars and letter from Sally in Michigan. A newsy sort of letter but what I thought was odd was this person who I had never heard about before this knew about me and my big project at the prison where I helped excavate the land. Nothing important in the next one, I will keep the letters I open in their corresponding envelopes, so I have the addresses if needed for some reason I don't know yet. There were so many letters, after getting through the first stack of them all from ladies I could see a connection, they exchanged tidbits of their lives, losses and tri-umphs traded recipes and their twist on a new treasure they had acquired, they all seemed to find joy in the brightly colored envelope with words of encouragement. You wouldn't think pen and ink could mean so much but after reading these letters I was enlightened and I knew I had to let these ladies know what happened to Charlene and thank them for sharing their lives with her and the good recipes and television shows we had all shared. I am almost overwhelmed by the letters and the genuine feelings this group of friends have shared over the miles with each other. The postal system undoubtedly gets its quota of money from all this correspondence. I believe that this is enough for one day, am hoping tomorrow to sort through Char-lene's clothing, it is time for that to happen. As I go to relax and sit on the red leather sofa that I seldom use I am satisfied, not without Charlene but that is a fact she is gone and I am alive, so I am satisfied I have made some accomplishments today, tomorrow is a new day. I think of this like saving money if you haven't started it is harder than if you have.

Sunday morning, I opened the closet, Charlene's closet that I have not ever been in before. This is all overly personal and almost feels like a viola-tion, she has it all arranged by color, has always said it was something she could control, she would match her socks, shirt and under clothing. Her colors went with her moods, she would even wear camouflage under her sweatshirt if she just wanted to have a quiet day and not be noticed. I start by taking some white blouses off the hangers then it hits me, what would I do with the hanger later. I went to the garage to get a box of lawn bags and came back again before I would change my mind about the process I am about to go through. I roll a bag out and cut a hole in the center of the bottom, wrap the bag around the pile of my wife's clothes that she hasn't needed in a long time and push the hangers through the slit in the bottom of the bag. I have checked all the pockets and found various candy wrappers, coins, tissues, and in the course cream-coloured winter coat with the orange and brown plaid stripes there is a white envelope with my name on it, Bob. Another small envelope, my life of envelopes, seems as if life revolves around them, this one is small, I am the addressee and fearful of opening it, it has been in this closet for how long, longer than last winter? Did she put it here years ago or days before her death, did she have a premonition? I am hoping it was all part of the plan from when she bought the vaults and didn't know or feel something before my knowing, that would have been a heavy burden for her to carry alone. I sit on the bed between the mounds of lawn bags that look like large plastic green boulders with metal hooks sticking out that could engulf me at any moment. I am stalling, knowing that I do not want to read a letter from Charlene, she is already gone and nothing that is said can change that, I open the envelope and read the short note my wife has left for me some time ago.

My dearest Bob,

You and I both know if you are reading this what that means. I figured if I was gone before you for some unknown reason you may want to know my wishes. Please take whatever of mine that you don't want to Gloria at the Seattle Women's Shelter in Belltown. She will know what to do with the items.

Bob thank you for all the years we shared. Please be happy in the rest of your journey.

Lovingly,
Charlene

I sat there after reading making the connection of Gloria and my walk through Belltown. The answers have been here all along, maybe I wasn't ready for them and they are surfacing as I need the clues. I am ready now, I will leave Gloria a message to call about donating Charlene's rainbow of clothing, for not it can stay on the bed.

door, more comfortable in this neighborhood than I and after moving my truck we entered the shelter. I don't know what I was thinking as we stood in the alley before this entry but certainly not what Gloria explained and what I saw inside, offices for obtaining resources, counseling, employment, basic housing, tables for schooling, meals, art activity, training, expanses of area for overflow on extra cold nights. Gloria explained there were three stories all had to be monitored twenty-four hours a day, people lived here, depend on them, there were other extensions of this place all over the city, the needs were far too vast for one building and one group of people. That is why it is so important and special when someone like Charlene comes along who knows how to touch the lives of groups of people and make them feel included, give them the confidence to step up and make a path for themselves. Gloria is careful what she says, she sees I am a bit shocked; I confide that I had no idea Charlene was ever here or what she did. I tell her of the note I recently found and confess that I have only started opening the stacks of mail asking if she is The Gloria from the note. She says she is and wonders if I would mind if she contacted Charlene's friends Marsha, Kimber, Debbie, Fawn, Tanya, Renee, Landy, Jennifer, Mindy and Olivia to go through her clothing first, I don't mind at all, whatever will help someone get through the loss of Charlene and whatever else they have on their plate challenging them. They all admired her and her style, she also had helped them when they picked out clothing for job interviews. I don't mind at all; I have goosebumps from my ears to my ankles learning of the things that Charlene did in-between breakfast and dinner. Gloria and I sit in her office as she reveals the significance of Charlene's time with the ladies, which in turn helped their families and children, Charlene and the snowball effect. All the paperwork she helped with for resumes, employment applications and questionnaires, college applications, housing program admittance, child/parent programs to regain custody, drug, civil and county court preparation, legal counsel applications and learning the importance of communication and correspondence, she also helped coordinate the schedules and deadlines. Gloria told me the favorite part of each day for the ladies was when the mail was distributed, they would gather around at lunchtime, listening for their name in hopes for a letter from someone. Charlene wrote them all but also taught them not to be afraid of how they spell, how to address an envelope, to make connections with someone important, write thank you notes for interviews, many of the ladies regained contact with a family member to tell of their progress and received letters back, this letter program was an act of bonding and organization. I told Gloria of the stacks of letters in the office and my plans. It was getting late and I am sure Gloria has someone waiting for her somewhere, I agree to stay in contact, remind her of my number and leave. I go to a café that is still open and buy an extra meal for the man in the alley under the dumpster lid, I knocked on his dumpster out of respect for his residence, he was grateful for the food and looked me in the eye. I get back in my truck and head north out of the city, I know I am not the same Bob Barton who drove here, I am a changed man, somehow there are more layers and depth to my being. I need to learn how to use them for the interest of others which will benefit me just knowing the little I know now. After meeting Gloria in that alley there is a platform to build upon, I am thankful for all I have and the opening of my eyes and heart.

2013

Bob

January 2013

I HAD EVERY INTENTION A FEW MONTHS AGO TO CONTACT THE PEN PAL CLUB OR whatever they call it with news of Charlene's death, time flies on our other activities. It is time now New Year's Day I need to draft a letter to all of them, I found address labels for each person already printed, envelopes, paper and stamps, right there in the drawer.

Pen pals of Charlene,

This is Bob Charlene's husband; Charlene did not stop writing due to lack of caring, I thought each of you should know what has happened. She sadly and suddenly passed away on March 25, 2012, of a virus. From the letters you have written, I have received them as they came in but was only able to sit and read all of them not too long ago. To be honest, I was and am continually broken over her death, your caring letters with Charlene sat in piles until recently. The piles sat, toppled over, I sorted them by size, color, date then started reading them.

I was not aware of any of the letters or you gracious ladies who so freely share your lives, ups, downs, new jobs, marriages, sorrows, divorces and deaths. Recipes, crafts and hearts, from all over the country, Cerritos, CA, Minneapolis, MN, Port Orchard, WA, Wald Port, OR, Macedonia, OH, Glendale, AZ, New Port Richie, FL, Gresham, OR, San Marino, CA, Reeds Port, OR, Lakewood, WA, Maryville, TN, Washougal, WA, Cheboygan, MI, Timpson, TX, Concord, NH, Warren, OH, Lakewood, OH, Fridley, MN, Camas, WA, Kissimmee, FL, Colorado Springs, CO, right here in Seattle and almost every other state, news of towns and cities big and small all filled with wonderful people who care. One letter included a poem I know Charlene would have wanted to share with you.

Pen pal, Pen Friend
We are friends across this land
Letters we gratefully exchange
I may never see you face to face
Our topics are from a wide range
We talk of family, friends and food
Tales of growing vegetables and flowers
sharing sorrow, sending encouragement
Friendship carved in ink and its powers
Some of us get married, divorced, move on
Others get tattoos of visions
New addresses are sent
Letters of new homes and life decisions
Some of you live far
Others very near
I love to hear of new places
Makes the world clear
One postage stamp affixed
On one enveloped weighed
Precisely taken to your home
On these pages our friendship made
Until we meet again in the mail
My box is always open for your letter to arrive
Questions answered and new news delivered
Our bonded friendship will thrive

Be safe and well
Until next time
Copyright 2004 M.V. Meadows

I hope this finds you taking care of yourself,
Bob

Bob

March 2013

I seems as if time has almost stopped since Charlene has left my side, this past year has been terribly long, the days aren't so bad as I can stay occupied and feel like there is a purpose. Since this is the anniversary month of Charlene's parting from this earth, I should go get some roses for her vase to celebrate the life she gave me, I celebrate our bonded life every day, the time we had and memories that flood my mind. We had nineteen years together, it seemed like such a short time, I almost think I need to come up with a tradition or something, just can't think of anything, maybe a small butterfly wreath.

I watch people while at work and it is interestingly unique to each person how a family celebrates the life or death of a loved one. The cemetery is an interesting place, I would have never thought there would be so much activity prior to my employment, on Easter, Mother's and Father's days there are traffic jams, the people flock in, will come twenty or more per family, they bring lawn chairs, tables, BBQ's whole families attending and to celebrate the life of their loved one, telling stories to younger generations of epic events that made them family, while others will be seen sitting alone on the grass with a bag and drink from a fast food place eating silently by a grave sharing memories, sometimes in words other times in silence, other families will bring countless sticks of incense and catch the whole bunch on fire like a fireball, still others come and have a drink or beer, then there are those who just stand vertical over their horizonal loved one, silently cry, say a few words or say nothing at all get back in their vehicle and leave the pain too much to bear, sometimes sitting in their car composing themselves for the drive ahead, possibly back to where their loved one lived. Last year the state of Washington was the first state to legalized marijuana since that has happened the smell quietly glides through the silence as it frequently crosses the lawns and headstones.

Grief is an individual thing attached to anyone who has lost someone, one moment overwhelming and the next moment gone. It seems as if one minute you can talk about your deceased loved one and the next the tears won't stop. If I am crying inside, I know not to approach anyone just in case they will want to speak to me. What would they think about the man who works there who starts crying? It is probably a good thing I have a job here where I can be alone most of the time because some days, I do not think I could function in normal society walking and working amongst the people so closely, afraid I would bear my soul and emotions. Maybe working here makes it harder to heal but I will not change this placement that has been chosen for and by me, it seems a destiny at this point in my life.

The idea and the actual event of the death of a loved one are as unique as the relationship was. Some people at the loss point become heroes in their family's hearts and minds, the obituary photoshopped for Facebook, they may have been actual heroes in real life or just ordinary people. The fact is just to live is heroic all by itself, you never know what someone is going through or what stage they have just left or entered, living is the hard part. Some things in life take you deep where you fight the battles within yourself using the tools you have allowed to be present, battles that may change you forever, for good. You may turn a corner in life or your mind and discover a place that is jagged and not know you were broken until you break again. All this is acquired by past experiences, good or bad, and the way the individual sees it. Now when I drive by the hospital where Charlene passed on, landscaped grounds, the building that is tall and making a statement of critical decisions, I watch the cars leaving, I wonder why they are leaving, is it bad news turned good, bad news turned worse or the end for someone. Remembering when I drove out after Charlene's death, that drive is a memory I have now but in the actual event was my mind there or replaying the words of the doctor who delivered the news, my whole life or my life with Charlene?

Gloria

May 20/3

I have been thinking in-depth about Bob and Charlene, knowing what has happened to her just over a year ago and wondering how is he doing? I will call him and see if he wishes to be included in our community donor's newsletter, the night he was here I could see his genuine interest in my story that included Charlene's part. Some of our donors are large corporations but others donate labors of time or talent. If Bob wants something to do, we have organized crews that paint, repair, replace and rearrange every part of our cherished building. We even have people who volunteer hours to cook for us, buy food, organize clothing, blanket, coat or glove and scarf drives, we try to have the people who use the shelter help when they are able but the community likes to be involved as well. It does take the whole city to make this operation a success. I generally train a client to organize the volunteers, so they have a life skill to take into employment once they have completed our program. We have a big promotion for local donors coming up and some serious revamping of the shelter before that, there will be supplies to track down and labor to coordinate and of course my favorite part, a party to plan. There are many stories of triumphs and failures that come across the threshold of this door, but the parties have always been my favorite. This is a place not many people set foot in but at the donor events they can see where we have used their money, materials or whatever they contributed and be pleased, it is our time to show off the labors of love that are performed here every day.

Bob

June 20/3

I RECEIVED A VOICE MAIL FROM GLORIA TODAY, WHAT A PLEASANT SURPRISE, SHE said something about mailing a donor letter, I will actually get mail addressed to me, monthly she said, I will be looking forward to that. This makes me realize that not receiving bills, mortgage notices or anything else for that matter in the mail makes life different than what I had imagined or lived before my marriage. Of course, then I would sort the bills and deliver them to the CPA, read the contracts and take them to the onsite project manager located in the shop trailer of each construction site, none of my mail had meaning. Now the money just comes out of the only account we have left or should I say I have left after closing Barton's Heavy Equipment, I have started checking to make sure it is the correct amount for each utility bill that comes to the company email or post office box.

As promised on Saturday my first letter was in the box, the stories were uplifting with the array of volunteers and it got me to thinking again about what I could do for the shelter. I will leave Gloria a voice mail over the weekend and am sure after she receives my call on Monday, she will have ideas, she doesn't look like a lady who sits still very long.

Gloria calls as I suspected, says they are going to renovate whatever they can with donated supplies and labor, then see what is left to do. The idea is to get this place looking as nice as possible and use it for an extension, classes or sell it to add funds for a new building. I was remembering the back doorway into the shelter, huge rooms and offices, that was only the level I saw, now wondering if the other levels had been kept up as well. She asked if I wanted to help or had skills compatible with any projects, if I had ideas, materials or manpower. I showed the following Saturday, I parked in the alley like I always went there, no longer uncomfortable, feeling happy and productive, not just existing but having purpose. There were sixteen of us, all had brought something to help, the idea was to use it, give it away or get rid of it, we used it all and needed more. We sanded, primed, repaired the walls, the next weekend we would paint and had a list of other repairs and materials needed.

Gloria would keep us updated with a list of which materials were donated, I decided to get doorknobs for every door. While shopping with Charlene for ours I learned a bit about the style of them. They would be like the gems on each wall, I asked Gloria if I could stop by some evening and get a detailed list of how many I needed and what kind, the local hardware store got on board and donated towards our project too. This got other people to thinking of who to approach with our needs, Gloria sent a special newsletter, shipments of supplies were being sent daily, a set of switch plate covers from one source, paint sprayer from another, faucets were flying in, local painter, plumbers, roofers, electricians and regular people showed up with a smile on their face and a tool in their hand with a willingness to help. I had to maintain my composure throughout the day, the goodness of people volunteering was overwhelming, I had no idea people did things like this for others. I didn't need a cooking class or any other kind of group, this was further into anything than I could have imagined.

The shelter was completely renovated in a month, some worked on a weekend only, others in the evening after their regular occupation, some ladies worked while their babies napped nearby, this is what has brought this community together, this building held together by helping hands. I think as I install the doorknobs and switch plate covers people from all walks of life are now sitting in their home or sleeping upstairs with a bit of themselves invested here, a dual benefit.

After we are all done Gloria send out a letter asking for food donations for an open house, what we don't know is that she had met with an architect and will propose a renovation of a new building at that open house. There are five floors, mostly open space right now but it would be ideal for sleeping areas which is one of the scarcest commodities in any city to come by. The food came in, the DJ, lights, tables, decorations, previous donors arrived during the 5:00 pm to 9:00 pm gala. Being as I had never attended anything like this, I was taken back that it was fancy, I don't think anything in my life was or ever has been fancy. You would think it was a grand ball, the whole experience showed me that no matter what your roof looks like or how many coins you have in your pocket there is always something to help with or a way to give back. I didn't think I could be anymore moved by this experience, then Gloria unveiled the front view of the proposed center, on the long oval banner that hung above the entry of two industrial silver doors, the sign read "Charlene's Place", it was written in gold script. Gloria told the story of Charlene and how she had contributed to this place and the women she had helped, in the place where I sat now, a place I didn't know existed a year ago, a place I now feel like I belong and am invested in, also a place where Charlene brought me unknowingly, I feel honored to be included in this, the groundbreaking of a new chapter of my life and Charlene's legacy.

I stay after and help clean up, as do many, walk Gloria to her car in the alley she has parked in for God knows how many years, she tells me she hopes the name for the new location is ok, waits for my response that is a nod, no words can come out I am still in awe, she thanks me for my service to the community, tells me of her grandson Carl III and her great-grandson who will be back from vacation in Florida next week. Then she closes her door, thanks to me again, I turn to my truck, turn back around wave goodbye with a salute to Gloria as she drives off, the lady of ceremony.

Gloria

October 2013

THIS YEAR HAS BEEN AMAZING, ETHAN IS TEN, I HAVE STARTED CALLING HIM double digit, he thinks that is funny. After school he doesn't mind hanging out here with me, the bus drops him off, we talked about other kids harassing him about being homeless, he said they know my dad works here, he has all his bases covered, that boy is as tall as me now, he looks like my daddy.

Next year is the year the shelter expands into another large building that needs some serious renovations but will triple the services we can provide. The system has gotten more stringent on rules so our success rate has skyrocketed, there are always those who aren't strong enough or willing to make the sacrifices needed to stay on track but our system is designed in small steps and the next isn't taken if the prior one is not solidified. Before entry into the program, there are criteria to be met, this is not just a place to pass through, many of the ladies that come through here have not graduated high school so there will always be a ceremony at the end of each step completed to acknowledge their accomplishment. We realize people are individual, this system isn't one set of rules with one occupation, it is a mutual agreement with our community members to screen everyone for natural occupational skills or schooling. Some of the ladies from here have opened businesses or gained high wage employment, I hear from them and many donate back to where they received their help. I love that we will call it Charlene's Place, she gave so much of herself to this community, possibly even her life.

I hear from Bob occasionally, he always asks if we need any help, we will soon. A new lighted parking lot, high cyclone fence around the perimeter and exterior renovation. Bob seems to have some community connections that came forward during the last renovation, I was quite surprised when the different businesses stepped up to help. For working at the cemetery, he has an extensive list of connections in city, county and national levels, they have called using Bob's name saying what they can help with, and that was exactly what we needed at that moment. For instance just over the amount of six-foot fencing we need, with black coating, all the hardware and posts, enough to extend out ten feet on each side of the building and go one hundred and eighty feet back and meet on each side one hundred and twenty feet across, a playground, picnic tables, heavy equipment with operators, paving material, paint, lumber, sheetrock, nails, the man is end-less in his knowledge of which rock to look under for supplies. He shows up and inspects the material like he ordered it, checks other workers skill and works himself like he is getting paid but acts like he knows nothing about where it came from, I call him the foreman, foreman Bob. We were blessed with Charlene and her skills and she inadvertently brought Bob to us with his abilities.

Bob

CHARLENE'S PLACE IS COMING ALONG, THE EXTERIOR IS DONE AND THE INTERIOR is mapped out with spray paint on the floors showing each area, the reality of this is staggering, how many lives will pass through these doors under my wife's name and be transformed into something that will make them happy, desperation to freedom will be placed on the lives of so many. I have seen some show up dirty, bruised, not forgotten by who put the bruises there, trailing a baby or two, only with the clothes on their back and baby without formula, looking so scared a light turning on startles them, the ever-present look over their shoulder to make sure they are safe. These are some of the people who come here, who roll paint on a wall next to me, it is what they can give in return, people who are grateful and changed by the services here. Gloria deserves whatever part of this I can make the transition easier for her. In all her years she has probably seen more cases than I could ever think of. Gloria doesn't know of my former occupation or connections, I talked to Simon and he agreed whatever time he puts in here with the heavy equipment will be billed and taken off the price of the business on my end, he can still get materials at cost so I pay for those or find them in the community in surplus from other jobs, this project may seem large but it is small compared to the places I have worked on before. I am glad my life is lining back up, it is almost like running a big production show again and my prior skills are being exercised, Gloria is great to work with, she realizes individuality, has even brought her grandson Ethan a few times and has let him pick what he thinks he has skills to complete.

I have a special project for the back corner of the yard if Gloria approves. I also have a secret that has been eating at me, for years before I met Charlene I had been stopping in and playing basketball Monday through Friday. When I started, I was young, had recently formed my business, it was a gentle way to stretch my muscles and increase my aim, plus it woke me up. I didn't have anyone in my life then so I just got up and went to All Star Gym at 6:00 am, then I met Charlene and it seemed an awkward thing to share with her at the beginning of our courtship and marriage since I hadn't shared it before, maybe like her pen pals with me, after she moved in I promised myself I would tell her, but I didn't nor did I tell her in almost twenty years we were together, it was the only secret I ever kept from her, a stupid thing I say now. Well, I am giving Charlene's Place a basketball court, this is the best thing I can do to release that secret, it never harmed anyone, seems strange I kept that in all these years, I will tell Gloria. She will laugh at me in my misery that I deserve to keep, keeping pieces back of yourself decreases intimacy in any relationship. There are people I have known for over twenty years and I learn something new about them every time we meet. I am starting to be more intentional about knowing people, what would they like, who are they, when is their birthday, just remembering what they say. Do they celebrate their birthday o'clock? I was born February 12th so every time I see 2:12 on a clock I should celebrate me, celebrate the gift of each day, of waking up even if it is at 2:12 am I am alive, celebrate that I am getting off work because I can work and have a job, celebrate, celebrate, celebrate you.

2014

Hazel

June 2014

HELLO, I AM HAZEL MARCENE SKYLAR BORN WITH THIS SAME NAME AND WILL most likely pass on with it too. Never met anyone that caught my eye long enough to add a ring and promises in all my years. Mom and dad seemed to hold what was perfect and I didn't think I possessed that quality, nor did I choose to or want anyone else to try with me. I live an all or nothing life, no gray, just black or white that keeps things simple and easy to make decisions. Maybe I was selfish, but I wanted what I wanted in life and there wasn't anything or anyone that said I couldn't have it, I could take on an assignment and be packed up at a moment's notice. Back in the day that is what a girl was supposed to aim for, a man that would keep her, I was born July 12th, 1940 in Eastbourne, England a magical place on the south-east coastal tip of the United Kingdom. I was born there, and Eastbourne was and is in my blood it seemed one day we were there and the next we were gone. Mum and I had a rhythm with her working and I off to school and keeping myself occupied.

My dad, Calvin Earl Skylar wasn't around most of the time he worked at the chalk quarry and when it was slow there, he had connections on the coal barges, always a capable man on the move, not scared of change.

There was one thing for sure he may not have been home much, but he always kept busy. Sometimes he would bring home big hunks of chalk for me that crumbled when you tried to write on rocks. I remember dad well, tall, chestnut hair and tan from his outdoor occupations. I was about fifteen when he was injured in an accident at sea and didn't make it home. Looking back, I don't think we took the time to mourn dad's death, just to survive took effort and time.

My, mum, Vera Violet Skylar was so in love with my dad, she lived for the moments he would be coming home, would always be embroidering new pillowcases and table clothes, saving the best meat and meals for when he was going to show up. Most of his absences lasted days but sometimes he would sneak in on us. Mum always came up with something special for him and he always brought his sweet Vera a bouquet for her special fluted multicolored glass vase that they had won on their first date at a carnival in 1938.

When I became school age, with dad gone so much mum became restless and started working hospitality jobs probably just for some social activity, she was an outgoing one always up for entertainment or to host a guest. Mum worked at Central Bandstand and at a newsstand outside the Eastbourne Railway Station. She would take me on the weekends or when school was out and let me walk the pier and promenade, where I watched people stroll along, sunbathe or whittle a sailboat out of driftwood. I would pretend there was a water dragon one hundred feet long out in the English Channel and it would disappear to the North Sea when anyone other than me would see it. My dragon, Halverson, was emerald green with a blue smile and huge teeth, flickering flames down its back that never went out, polished black scales like coal and yellow glowing eyes that saw everything.

The people would saunter by as I studied them while they were unaware of my presence, all their clothing appeared to me as costumes, it would sway in the wind, the light would magically shine through all the satiny fabric and yards of lace that were attached to the edges of skirts and brims of hats. Our home life and family was simple with plain clothing and furnishings, the bare necessities of life. The people I saw going into and coming out of the rows of bathing huts wore amazing clothing, girls with swimming clothes that had flamingo's, polka dots, cherries, gingham and raised lace flowers. These ladies never went swimming just laid around on their extra-large beach towels for the eyes of the gentlemen wearing the strangest clothing I had ever seen any man wear. Most of the men's attire was blue or red and had stripes, the shirts almost always matched the bottoms, some of the men's bathing attire had wide suspenders. They would all be sprawling out on the beach, men all wet, women acting surprised when the man would drip puddles of water on their backs. The women may act surprised, but I had seen this show before in my many afternoons observing the beach, I never grew tired of the crowds or their reactions, different faces the same stories. Predictable for me, vacationing memories for them, seeing people that were normally in a routine but were there to let loose and have fun brought joy to my life, almost like I was on vacation with them.

When Mum would work at the Central Bandstand I heard all the newest music and paid close attention, they never asked me for my ticket into the area by the great pillars and dome that was just as magical to me to be in a sea of people that I didn't know who they were, all here to see the latest musical production. All the modern big bands played there, I always felt it was like a secret I kept that my parents weren't with me and I had the run of the place, a child and her imagination alone. I would sneak back and look at the band members that became nearer to me than the people who paid entry fees; they had some extreme clothing to attract the attention of their audience, mostly men with polished shoes and brass instruments and they put on a full show, music like I had never heard. Every weekend the band seemed to outdo the performers from the week before.

One sweltering summer day in 1955, mum came in and said pack your Globe Trotter and let's be gone, I had no idea what had gotten into her, she was extremely routine. She had started working for the Clayton family a while back and now said we were moving to Boston, MA, USA, I didn't have time to process this as we packed and left all in one small increment of time. I had seen so many of the Globe-Trotter suitcases by the pier as people vacationed there regularly, about a week or so back a tall blonde lady saw me admiring her magnificent case and asked if I wanted it, gray leather with silver latches that even had a key to open the latch on both sides. She told me she had traveled as far as she wanted to go and had found her home right here in this magical place. I told her about Halverson as she handed me the case and keys, he was our secret. I had always wanted a Globe Trotter, had been studying them for years. It took months to read the name as it was inside the lid, like a certificate, made the case seem proper and important like it had a connection to the owner. I came home with that suitcase and packed it with my finest possessions, books, pieces of ribbon, letters that had been written and not sent, some clothing that I had outgrown but had plans to make a pillow. Now a week or so later we were heading to Boston. I am not aware I have ever thought of living elsewhere, Mum was certain of this move, we were heading out immediately. We flew over with the Clayton family, the airport and plane ride being our first was unsettling.

We arrived in Boston which was just as hot as Eastbourne, summer went, and Autumn appeared with leaves of gold, orange and red, there were so many American flags displayed outside of homes, this was an odd feeling seeing so many flags that weren't the ones we were used to. The Clayton's had us settle into a place they said was their first home, I have never seen that much brick in one city. The view of Boston Harbor was wonderous and comparable to Eastbourne in the way I could walk along with the saltwater, just on the flip side of the Atlantic Ocean. We lived on Commercial Wharf adjacent to Christopher Columbus Park, I didn't know that life could be so elegant. The furnishings with brass finials and glass knobs were above anything we had ever owned or dreamed of having. So, this is where my Globe-Trotter had taken me, maybe it had something attached to it that was passed on from the kind lady whom I had received it from. Boston would work for me until I started my obsession with the sea, I joined the US Navy in 1960. That enlistment took me far and wide; I was mostly assigned to a ship and then shore duty, I saw places such as Spain, Italy, Greece, Guam, and Japan, I even made it back to Eastbourne while on leave. It is diverse in the evolvement of a place when you haven't seen it in years, it's close to the same but that is not what you see, you focus on the differences from your last appearance in that location, you are even a different person upon arrival because of new experiences and travels you have been through.

Upon arrival the second time, I knew I was not who I had been previously upon departing from the only place that my life had unrolled from. Now I had seen many seaports, been a WAVE and ridden across the oceans in self-contained iron ships larger than an apartment building. Eastbourne was and always will be special to me, it is where my love of the sea and Halverson were born, it is a place no matter where I am, I can be in Eastbourne mentally, my anchor.

As I got older my need for warmth was greater than my love of the Atlantic Ocean, I retired in San Diego in 1992 but didn't think I could get used to that climate. Palm trees, heat, the Navy Pier, the beach all wonderful attractions but I need days of dark and dreary, I need rain, maybe it is in my blood. There was still much of inland America I hadn't even laid eyes on, but my heart followed highway 1 and 101 in my new Lincoln Nautilus up the coast, through Reedsport with the picturesque dunes, onto Waldport with exquisite beaches, this country has some spectacular views to the furthest northwestern tip of North America on the Salish Sea. My schedule was nonexistent and had no idea where these roads would lead but knew in my heart when my Globe-Trotter and I were at our destination then I would stop. I headed over through Port Angeles where the waters were clear and green to Port Orchard where I felt at home with the marina, I knew I was getting close. Heading through the ports by land was a different experience for me, I saw lights across the water one night from my motel room and took the large green and white ferry across to Seattle and knew I was home. It is now 1992, in all probability I have seen more water than the average human being, have traveled for forty-two years and know I am at home now. Maybe mum will choose to visit me or stay on in this new place to explore, Seattle, WA. She agreed to fly out as usual and stay for two weeks, said send me the tickets, it was our system.

As it turned out Mum had developed a special relationship with the Pacific Ocean, it was like love at first sight to her, I think she had decided to move here before me asking. She flew back to Boston after her two weeks stay and the following month, I flew into Boston Logan International

Airport to retrieve her. I never liked to return to my places of residing, once I leave, I want a new adventure. The Clayton's had always honored their many year contracts with mum, we packed what little mum wanted, had a final thank you dinner and going away party with the Clayton's and a few select friends, turned over the keys and called for a rental car. There wasn't a schedule just a destination to arrive at when we were done exploring. Saying goodbye to Boston and friends mum had established in the thirty-seven years since arriving was hard on her, I could see it on her, usually strong but ready to break. She was unusually quiet as we veered toward the west on I-90 passing through Albany, Buffalo, detoured to East Aurora to see the Roycroft Campus where we learned about the craftmanship in America and stayed at The Roycroft Inn, the dinner and breakfast was more than we could ask for. I asked mum if she was sure about this move, she said, "I have been waiting to be with you, you are ready now, so am I." I never knew it mattered much to her that I was here and there in the world. Looking back, in truth I was all she had, it had been 32 years since I left for the Navy, we had visited in different places but that is not like living close and sharing a life, it was more like sharing a vacation, the highlights of discovering the new.

The days, miles and sights passed us, we were tourists in America, Cleveland, Toledo to see The National Museum of the Great Lakes, we stopped to see the main attractions; the Great Lakes were a special attraction to us, as we both seemed to be drawn to vastness of large bodies of water.

Chicago, Madison, Minneapolis where we saw my friend Suzanne, Alexandria, Bismarck, Miles City and Billings. I know we need to move on, but this seems like the last big adventure mum and I will have. We decide to stay a couple of days in Billings, I hear we should be happy it is not winter in this part of the country. We visited Moss Mansion with the spectacular architecture and Rimrocks sandstone cliffs, neither mum nor I knew that water flowed through there from the Gulf of Mexico to North Atlantic. After our stay in Billings we knew it was time to get to real life and head to Seattle, the miles fled behind us as we passed Missoula, Coeur d'Alene, Spokane and Ellensburg, one last stop for cherry pie in Cle Elum. Arrival in Seattle was late, and we were tired, walked in, set our bags down and went to sleep.

The next day I think mum and I realized what we had done, we now live together, we were both used to our independence, we had not lived together nor got into each other's business for many years, this would take patience on both our parts to make this work. It seemed to fall into place most of the time, Mum loved the transit system, she figured out how to even get to Ocean Shores and Westport on the bus, she would frequently take bus rides to Tacoma to explore, learned all the routes around Seattle, Bellevue, Redmond and Issaquah. She had unlimited time on her hands and was like a child with a new toy. We rarely saw each other for too long, sometimes we would explore together but either mum liked to be alone or didn't want to be a burden to me, I know she had more energy than I did with all her activities.

Mum was slowing down a bit which I thought she would have done someday; she was home for dinner and was up for rides and vacations with me. It was almost like she was a teenager when she arrived in Seattle now, she has short outings, not all-day excursions. Parades have always been her favorite activity, the floats, bands that remind her of home and the creativity that goes into the mastery of one. She had attended the Daffodil Parade every April in Tacoma, Pride Parade on Capitol Hill, Torchlight Parade by our home in July, Bumbershoot, watched the Macy's Thanksgiving Day Parade downtown and on television from New York and the Puyallup Santa Parade. Looking back mum's life was a celebration of parades to each season, she genuinely enjoyed watching the festivities and being able to say she was there, but she adored watching people be happy and celebrating with them, she was raised like that, so she felt at home in a crowd. This was an activity that ultimately cost her the life she loved, Vera Violet Skylar died at 94 years of age, doing exactly what she loved, and I wouldn't have wanted it to be any other way.

Mum had gone out, as usual, to do whatever it was she was doing that day, she had friends in every part of town, would tell me she saw so and so in the U District or the nice young gentleman in Bellevue. She shared with me what information she wanted me to have, I never feared for her safety but insisted she carries a cell phone. On June 30th, 2014 it wasn't a call from her but someone else who said she was dialing me after she had been knocked down in a crowd heading towards a parade. Mum raised me to never dislike anyone and mind my own business, there was much to see in the Navy that I could have put my nose in but always remembered mum asking, "is it your place?" She had stopped at a street vendor for a hat, boa, sunglasses, cookie and the American flag, turned around and the protesters of the parade shoved her, told her to go home, she went home alright, straight away to Heaven. That night I wondered if I had done the right thing bringing mum here to Seattle, she had twenty-two glorious years here in this wonderful city. I received a call from City Square Funeral Home the next day telling me of her wishes. I guess they knew her here too, said she had attended many funerals and planned for her own passing years ago. There was quite a bit of information I didn't know about her and now this call. They asked if I would like to view her body, they said they thought I would, that is not a thought I have ever had before this moment. As I drive to the cemetery wondering what mum will look like in this state and after being injured, was I supposed to bring her clothing? I arrived and didn't want to go in, I don't even know what is the proper way to act now, if I didn't get out of my car this moment wouldn't happen, this is not the last picture I wanted of her, she had requested a closed casket ceremony with just a few people to attend at the burial and a large celebration of life at Atlantic City Boat Ramp off Seward Park Ave. South. How had she gotten there to know that is where she wanted to have her celebration? Maybe she hadn't been there and just loved the name, a return to the Atlantic, the closest she would get in Seattle. So many questions of mum, it appeared she knew everyone, and everyone knew her. It was just like mum to have the end of her life planned without telling me, everything was done and set into place, down to the catering, entertainment, a speech she had written. There were people in attendance from every culture and I didn't know any of them, they all seemed to know me and how grateful mum was that I had brought her here to Seattle a place she fit right in and loved exploring until her last day.

I exit my vehicle and head in, they seemed to recognize me as I entered the facility, how? A mortuary was not a place that I had thought of visiting previously, I wasn't mentally prepared for the viewing, they ushered me to an office and said this was normally where decisions were made, I wasn't prepared for the stack of forms to sign as they were explaining each one to me. It was all set-in-stone by mum, no room to budge, she was specific in not wanting a thing changed, said it was her life and her death. I signed the stack of forms on autopilot with the blue pen they handed me, I was thinking my signature seemed unfamiliar since I always used a black pen in the military and since retirement, I still have a stack of military issue pens at home. They have tactfully laid out my mum, she is covered in a high-quality sheet and doesn't look like she has clothing on under it, this is the last time I will see her and don't even want to for sure not like this, the bottom of her feet and bare shoulders are sticking out, exposed beyond the sheet. The man introduces himself as Darian. Says he has been taking care of my mom, strange for her to be with this man and being called the American name and that she is being taken care of. He said he has found a few items on mum's body and suspects I didn't know about them, this has me baffled like maybe someone has been hurting her? I must have looked shocked because he asks if I would like to proceed, I respond with a nod of agreement even though that is not what I feel inside my head / thoughts, heart/feelings or spirit/being, all these places in me were in a hyper conscience mode unlike any other time or place in my life. I am uncomfortable with this man and mum in this cold room. He slowly lifts the sheet with all concerns of modesty being fulfilled. On the inside of her right thigh is a tattoo of The Eastbourne Pier this takes my breath away, memories flood back to me. When did she do this, we all have secrets, but this seems like a large one for a ninety-four-year-old lady? Darian says there is more to see, on the outer almost back of her right thigh is an alleyway I recognize from Boston, where we had been so many times to a café in the brick district as we called it where we sipped tea and hot chocolate, Darian asks if I am ready to proceed or do I need a chair, states there is much more to see as I mentally prepare myself to meet mum in her whole being. On her left inner thigh is a float from the Daffodil Parade, Mt. Fuji on her left outer thigh where we had vacationed while I was stationed in Japan. There was a world globe around her belly button with my name, Hazel Marcene Skyler circling the globe, on the sole of her left foot was a tattoo of my Globe-Trotter, sole of her right foot one of the Navy ship I had been on. This was inconceivable she had lived her life and cherished our times together so much to get these permanent reminders inked on her body and I never knew, she must have gone to great lengths to hide these from me, things like always saying her feet were cold. On the left side of her stomach was a lady in a Flamenco dress from our trip to Spain, on her upper left arm is a sunset with Guam over it, another place we had been together. This was all quite emotional to me just knowing her secrets, the Leaning Tower of Pisa and the word Italy on her upper right arm. Darian was extremely professional despite the strange circumstances; he would stop until I was ready to continue the tour of mum's mapped out body. My stopping mostly had to do with memories of all these places, mum must have spent an extravagant amount of money on this artwork, this explains some of her appointments. She had a wave tattooed on the outer side of each breast, on her back The Space Needle was crafted skillfully to the length of her spine, the shading made me believe it was a picture from sunset. On her lower right back sits some autumn leaves and the word Vermont, on her left lower back a palm tree and San Diego. I thought I couldn't be any more shocked but here it was on mum's right shoulder a sea dragon with the name Halverson under it looking just like I imagined him to be, our own special dragon.

Vera

June 2014

I ALWAYS MISSED THE COMMOTION OF EASTBOURNE AFTER LEAVING, IT WAS where I was raised, the only place my heart knew. While growing up the town was always hoping, as our family was involved in the entertainment business, we worked at all the events that rolled through, whether a song, circus, dance or other shows, the pier was a popular destination that many families relied on for a memorable vacation every year and in town people loved the star attractions that Eastbourne brought our way. Being on the coast and having the spectacular pier so many tourists would flock into town to see the newest bands and entertainers, even if some were just jugglers, clowns and mimes it all appeared magical at the seaside. The children's faces would light up as the entertainment would roll by one act after another. I felt privileged to raise Hazel in such a colorful environment, we were not a fancy family at home but that made the outside world noticeably more exquisite, this enticed her to seek out the good, be flexible and learn different cultures.

Upon moving to America with the Clayton's in the deeply historic city of Boston I had no idea that Hazel would move away for the Navy, her leaving was not a thought of mine. I had figured she would stay and enjoy this new space that we landed in just on the other side of the Atlantic Ocean. With all my work and only connecting to my daughter in the evenings, it caught me unaware when she said she would be leaving. I guess I never truly and deeply thought about how the death of Calvin, the move to America, culture shock, even the language could have affected her. She always appeared fine but perhaps that was due to her studious ways and self-entertainment, we spent our weekends exploring the new city. It was on one of these outings in late May 1960 that she told me of her plans, I couldn't stop her, she had already signed the papers and was planning on leaving the next month. If I had been paying attention I would have noticed all she remained in her room were clothing that would fit into her famous Globe Trotter, a faceted turquoise bracelet won at the carnival during one of our last weekends in Eastbourne and a small wooden boat carved from the beaches in Eastbourne that her father had given her, these were the items she would start her journey with. Of course, after further thought she was probably more like me that I would care to admit, I had the clothes on my back, a couple of knickknacks, a bit of jewelry from mom, Calvin and a suitcase that I purchased at a second-hand shop and had only used once in 1960. It broke me when Hazel left, she was all I had.

Looking back Boston was my kind of place, similar waterfront activities and the salt air drifted in at different temperatures. The summers torrid heat raising from the city, saltwater evaporating and winters wind brutal blowing of snowflakes to make wishes on, the weather forcing you to change and never become stagnant. Spring was a beautiful time of year with the new growth on the Copper Beech trees that bring my mind back to home. How I miss England, of course, there is no one there for me just my thoughts of who I was then, I shall not return for now since I am no longer that person. I am who I have become here in America, the new me on my own, awaiting news from Hazel. Last time she sent me a picture that sits on my end table facing the living room. I have placed it in a location I would see it the most since many of my evenings are spent seeking ships in the harbor with my telescope and reading adventurous fiction to pass the time.

Visiting Hazel in her various locations worldwide has become one of my yearly pass times, my only chore is to show up at the right gate at

Boston Logan International Airport with the ticket in my hand that Hazel has mailed me a few weeks prior. I am in truth a sentimental person but in my upbringing that was not a trait we focused on. I still carry the book with me from childhood being selective beyond measure with the things I record or adhere on the pages. The book has been repaired many of time to keep the pages from flying free with my treasures of sayings and poetry written so small I can barely see them and the pressed flowers and leaves to remind me of a journey or location. At the beginning of my travels to see Hazel she asked about the book, I have always carried it on our meetings and added a treasure or two but now I have new ideas of how to record my adventures.

I had already retired, and the Claytons allowed me to live on Commercial Wharf for as long as I chose, I was fortunate for that benefit being as it was my only home, the only place I had lived in the USA. My whole life was filled with work and must complete tasks, resting and walking the wonderful city of Boston, driving was never a necessity for me on either side of the Atlantic, we are who we are no matter where the road takes us, working and other tasks just fell into place in all my years. Midway through 1992, Hazel called to see if I would like to visit her in Seattle, she said she had just located a spectacular residence on Second Avenue downtown, right in the activity of the city and knew I would love the daily commotion. I flew straight into Sea Tac International Airport nonstop, Hazel picked me up at the gate after I had ridden the interior subway system to find her. Before leaving Eastbourne I had not been an adventurer but have learned to be confident in my travels as I am the only one knowing where I am supposed to arrive and at what time if I get nervous my internal GPS may not function to true north. I have only traveled to visit with Hazel so wouldn't want to end up in the wrong location.

We start just south of the city of Seattle heading north on I-5 gliding past some of the largest evergreen trees and a view of Mount Rainier that is stunning, Hazel says you wouldn't even know it was there on cloudy days. We enter the city proper just as dusk is setting in and the lights pop on as we drive through town, twinkling as if to greet us, another place for my map and memory. We drive to a small place on a side street in Ballard called *Delancey,* are promptly seated outside at their quaint tables right on the sidewalk and have the best wood-fired pizza I have ever experienced. The Brooklyn it's called and Hazel says is the best pizza in town. I am almost sure I need to move to Seattle just for this cheese pizza, and the attention to detail that this city has shown me already, the eatery nestles up in a neighborhood welcoming you like a home would and drawing you in like you are truly their guest.

After eating and being overly excited about seeing Hazel again, who looks calmer now than at any other time I have visited her, maybe this city is her true home. I am tired, feel I need to rest and ask to see her new place. We head out of Ballard I can't relax because every time I put my head back there is a view of the water and then the Space Needle, what a breath-taking bit of architecture. I see there are many places to research here, it is like entering an entirely new world connected to another ocean that is still unseen by me. Hazel and I haven't spoken much on the ride, the scenery is staggering, so much like Eastbourne, so much like Boston and many other places we have visited, water is the common denominator to all of them. We slip into an alley with dumpsters, and various debris, heat transferring off the surrounding buildings, I am unsure this is safe being new territory to me, but know Hazel knows exactly where we are going, she has always had a true sense of yes or no, that is why her occupation in the Navy suited her, maybe she gained her wits during her childhood in Eastbourne, all the hours alone on the pier. The echoing sound of her remote in the enclosed space of her SUV chimes, one of the largest garage doors I have ever seen opens and we are in a parking garage without natural light, the fluorescent bulbs humming, concrete surrounds us as our steps echo behind while heading towards the elevator that will take us to the sixteenth floor. We arrive at Hazel's place, I have never been this high in a building, always been a land dweller, she describes each attraction as I stare out the wall of windows in wonder. I turn and see a staircase looking like it was relocated from the dock by the pier, leading up to where we will sleep, still farther up, another floor to go before rest. Hazel asks me if I would like anything and says she would love to talk tomorrow, she has a plan. I kindly accept her tequila slammer and head up the metal stairway to rest and reflect, tomorrow is another day, possibly another life to start.

I am in Seattle and with Hazel for two weeks, the weather is not as brutal but changes frequently, the rainstorms are comforting, this place started growing on me, already after one day. During my visit, we toured the waterfront and all the quirky stores, have some of the best fish and chips since leaving Eastbourne, go to Mount Rainier, take a couple of days and go to West Port, Ocean Shores, pass through small towns such as Hoquiam, Aberdeen, McCleary. It seems there is an Aberdeen in most places. This brings memories of being a child, for some reason we had to retrieve my Uncle Jack. He was in Aberdeen, Scotland, we traveled to London and I saw more activity than I thought was possible then headed north many miles to Aberdeen. That trip always stuck in my mind, it was the biggest adventure our family had ever gone on, I don't remember coming home or getting Uncle Jack but I do remember Aberdeen and the towering gray buildings with such detail and height. Here I am again in Aberdeen, life circles around to bring our memories to the surface and reminds you to be grateful for the good times that you had. My first view of the Pacific Ocean was breathtaking, what a calming effect, being able to drive on the sand, while living in Boston I saw water daily but not like this, there may not be words to describe the process that is happening in me but I know beyond a doubt that Hazel will be asking me to move here and there will be no more thought about my relocation, it is already done in my mind and she hasn't even brought up the subject, I am seventy-two this year and feel as if I am just getting started. At our spectacular hotel with the grand swimming pool and views Hazel starts her intro speech of why I should be here, I interrupt her during her second sentence and say yes, I will move to this beautiful location, we discuss the options of how to move me here and decide on a road trip across the country. We return east on highway 101 to Olympia and tour the state capitol, there is different history in Washington than anywhere else that I have traveled, it is a younger place than most where I have existed or passed through, I always tour the historical sights. We have dinner in Tacoma at *Frisko Freeze* a walk-up diner with fabulous burgers, fries and milkshakes, right in the heart of historic Craftsman houses. We take our food to *Wrights Park*, eat at a picnic table and watch all the dogs, pets are not something I have ever felt the need to own but I love other people's animals. Dogs are an interesting bunch, they seem to say to anyone who sees them, "I am out here on a mission and it's important." After touring *W.W. Seymour Botanical Conservatory* a historical greenhouse with an elaborate variety of plants, plants like I have never seen, orchids, elkhorn ferns, pomelo trees and while walking the lush trails of the park there is an array of trees, most labeled with the year and species. We must head back to Seattle now it is time, but I know I will be back to explore this gem of a park soon enough.

Hazel

July 2014

MUM IS GONE, I HAVE TO KEEP MANUALLY PLACING THAT IN MY HEAD, SHE IS NOT past tense to me yet for some reason, her vibrance still lives with me or in me, certainly in my house and as I maneuver through the city. I was thinking a few days before her death as she was going out the door in her fluorescent yellow spandex outfit with a multi gemmed parrot pin on her collar that she seemed to be regressing to her teenage years or finally living them and was wondering just how many more years I would be blessed with her presence, the older she got the more speed she had, on her birthdays she would switch the candles around, last year she was thirty-nine years old. I found it enlightening but sad at the same time, she was always on the run, would meet people at dawn for bird watching or come in at dawn on other mornings from an all-night cruise or watching the night divers in Puget Sound, magically telling stories of starfish and orcas that the divers brought to the surface for her viewing. The life of everyone's party, some days I was lonely wanting to spend a day with her, she had her days planned out and didn't seem to need my companionship, that was most likely from the time I spent away from her traveling the world, quite possibly she didn't want to get in my way, in reality, I had nothing on my agenda for the first time in over thirty years. Mum was who I received my adventurous ways from, this is how she must have felt while I was in the Navy.

It feels as if my world was never real, mum was out and about and now is gone, the tattoos were shocking, to say the least, maybe I should get one or not, there have been meetings with the detective in charge, I can't remember his name. I am thinking it may not be necessary to remember anything since it is all different anyway, the facts keep changing all but one that matters the most, mum is gone. The detective was a nice young man, he was concerned about my comfort and privacy, asked if we should talk at my residence, anywhere I chose or at police headquarters. I chose home due to the fact he may need something of mum's, I couldn't imagine what but if so, it was there. When he called with his condolences, he explained that he was on the gang task force and was assigned the Vera Skylar's case because her death involved a hate crime, I bet he is glad he didn't have to notify me of her death, whoever the person was that grabbed her phone confirmed it. Before his arrival tomorrow at 3:00 pm I should go through all of mum's things looking for clues if there were any, I suspect not but better to be safe after the surprises she has left behind. I find her notebook of pressed flowers, sayings and memories of her life's travels, the binding coming undone again, I believe the book was a homemade one, the pages yellowed from almost a century of use, some with hand-drawn lines for her writings so small you can barely read the quotes. One of her final entries was about the park system in Seattle and how she only had three more to go, there was a detailed Seattle map of all the parks under her book and a decorated composition book under that with dated written records, observances of nature and people she had met along the way. Mum didn't just go somewhere and pass through she stopped, existed her entire being wherever she was, took from nature, returned with words of the blessings and seasonal wisdom. She was a free spirit that life didn't hold down, she took care of what she had to but didn't carry any baggage for long if at all. I know she mourned the loss of my father possibly forever this changed her, this never-ending exploration was her way of coping, maybe she shared her days with him although he had been gone for over three decades when she relocated here. The times she would sit and read, she was more at peace than anyone I knew, am sure she was truer to herself than a person could imagine. I can sit and read for hours but if there is a problem, I take it in the back of my mind to the storyline, I cannot disconnect from troubles as easily as mum. She always said, "worry not, not now, not ever."

The intercom bell startles me from being lost in thought, Detective Munser enters, he seems troubled and walks to the window like it is beyond his power of not going there. A few minutes pass, I think if I had married and had children they could be about this age, I had never in all my traveling years thought about being solo, felt alone or wished I had reproduced, this was my first time exploring this thought, it is quite shocking. He must have felt me staring at him even though it wasn't intentional, turns suddenly and startles me, I was abundantly lost in thought, not even sure I was in this room but watching a movie of my life determining if children could have entered. We both introduce ourselves as he apologizes for his rudeness, I tell him he was not rude but not what I had been thinking, he seems a tad awkward in this space or it could have been the lapse of time that we were each suddenly aware of, both of us have secrets from that moment that could or could not have to do with this case, I wish it weren't a case and that it was closed. My thoughts can't focus or stay still, Munser is asking me questions, like who mum left with, I don't know, just like always she just left and gave me an approximate time of arrival home. He is telling me facts like she was pushed, making statements of possible hate crime, things I am having great difficulty listening to, not because I haven't heard it before but because I just realized I am alone and need to be alone to process this. He said there was video footage from a store close by, stated in any city there would be people that protest other groups of people at any given time and made reference to being able to catch the suspect, I thanked him, he left and I was alone finally, I didn't know before he arrived that I was alone, moments change us, what a shocking emotional experience to have when a stranger walks in your home, one he had nothing to do with but it was drawn out of me nonetheless, now it is out in the open and I need to deal with my new found discovery.

I am not entirely sure how I will change the fact that I am alone, mum was never alone unless she wanted to be and that was usually after a long day of digesting and exploring the city. Mum put all her energy into her days, not a moment left over for waste, perfect balance of learning and resting. After today's visit with Munser I can't even remember what I have been doing since the funeral/party mum planned. I hope the case can be solved soon and I can figure out what to do besides watching ferry boats head across the sound.

Detective Munser

August 2014

It was an odd experience meeting Hazel, after being handed the case of a woman in her nineties I was taken aback, this wasn't the type of case I usually investigate, all of my clients as I call them have been much younger. These were British people, apparently with tattoos, someone who just went to a parade that died from the hatred of someone who didn't agree. This happens all the time all over the world but this lady was just having fun, she had a black and white cookie in one hand, and an American flag in her right one, had just told her friend that the cookie reminded her of Eastbourne and the baked goods from home, was observing the costumes she adored colorful displays and people. Then she was pushed, hit her head on a curb and was gone from this world, just like that a few blocks from three hospitals. Vera traveled light, they thought her purse had been stolen while looking to identify her, that was not the case, she had pockets sewn inside her spandex waistband with her identification, security entry card, money and a house key. Vera Violet Skylar born June 9, 1920, gone just like that, not from any other reason than hate. This is a case I need to solve for the sake of this community and her daughter, why can't hate just walk away, run from this continent, this world, why can't we coexist and let others be who they are without killing them, now I will have to arrest someone who is most likely an upstanding business person, who does community outreach and good for this city. Take them out of their home or business, possibly in front of their children, neighbors or coworkers for killing a lady, what part of that is correct except it is my job to do this for the sake of the same community that is a different place due to Vera being taken from us in ill will, someone trying to forcefully make someone else believe what they do, we all have a free will to believe what we wish, just not to force it on someone else. There are entirely too many people who want to police others actions when in reality the actions probably wouldn't harm them if they just let people be, it wasn't like this parade was being detrimental just not something some people believed and they were willing to kill for it whether they knew it, would admit it or not.

As I scan the video footage from the store, I see a group of about a dozen people with matching blue shirts and a circle logo with the letters QDIN, this is hard to watch, here comes Vera with her cookie, the shove and the whole group turns their head like they didn't see anything, not one goes to help her, no one bends a knee or calls 911. Instead, they unite like eggs in a carton in their matching shirts and narrow minds, not only turning from their self-created crime scene but running from it like it didn't happen at all, there isn't a dead lady on the storm drain. I sit back in amazement, knowing I need to rewind the footage and attempt to identify these murderers disguised as do-gooders or persuaders, this may be their only act of violence but to turn away and not render assistance, even call 911 for a lady they caused to fall on the ground is unimaginable, unthinkable, detestable, unhuman.

I scan the tape again and notate the times of the event which was under a minute for the whole scene to happen. I recognize the man and woman who shoved Vera from a community fundraising event, two people did this, actually, all twelve were accessories, head turners turned to guilt, we will need the addresses and a paddy wagon or simultaneously pick them up so no one notifies the others or runs. You never know what people will do once they are pushed into a corner, my old boss used to say, kick their bucket and see what they are holding. Brent Solis and Elaine Curry are the first two I pay a visit, see about their story, does it match the video and then bring them in. They are guilty of felony murder no matter what their story is, the charges will undoubtedly be dropped to involuntary manslaughter and the rest of their crew being accessories will probably get misdemeanor manslaughter.

I sit in my squeaking faux leather chair, at my metal and wooden desk with my feet on the steel government issued trash can, organizing notes and scheduling this mass arrest, we wouldn't want them all to know we are coming to escort them with our fine silver jewelry to take part in a series of statements in our interview rooms and give them sleeping accommodations for the night. In one day, not something I am proud of, just part of my job all these upstanding citizens will have obtained a record for themselves that will change their life forever.

After the heartfelt interviews and confessions and tears of guilt, all were locked up for the night, waiting for arraignment in the morning if then, if there is time on the docket. I am glad this happened in the summer Vera is the second to tell of the arrests, the first is Hazel who I will call on the way to the cemetery to tell Vera out of respect at her graveside.

I had been to The City Square Cemetery on many prior occasions, make a habit of attending the funeral of the victim and the gravesite after we have solved the murder. This is all I can do for the victim and family but it is something, these are people I get to know after they are gone, their life, habits and family put in front of me like a puzzle and if I am fortunate enough to locate their killer that is a bonus. It is just starting to cool down, as I leave headquarters and make the call to Hazel, the call that should have never had to of been made, apologize for the lateness of the information and tell her of the dozen arrests, she thanks me and asks a strange question, is the police department needing volunteers, I assured her I would look into that, give my condolences and hang up. I steer my undercover police cruiser into the cemetery bearing the bittersweet news for Vera of her dozen murderers. From what I have learned of Vera she would hang her head, sad with the news of hatred being the cause of her death but knowing she had loved all, rest easy Vera.

I stand over Vera's gave for a bit feeling mixed emotions of turmoil and relief, turn to get into my car knowing it will always be a long night in the city, in summer. I catch a glimpse of a long car, Bob's Pontiac I wave as he leaves for the night, a man I have seen here for a couple years or more, he is unmistakable in the old steel car, he waves back happy to see a familiar face. Both of us knowing this will not be the last time we will see each other at this location, we are just fortunate to be on this side of the soil helping the ones who aren't.

Hazel

October 2014

IT SEEMS LIKE YEARS SINCE MUM HAS BEEN DEPARTED. HER CLOTHES AND EARTHLY belongings are still as they were the day she left. I don't have a reason to claim that room, my intentions were for her to live there forever. My thoughts never veered towards her death, especially at the hands of another, a do-gooder at that. Some days I wonder if I should have moved to Boston and this would never have happened, I try to convince myself that when mum moved here it was like she opened a present with many levels, in twenty-two years she made hundreds of friends, did she have that many when she was in Boston, I will never know. I always saw her as outgoing but rarely with anyone, I assumed that she lived a lonely life, it seems that her move to Seattle was a turning point for her to open up and explore but I honestly have no idea what she did in Boston once she retired, or really in Seattle just tidbits of her activities. As children are, I led my own life and never asked what she did, only how she was and then she would always say she was fine. Fine may have been a deep word that contained a full spectrum of emotion, she may have been lonely or sad, possibly fine.

The weather is starting to turn here and feel more like my memories of Eastbourne, my memories as a child of the ferry crossing the sea led me to buy this place, although they were rebuilding the city from the war in the 1940s, there were still peaceful moments and the people who were left in town to survive needed transportation with the railway being rebuilt and also entertainment even if it was to watch a boat bob in the water heading to Queen's Wharf and back again, the same fixation is upon me here Seattle to Bremerton, Seattle to Bain Bridge Island and back again. This thought has never crossed my mind before but the past few months I have had a ferry obsession, watch them for hours on end from my window, even have the schedule to see if they are on time, then if I leave home and drive across the West Seattle Bridge to Lincoln Park to watch those ferries, then onto Alki beach to watch them from there. While on my weekly outing across the bridge I call the ferry run, the wind whips water out of the Elliott Bay into my face, something I miss from my Navy days, I also miss our November Harvest Festival celebrations as a child, mum would decorate the house with the produce we had grown or bartered for other families in town. I would arrive home from school, peppers would be handing from the light fixtures like an emerald chandelier, carrots laid between our dishes in the yellow open cabinets without doors, stings of bean and peas formed garlands strung throughout the house, apples placed on the wooden carved mantle top like giant ruby's, heads of cabbage lined the kitchen counter like people in a row, a pumpkin in the center of the table waiting for company, onions of yellow, red and white lined the stairs, corn standing stately ears at attention, tomatoes placed amongst the rest, pears giving off their musky scent and vibrant color, ripe and ready for our Harvest Festival. Mum would be singing songs of praise for the harvest. This year I missed it, I missed the date September sometime at the end, you will have to forgive me for not knowing the exact date, mum took care of that when I was a child and we celebrated on a couple of occasions here when mum saw the fresh produce. On my way home I will stop at Pike Place Market and shop for Harvest vegetable, I am missing Mum's Harvest Soup.

I reverse my trip back to my side of the Puget Sound, winding my way along the water catching glimpses of the ships and cranes as I head to HWY 99 Northbound, getting off an Alaskan way and turning onto First Ave. I am lucky today, there is an open parking spot, close enough to walk and retrieve my produce for the decision of the soup and celebration. I head west on 1st and enter the market, the people, the colors and the vibrancy of the city are almost overwhelming. I realize I haven't been out in a crowd since mum's funeral. This is the first time a crowd has had this effect on me, I used to live on ships sailing with their own crowd, two thousand people in one location close to each other was never a problem before this moment. I was the peacemaker the ships, the person who reminded you to follow a set of ethics and codes set by our government, I was part of a unit of Axillary Security Forces that worked with the Shore Patrol and Masters at Arms when needed, generally, I stayed on a ship for a year, then onshore about the same duration and back to the water. Many years, thirty-two to be exact I did my best to protect the seas, our nation, the equipment, bases, the other enlisted personnel and officers, it is in my nature now to observe and respond with dignity and diligence, this crowd is peaceful just more people than I had experienced recently.

I watch the crowd expand and recess, they pass through the aisles and levels with ease unaware of my presence, I am suddenly grateful that I can shop for my necessities on the exterior aisles and breezeways of the market so as not to enter such enclosed spaces, I start picking carrots, other vegetables and fruits from various vendors all to the tunes sung by a street artist playing the accordion, sporting a black velvet jacket and baseball cap, and a dancing cockatoo, songs he has written come out of the instrument and his being, magically into the air surrounding the produce, people and dogs, mingling as if it belongs there too because it does. On my way back to my car I purchase his home burned CD, knowing this is what I will be listening to as I prepare for my own version of the Harvest Festival. I head back to the parking lot and am truly appreciative of mum, the farmers and vendors who have allowed me to travel the world and come here for my goods to celebrate at this moment. I head home, take the elevator up with my newly purchased CD, hoping the elevator can handle the weight of my harvest, I enter the door as I see the three o'clock ferry heading east to Bremerton. I place all the bags down and start my soup, Mum's Harvest Soup, as I slice the carrots I know what is left over will decorate my space tonight as I watch the lighted ferries glide by.

After the soup is on and simmering, I notice my phone on the end table that I seem to forget at home most days since no one calls me, it has a voice mail alert. I enter my access code and am surprised Detective Munser had called, he recalls my last request of him that I had forgotten, asking about volunteer work. He apologized for his late response and says he isn't sure of my background but there are some paid positions and some volunteer ones. He asked if I would like to meet him at the precinct downtown to discuss the options of my liking and see if anything will be a mutual fit.

I left him a message with the time to meet up with him, he is the one with a schedule, all I have going is the ferry schedule, he calls back the next day, we agree on Thursday at 11:00 am. For some reason I pack up some of Mum's Harvest Soup and a couple of rolls, thinking he would like to see a portion of mum's happy life. I drive the couple miles with the soup balancing on the passenger seat and rolls helping it stay upright. After parking in a paid lot on Fifth Avenue and walking south the three blocks, I was feeling confident about being out and in a crow. Detective Munser met me in the lobby, we went to an office that had files in some sort of order I presumed it was his order of cases. He had print outs of positions available, told me of their pros and cons, we talked of my experience in the Navy, we had both assumed I would want something inside and not on the streets. I found one that was of interest; a Records Request Clerk, a paid part-time position, one my prior experience would help since I knew the terminology. I applied on the spot with Detective Munser's computer as he ate the soup, he had warmed in the microwave. I felt a weight had been lifted off me, one that had been put there upon retiring so many years ago. At that point, my life was to take care of mum, like we were on her holding pattern to help her through each day, and that I am grateful for. She added the vibrancy to my life. Every day was enjoyed as its own capsule. Life is hard as you lose people that you love, these last few months since mum has been gone, I realize how she felt when I went away so long ago. I am thankful for our time together and if it had to end this way, this is the way it was for mum to go then I need to be grateful the case is solved and I may have a new job helping others.

One more piece of mum's case is on my mind, what does QDIN stand for? Who were these people that would protest against a lady out enjoying a parade? Detective Munser states they were a company who helped people dial in on their destiny, people who made you aware of the stresses in your life to eliminate them so you could focus on your natural talents. QDIN is a twist on cued in, they have a clock for their logo that says timing is everything, adjust it. I don't think I would ever make the connection from that business of focus into violence, but this sad act has happened and cannot be undone.

Detective Munser

January 2015

I APPLIED TO THE FORCE, YOU HAVE TO BE A PERSON WITH THICK SKIN OUT HERE, I started this gig when my band *The Green Pyramid* parted ways. We were really onto something big and our lead singer disappeared, it was never right after that. I already knew the other side of downtown and what happened there, not the police side but the one where the music came from. When I started on foot patrol it was Halloween night 1994. I was 21 years old, dressed in an officer's uniform for the first time on the street and at that stage I felt like I was the one in costume. Flipping of rolls, an adjustment of plot, changing hats, that I wasn't mentally prepared for, I was patrolling on foot in Pioneer Square the same area my band always played, no one even recognized me of course, when you join a group of people all dressed the same you just become one of them, like a branch of the military or a sports team. No one is distinguishable unless you are searching for a particular person in the crowd. The first few weeks were brutal, me thinking I would know people and it would be the same since I had been around for quite a while. That was not the case at all, no one seemed to realize it was me, from the stage, I could scream out a lyric and everyone knew me, but now, in these trousers, polished boots, basketweave belt and waist carrying pounds of gear, that wouldn't be right. It seems as if what was normal and proper for me before in life was now taboo. The bands come and go, some make it, most change members frequently, each piece of the band meshes with the rest so if one segment changes the entire dynamics evolve into something better or they split of ways.

Many crimes and faces have gone before me in my time on the force, most people are just trying to get by, but some go too far. Others now are amazingly twisted in the brain or heart, not sure where that started. I study them or the crime, occasionally I see the criminal first, other times, the crime scene with no suspect to be found, like poof it's happened but no evidence of why. Cold, wet nights are the worst, victims left lying in the street or if they are lucky enough to be still alive, left on a curb shattered mentally or physically, possibly both, possibly hit in the head and robbed, or fell and said they were robbed out of embarrassment. My job is to help locate the truth. I wonder why people lived after a horrific event, at the scene they look like they won't recover from it, but something will jump out and remind them of the particulars of their crime at every turn from this moment on. I try to be gentle with the naïve crime victims, act like we are related or something, they don't know I have feelings too because I can't show them. My approach is generally from the outside, they have no idea who I am, as I introduce myself as Seattle Police. They shrink back knowing they don't want to acknowledge whatever just happened. I am not the problem they just know they don't want to be there or connected to anyone in any way that has a connection to this scene but I am the only connection. Many times, they will spill the story faster than I can write, they just want out of the crime scene. That can't be the way it works though, the assailant may be right there still and them having sat down from the shock of the crime they may have missed that they are being watched by the person who caused the entire incident and they don't even know it. Handling people, victim or criminal is a tricky line, there are times the criminal looks upstanding and the victim looks shady, the victim and the criminal may even be the same. This is a profession that you need to learn to read between the lines and listen to what is being said, there are always clues they just may be twisted. Now twenty-three years later I am a seasoned Gang Task Force Detective. That doesn't mean I know it all but have seen almost all until something new comes up, more than I can take some days, days I need to erase it all from my mind and the back of my eyelids like a whiteboard.

Detective Munser

April 2015

SINCE BEFORE MY TIME IN THE GREEN PYRAMIDS MUSIC HAS HABITUALLY BEEN the outlet where I get lost for hours. Seattle seems to be a music incubator; the number of bands has inevitably been hard to wrap my mind around. When I would go out on patrol or now on the way to a case, my head is consistently banging some tune, I am still a heavy metal fanatic at heart. After I became a patrol officer, there were still a few people I knew from the bars and had met more people in the music industry since. My transition to the department was tricky at first but meshed well as time went on, the streets were a natural place for me.

One cold night around Christmas at about 2:00 am I was called out to an old two-story turquoise house in south Seattle at the end of a road, it seemed this was county territory, but we were called in for some reason. The night was stormy, the wind blowing everywhere, trees were bending in the rage of the wind, pine scent in the air, the alder tree in the center of the yard by the community barbeque pit was bowing down so low I thought it would snap, you could hear the creek running by near the back yard slightly down the hill, cats were scurrying about, their suspicious eyes glowing. There was also a band playing some heavy metal music deeper than I cared to get into, it was loud from the storm, but the music was at a decibel suitable for a venue, right here in this neighborhood, apartments on either side. This was one of the scenes I remember vividly because there was an extreme amount of action going on even though I had no idea what was happening. The yard was void of grass it was a literal mud hole, there were cars parked all over the place, mostly imports. Parts were strewn throughout, doors here, hoods there, stacks of motor pieces all around and the stench of motor oil, gasoline and 90 weight oil were blowing up from the mud as we walked, I knew I would need new shoes after this night, maybe new ears.

There was a short, blond, curly-headed guy, too thin to hold his up pants that were stiff from car oil, he was covered in grease from head to toe. Probably would have slipped right by us if he had not emerged from the side of the house going 100 mph as we were passing on his left, looking for the body we had been called out to locate. I imagine it must have been a respectable garage at one time, but now there was black car sticking halfway in, halfway out, an extra-large speaker playing some slow jazz conflicting with the metal, a bulletin board with black marker scribbles and appointments, a propane heater running full blast too close to all of this, a spotlight hanging from the rafters and the craziest door I had ever seen made out of a stove and old refrigerator racks; recycling at its best. There was a stack of used up appliances piled two stories high on the side of the house. Do these people get rid of anything? They must have seen me looking because they explained without me asking that it was a scrap pile, of course, their truck didn't have gas or tabs, maybe next week. We were called out for a homicide but when we arrived this is what we saw and no body. The neighbors just called in a body because they wanted the band to be silenced and had seen someone laying in the mud. Places like these keep my mind going, knowing something is up but there were too many variables to place what was happening, like contained ants in a farm. Many crime scenes are sketchy this one, no one has identification, no one saw anything. I get it, once you are connected with ID you are on record for being there and if you did see something that is on the record too so the victim or innocent bystander becomes the target which creates another crime scene in the cycle of what happens every day, in every city, everywhere. We were able to identify the mud laying gentleman who was proudly wearing his new layer and we left the scene knowing he was alive.

Frederick aka Kobus

August 2015

HELLO, MY NAME IS FREDERICK ARTHUR TUFNELL. I WAS BORN IN SUSSEX, UK sometime in November 1939 I believe, give or take a year. I have a younger sister named Trillium, never met my dad. My daughter Holly is typing this as I have not once, in all my years, turned on a computer, nor can I read or write except for my address and name. I started coming to the City Square Cemetery because it felt comforting, the scenery always changes here for the living. New flowers, leaf color and people come and go, it is a good place and I feel closer to Gabby here. She has been gone just a short while, a week or two physically, but mentally a couple of years; we couldn't afford to bury her, so I drive around with her next to me inside a teddy bear seat belted in my car.

I was born with a club foot, and my family was not able to afford the extensive treatments to correct it. So, to this day I still wear leg braces and crazy hot boots to walk, constant pain overtakes me due to my legs being so weak and the various surgeries that have been done to correct my deformity. The pain is also due to the work I perform since I can't read, I must do what I can, that requires standing and lifting all day, I accept donations to a local charity in an affluent neighborhood. It always amazes me how happily people are willing to give away so many items of value that they couldn't wait to purchase weeks or months before, things I could never afford.

My story is tragic, but I am a modestly happy man and see the good in all people, I have learned to be grateful for the small things even though I may appear down and grumpy, that is just the old man inside of me with regrets and frustration circling and lashing out. When the possibility of war invaded London in the 1940's I was very young, but I do remember Mother packing two small bags, one for me and one for sister and taking us to the train station where all the children went away for safety. When we arrived, we were given a health check and Trillium went to a home for girls. I was not given a bill of health, so they put me in a hospital for boys. The building was a menacing tower, four stories tall, brick and cold, boys everywhere. Still to this day when I see a big, brick building my insides start to shake and I remember the deep shivering of childhood, hunger from measly portions if there were any at all. There were over three hundred boys with a physical problem, it was the first time I really felt a connection to other people outside of my family, this was because I was a burden to my family, but everyone here has physical adversity, you should have seen some of them, all twisted up. I was always made fun of for my leg braces, now I look rather ordinary compared to them. When I sit down you can't even tell I have an issue with my feet, after all the surgeries, maybe I will walk with a normal gait and not quite so noisily.

I think this is where I lost connection to others. I knew I had to rely on myself to be safe but so many came and went, just like mom and Trillium, that I was afraid to form a connection. I guess that lasted a lifetime. Now in my senior years I have never fully understood what being a part of a family unit is so I could never have taught Holly what that means. I have chosen other things over family, whether it was Holly or mother all my life, not sure how to change that but will try in the years I have left, if I can. When I attempt to be normal it brings my shortcomings to the surface and I am the one to suffer, I cannot just forget I was not the person I was supposed to be by societal standards.

During my stay they performed a few surgeries to correct the angle of my feet, I was raised in this hospital for approximately eleven years. The thin, gray porridge was scarce and hard to get to since I couldn't walk most of the time. After my operations I was in a bed with my legs in the air so if other children didn't bring food to me, I went without, I had some friends there who helped me. We learned to play checkers and I always won, strategy was my calling, there were countless hours to think about it. The hospital did not provide any training in mathematics, reading or writing, many of the children left after we heard the war was over, parents were required to get their children, no one came for me, I was on a floor for forgotten children. Not sure if it was because of my legs or just the way they were, maybe life was easier without two children, maybe Trillium didn't go home either. I had no way of knowing; I only knew I was there alone; the beds were mostly empty; you could hear nearly silent cries in the night echoing off the brick walls. In the morning you never knew who it was that needed comfort in the night hours and held it in all day but when the lights went out it was a recurrence of the prior night and each one before that.

I am not sure of the year or date but a lady who I did not know came to the hospital to claim me. She had the correct paperwork, a husband in a uniform and a girl named Trillium. We went from the hospital to the dock to board a ship. I had never seen a colossal ship before, and I didn't even know the people who were taking me, Trillium did not look like the little girl I knew, I didn't realize I had also grown taller until then, in my mind I was still a little boy, I was the small boy who entered the building. As we boarded the ship the lady who claimed she was my mother handed me a small valise. There were stickers all over it, it was used by someone else before the departure of my homeland. When we got to our cabin there were stacked beds. I could only remember sleeping in a hospital bed, I had never been anywhere that moved like this. I opened the valise and there was actual clothing, before this strange event I had only worn unclaimed children's standard-issue hospital wear. It makes me laugh now at the combinations of clothes they gave us; I had a pair of green tweed pants that I was fond of. We were on the ship for days, it was good to have real food but unnerving to be with these people who I did not know going to somewhere I had never heard of called America, I wondered if this was a place or person. I figured I would know soon. After being checked by police officers in a city called New York with many tall buildings and noise we were escorted to a train and rode for a few days to meet America. When we exited the train, a car was waiting for us and we were taken to a fort called an Army base in America. So, America is a country, the fort is an Army base in the United States. I wish I were able to attend school at the hospital in the UK so this process of moving with strangers would be understandable, all I could do was look and not read. I must believe what they say it says and what they tell me, they also inform me it is important to use the new name, Kobus Porter Elliott. My mother says her name is Ellen, dad is Easton and is in the Army, we are the Elliott family. They seem to have a connection, I feel as if I'm an add on, the fit is just not right, they have a natural flow of family and I have not had that.

A few days after arriving I rode the bus to school; I was sixteen years old and had never been to any school before this. Upon entering my classes I had no idea what all the books said or what the teachers were referring to, I still don't know now, decades later. Occasionally they would reference the war and the UK, but their stories were all wrong. As we were not permitted to talk in class, only listen, I could not correct them, they thought I had a learning disability and put me in the lower classes, as they say, that still didn't help, I couldn't read. They passed me on to eleventh grade, I learned how to help the sound man with the mixer board, excelled in the gym, made a few friends and attended church, the Baptist church where I still attend. In my junior year, I met a short, cute girl named Clary. We had so much fun, her dad Phillip taught me to drive, I was more of a person than I had ever felt before this, we went with her parents on trips to the mountain, Oregon and the Pacific Ocean. Her mother, Amanda, always baked chocolate chip cookies and bread pudding. Life was better than I had ever experienced, I think I had a connection to this group of people, they treated me like one of their own. When you haven't ever fit in it is hard to distinguish when you genuinely do.

One day after school mother explained to me that Easton had gotten military orders and her, Easton and Trillium were moving to Germany and would be back in three years, she felt it was best that I stay with Mrs Olmstead from the church, it was all arranged. One year with my family in a new country and now onto Mrs Olmstead's. She was a nice lady, lived on the lake, drove a green Lincoln Continental and must be rich. She was the only person I knew who lived on a lake. I think she owned half of the town and a real estate company, I am not sure I was used to this "America" thing yet in my heart "trucks" were still lorries, "elevators" still lifts, "garages" still car parks, "French fries" still chips, my accent always gave me away. I spent a lot of time on the dock alone, at church or with Clary and her family.

After graduation I was on my own and still didn't read, they just pushed me through and gave me a diploma. I got a job at a bowling alley putting the pins back up, that was brutal, I had to change that position fast, too many bruises. I went on to be a dishwasher at a swanky restaurant. I was still seeing Clary, she wanted to get married, I don't think I was ready, we had a big wedding, all the yellow flowers, white dress and suits. I had met Penny a waitress at the restaurant downtown where I toiled in the hot kitchen. I suppose this is where it started going wrong, where I seriously got off track, if it was ever right to begin with, looking back I shake my head in wonder that I am still alive. I was at the altar with Clary and in walked Penny, she sat in the back row on the aisle end of the seat in a spot I could see her, I didn't tell her about the wedding, someone must have told her from work when the vows were being said. I was a married man and I would have to walk right by her. As Clary and I were leaving, Penny caught my eye; I could only imagine being with her and wondered what I had just done. I told myself the marriage was the right and normal thing to do, I had said my vows, posed and smiled for pictures, ate the meal and cake, drove the old blue Chrysler Windsor with cans attached and writing on the windows to the quaint little motel at the ocean, it was a sweet place, I was happy and so was Clary. She was talking so much of our future; my head was full of Penny and the one night we had spent together not long ago, looking back everybody can be on their best behavior for one night. I got Clary in the room with her suitcase, told her I was going to get ice but got in the Chrysler and drove off, miles behind me as a married man I found Penny, knowing it was the wrong thing to do but normalcy was not in my blood or heart. I hear years later Clary called her brother Liam after two days, broken-hearted and asked for a ride home to her parents' house to recover if that would be possible for her ever, I am honestly not sure what happened with Clary in the next couple of years. This story is about me and that is really who I want to talk about, I have not been a priority to anyone all my life, so this is about me, Frederick Arthur Tufnell aka Kobus Porter Elliott. Of course, I have never made anyone a priority either and don't think I ever will, moments are my solace, moments to pull out and examine when I am alone, no one that means anything to me knows how much they mean. I am afraid of connection and prefer the feeling of my sassing link to rest upon.

Since I had a few days off for the honeymoon I called Penny, we went for a ride to no designated place, this was my mistake thinking she was free-spirited and wishing I was back at the motel, but I couldn't return now, Clary would be devastated and never let up on me. We stopped when we wanted, ate when we wanted and were free, so I thought. Penny wanted to get married too so I had to take her back, change jobs and become me again. Drinking became my priority, working at the country club allowed me to meet some influential people, I met a tall, dark-haired man who came in to eat and would slip over and play the piano, his name was Robert, he always wore a black suit and drove a long black elegant car. One day he walks up to me and says, "Hey you, you can drive right?" I nodded, as the staff weren't allowed to interact with patrons unless addressed. He pulled me aside and we agreed on a place to meet right up the block at 11:00 pm. After that meeting, I was taken into a whole different world, the drive and shut up world. I transported cars for him loaded with things I couldn't ask about but I was paid well. I was set up in motels across America (where I got to know the people well) and drank my nights away forgetting about Clary, Penny and the women from towns gone by.

I figured it was about time for mother to come back from Germany, so I drove around and decided to go by the church, Clary was there with her mother practicing the organ. One thing led to another and we were in the same motel as the honeymoon picking right up where we left off two years prior, that is where Holly came about. We had been married three years and had not spent one night together except that one. I irregularly kept in touch and Clary said she was pregnant, I couldn't leave her again, even though my mind said run, we were still married, so we got an apartment downtown by the park and hospital, I went to work at another restaurant, and we were happy she thought, I was playing the game the best I could, the only way I knew how; the wrong way. In August of that year, Clary's dad, Phillip, became ill, by December he was gone. Clary was devastated, the baby was due and was born on the same day as Phillip's funeral, the first day of winter. Clary hated that little girl with a passion, she had it in for her, the baby kept her from her fathers' funeral, and I suppose she blamed the baby for what happened with me.

On Christmas Eve Clary was released from the hospital with Holly, who the nurse named since Clary chose not to name her, she was given the last name of Elliott, a name that wasn't hers or mine, and now Clary has it too, Easton sharing his name with all of us. I drove Clary and tiny Holly on a cold Christmas Eve morning to Amanda's house, dropped them off and said I would be right back, but we all knew I wouldn't be returning, we just all knew as we looked at each other. I stopped at the local bar and got a drink; the festivities were in full swing being as it was Christmas Eve; I have always loved Christmas, everyone is included, a moment to step into. It's a time to be happy and no one expects anything if you chose to not have anyone close to you. This is a time to enjoy the lights, music (that I sing all year long) and everyone says hello, there is no other friendlier time of year.

The next couple of years were blurry, a minuscule job here and there, lots of drinking and parties, I was driving again for Robert. On Holly's third birthday I knocked on the back porch door of the one story yellow house at the end of the long driveway where I had last seen her and handed over a tea set wrapped all fancy with a shiny bow by the pretty girl at the department store wrapping station. Clary was coming behind her yelling, I drove away again, this time for six years.

About five years later I married Doris, she was a huge lady who ran a motel at the ocean, would take up a whole room. This arrangement worked for me, it gave me a place to stay and was close enough to see mother and Trillium occasionally and drive by Holly's to see if she was in the yard or window for a quick glimpse of her. When she was nine, I got her a Ken doll and a Mickey Mouse watch. I showed up unannounced, but Clary let me in and there are even pictures of that day. I just am not capable of keeping a connection, I didn't see Holly again until she was seventeen, said she was on her way to Los Angeles.

I couldn't keep it together with Doris, she wanted more than I know how to give, so I took off and got a job at a Chevrolet dealership, Robert even gave me a perfect reference for driving for him. That was when I met Gabby at the restaurant, she must have loved me or appreciated me or something. It was on my birthday I was out alone, and she was eating with some older children, I later found out it was her birthday too. She was so tall, legs a mile long, I am a short man, she had seven children. Little did I know those children would keep coming back home again and again, all wanting to live there at some point or another. Only one of them drove an automobile, they all seemed a little off, I was used to that from the hospital where I grew up so putting up with them and finding humor in their idiosyncrasies as I do in mine, was easy. Gabby and I had a thirty-six-year love affair together, we were strong, witty and traveled western America, we worked through it and needed each other, we were a good fit. She got me off the booze and settled me down. In 2013 I knew she was leaving, as her mind would wander and so would she, the police would bring her home sometimes from the streets at night while I tried to sleep so I could work to keep our roof. I couldn't leave her alone to go to work or at night, they called it Sun Downers syndrome. Her daughter would stay with her in the day, but she was on pills so slept and she would get away all the time, she became an escape artist. I am sure there were resources, but I can't read, and the doctors were of no assistance. Even though I sat at the hospital for two months with her waiting for a transfer to a nursing home, it was still so unreal on August 12th, 2015 when Gabby was gone. I didn't even know how to get through this she was the only person I had had any real connection to in seventy-six years. She had my heart, did my reading for me and my world was absorbed in her.

I am not sure I will make it much longer myself, there is something wrong with my heart but that will have to wait. As I sit at her funeral that only three of her children attended, who knows where the rest are? I sit with Holly at my left side and Sage, my granddaughter, on the other when she is not chasing Mercy, my great-granddaughter, I knew this story had to be told, no one really knows my version because I have remained mostly invisible with my life on two continents. My family is large, I see them only on holidays and other events since I am not sure how to have real emotional connections, these are celebratory times, I mostly see them at Christmas, my favorite time of year. Clary who I haven't seen in 40-plus years is at this year's party, she tells me of all the people attending, Ava my oldest granddaughter, her husband Jeff, my great-granddaughter Azalea, Sage, her boyfriend Kyle, Mercy their daughter, and my only grandson Micah and his girlfriend Rose. The list goes on, Clary is still chatting up a storm fifty-five years later. I only care that it is Christmas Eve and I have family and have lived long enough to see them, I carry all of them in my heart every day and imagine the group happy as they are now, they are all beautiful. I am a blessed man. America is a person and a place. I am a person in a space.

Gabby

HELLO, I AM GABBY, FRED AND I MET IN 1978 AT A RESTAURANT IN THE NORTH end of the city, it was on a blustery evening, our birthday November 26th. I was only there because my children insisted that we go out, I would have been happy to finish off the turkey from Thanksgiving three days prior. He was alone and I was with my three youngest children, the rest were off living their lives, probably calling me in the time slot their life allowed around the same time we left for dinner. You can't always sit and wait for the phone to ring, life must be lived, especially on a birthday. You could tell the man was comfortable at the table across from us and probably drank coffee by himself frequently, his corduroy pants, cotton button-down shirt with a thermal underneath and boots all seemed worn and comfortable, as comfortable as he was being there. That past year had been hard on me and my children, their father had passed away, the others were grown, seven in all. Seemed like I was only a child when I started having them, nine people in a small space was too much to bear sometimes, our living quarters were generally a small apartment or a 1950's run-down trailer that had seen better days before we arrived, children ran in and out of the doors faster than I could close them. Their clothing was handed down three or four times before it went to rags, of course for me to clean, work never ended. Occupying that many people and attempting to make them happy was near impossible, someone was always complaining, in my mind that someone was me, I was finally starting to enjoy myself with some of the children grown. I never had my way, Dale, my husband, was a drunk, he would always want things different once he drank, the kids acted like kids, so that left me, mom, a woman with her true identity hidden under all of the mopping of physical, mental and emotional messes laid in of me to fix after the tirades of others.

After our meal, my children and I nodded to the stranger I had smiled at earlier, I paid our bill with the last of my weekly allotment and we stepped out into a windstorm and went to meet the northbound bus. For some reason, the bus didn't arrive on time, we were waiting that windy evening and a turquoise colored GTO pulled up to the curb, there was the stranger we'd seen drinking coffee, he asked if we needed a ride. Even in my uncertainty, I told my children to climb into the back seat of that two-door, shiny car, as we inched off the curb and merged onto north Interstate 5 towards my little house with bedrooms as small as a refrigerator, where I had raised all my children. Thank God some were on their own, the tension eased as more room became available to breathe. That day Fred did not know there were four more children and I didn't know he had Holly. That ride started a journey that I am not sure either of us would have survived without each other. I had the house and he had none, he was just relocating from down by the ocean and had recently started a job at a car dealership. He said he does things one step at a time to get it all right, finding permanent shelter was his next step. I'm not sure where he slept that night, or the next, but on November 28th, days later, Fred moved in with me and my children, I didn't know his story, but he seemed to appreciate the roof, meals, and love that we instantly had. I was concerned he may be running from something or himself, but he seemed harmless as he sat back and laughed at our stories.

My children were skeptical, especially the ones who were grown and had moved out. They didn't have any trouble with Fred when they needed rides or moved back in. Fred was good about their unforeseen return to home on many occasions he would shake his head and laugh throwing his right hand in the air, maybe he was better at this than me, I had been at it a long time and was tired, it was as if he had never lived like this before, with people. Our time was always when we would go for a drive, we would leave all the adult children at home, however many had returned. We moved from my house to an upstairs duplex, then onto a string of apartments and a couple of trailers then to the last apartment upstairs, this one was my favorite because it was just us, finally, they were all grown and gone, oh finally. Seems like we always had financial troubles, I never worked outside the house, not with seven children, so I wasn't much help to our pocketbook, nor did I have any marketable skills or transportation. Fred used to love taking me to the beauty salon to get my hair dyed all different colors, I think he knew it made me feel special to come out with a new color and style smelling of all that hairspray with hair as stiff as bristles, he would stand back looking at me, proud to have me as his wife. Afterwards, he would always take me for a long drive and out to eat to show me off, we always went the same places that were far from home, he knew the way there and back, Fred was always good to me on our journeys.

When I got sick and started forgetting none of my children were any-where to be seen, I was coming in and out of reality, in the end, more out than in. One second, I was talking with Fred about a television show we loved and the next had no idea who he was or why I was even in the little upstairs apartment, that is why I ran off so much. The last few months were the hardest on everyone, I know it was hard on Fred and my children but it was hard on me too not knowing the normalcy of my life. I would come back to reality sometimes attacking Fred because he wouldn't let me leave in the night, other times in a hospital, out on the street at night, in a police car or just talking to people I probably had no business talking to, I met some strange faces during those times, evaluating if they were part of my world or not, this depended on if I was in reality or had slipped out. I couldn't control what happened when I was out of reality. They took me to a hospital, Fred couldn't handle me anymore, no one could figure me out for months while waiting in the hospital for a nursing home, I slowly passed away, went all the way out.

Bob

September 2015

AFTER WORKING AT THE CEMETERY FOR A COUPLE OF YEARS, I STARTED RECOGNIZ-
ing the people who frequented the graves. There were also fitness walkers
and joggers and photographers. In a place like this people generally like their
privacy, don't come here every day or stay long but there was a gentleman
that started coming almost every day last month, he showed up every morning like clockwork in a car that didn't have much to be desired, front end all
beat up with a padlock holding the hood in place, the windshield had a crack
running across it. He was different than the rest, he would be here and there.
Never stayed in the same spot, at first, I thought he was homeless, but he was
always clean, wore button-down cotton shirts, slacks and work boots, and
his car wasn't full of stuff, just a few stuffed animals. He would walk around
sometimes like he was exercising and other times I would see him napping.
One day he approached me and I found out his name was Frederick, he said
to call him Fred. There wasn't much to him, he was a short man, just skin and
bones probably nearing eighty, he had a smile that was so grateful to have
made a connection somewhere in life.

Fred and I got to know each other a bit, he said his Gabby had passed
away last month and he was raising money for her burial, he walked around

looking for the perfect spot, this explained his actions. He confided in me that her ashes were inside a large white bear in the passenger seat, someday he would lay her to rest but even if he had the money now, he wasn't ready for that. I told him about Charlene who is up the hill and why I work here, explained she is my wife and has been gone for just over three years. When I said that Fred smiled. It made me wonder why, then I realized he was a lonely man and had found a connection with me. That's when I told him the story of the flowers showing up mysteriously, he liked that someone cared for my wife enough to leave flowers, he seemed sentimental. Fred and I talked through Thanksgiving, Christmas and New Year's almost daily, he was a comfort to me, someone else just trying their best to get through the season of celebrations in a new way. One day I brought Fred a coffee, he said the next one is on me and was true to his word.

2016

Frederick aka Kobus

July 2016

I HAVE BEEN OUT FOR ONE OF MY LONG DRIVES, DRIVING IS SOMETHING I CAN usually control. Of course, there were the three accidents in the past year, truth be told they can only prove one was my fault. The other two totaled my cars and left me sore, but no closer to Gabby. They were just freak accidents, something that happened. At least the people had insurance and I got two new cars, new to me anyway. The discount insurance that Holly had found for me was canceled due to being involved in three accidents within a single year. They said "it was their policy", I thought the insurance was my policy? Sometimes words throw me off balance, as I can't read it's hard to grasp their multiple meanings.

It was a beautiful crisp day; the leaves were just starting to change, and you could smell the snow on the mountain, the beautiful mountain where I always felt a connection to my wife. Gabby and I had an agreement that whoever went first would scatter the ashes in our secret location, one that we went to many times for our picnics and other activities. The first of my accidents happened near this location, this is the first time I had been there without Gabby physically, her ashes were in the front seat next to me. I figured it was best to scatter them before the snow fell, I couldn't bring myself do it and as I left a car came out of nowhere, totaled the last car Gabby and I had together, it still had her name on the documents. We purchased many cars in our time, they were all special since they gave us freedom but this one was our last car together, the last one she had ridden in. I removed what I could of our personal belongings, the big stuffed bear Gabby insisted ride with us everywhere, her beaded necklace that hung from the rearview mirror, her shoes, our blanket and picnic basket filled with fast food, today just a couple of burgers, my thermos of coffee and her ashes. As I got into that big tow truck with our car on the flatbed, I kept looking back knowing I needed to look forward but didn't know why I couldn't do it. Somehow this made the second broken connection from our life together, the first being her death. All the pieces of Gabby that remain are in my arms, my memories and photographs. I thought I could do this today, the ashes still with me and couldn't release them. Now look at what's happened, maybe it is a sign to move on, it is a nice day, Gabby would want me to move on but I can't grasp the reality of what the picture would look like without her in it, she is with me in this truck.

All my boxes are packed, I can't afford to live here anymore without both of our incomes, she had finally qualified for disability benefits. My job is lost due to health problems and old age; the heart and body are not what they used to be but keep going for some reason. Funny how a small one-bedroom apartment, the basic box, can cost so much. We struggled to hold onto this for years, neither one of us could navigate the stairs to the second story, we would watch each other as we took each step but knew we couldn't afford to move. We also knew if the other one fell, we would be unable to catch them. We must have had angels watching over us on our continued flights up to home. When Gabby's mind started going, she didn't know how to cook anymore or do simple things like laundry, I cooked for the first time in my life. Never had so many sandwiches, hot dogs and potato salad, Gabby didn't complain, I was lucky she ate at all, but it took me a while to discover she wanted it cut up. One day she left with our clothes in the laundry basket headed for the community laundry room in our complex, I couldn't find her and I was so worried when the hospital called me saying she was there with our laundry and detergent, the detergent didn't belong there. Which hospital? I hadn't caught the name and we didn't have caller ID or voice mail like the rest of the world, I went to the one not too far across town. There Gabby was, still holding our laundry, she wasn't setting it down, seemed funny she was in that room with the laundry and was worried about the detergent and didn't have a clue that she had been lost, had ridden in an ambulance, that she was in the hospital or that I was worried. It was things like this that made me wonder if it was my mind or if I was living in an alternate reality. She had been taken by ambulance after she couldn't tell the police who she was, where she belonged or why she had a basket of men's and women's clothing. Me not being able to read did not help, she had always helped me with things like the mail, paying bills, employment forms and health insurance. We had spent hundreds of dollars on co-pays and the doctors kept saying go elsewhere for testing, we didn't have any more money for all the co-pays without answers, it seemed no one was there to help, she looked healthy but was slipping. She had never worked outside of the home, and I didn't make much working for a local charity. An elderly service tried to help but I think it was too late in the day, her mind was already deteriorating past repair or reason. I would be paying for the groceries or looking at a can of soup and turn around, Gabby was nowhere to be found. She would already be out the door of the grocery store and across the street, as I ran out on my unsteady legs catching a glimpse of my silver cart of groceries, left abandoned and taking off to chase my wife or at least attempt to locate her.

So now I've moved in with Trillium, this is a strange arrangement but is good for both of us to at least have someone to check on each day. We haven't lived together since we were sixteen and seventeen years old, we are now seventy-five and seventy-six. How could sixty years have gone by so quickly? For now, this is the best for both of us, I rent a room in her house, with my three boxes and a different car to park in the already crowded driveway. The location is handy for my work just across the bridge that I may be able to go back to, it is my freedom, allows me money and to smile at the people giving away their possessions that they only purchased last year. It's an outing for me, a purpose and I get money. If I couldn't work anymore, I am not sure what I would do.

Gabby

November 2016

FRED INSISTS I AM WITH HIM AND HE IS RIGHT, IT SEEMS WE ARE SEPARATED, AND I am separated but a part of me is stuck because he isn't willing to let me go, he knows I am gone. Like when he went to spread my ashes and couldn't, our life and everything in it disappeared. I watched him one day when no one was looking, he had my urn under his bulky brown winter coat and was walking with a tilt on his unsteady booted feet as he went across the imperfect lawn. He stopped by a tree, the biggest one in the cemetery, probably so he could remember exactly where he had left me and he dumped my ashes around the base of that tree, the tree without leaves, it was standing tall and bracing itself for winter, the day right before Thanksgiving. I wonder what he will do this year but then I know, he will be here looking for me but I am gone and if he would only move on, so could I.

It feels unsettling to be here and not be here at the same time. Maybe it's me who hasn't let go? It's hard to watch Fred as he goes through his days with nothing to do, he doesn't understand how to return through to the normal rhythms of life, he stays steadfast in the alternate reality universe just for the sake of me still being here when, in fact, I am not, I am only here when he pulls me back from a memory. Of course, he has lived in an alternate universe among the other humans all his life, his system works for him but doesn't fit into the reality of what happens here, maybe we all have a predictable sequence that works for each person.

Bob

November 2016

About the time I met Fred I was starting to heal, beginning to see an impact from the job I was doing. At first, it was just being there, close to where my heart drew me and a job, now I see it is so much more. People recognized me, appreciate my efforts in keeping the grounds clean, they like my distance in their own form of grief so they appreciate my distance and sometimes wave as they drive out. I know there are grief classes, but could never bring myself in all these years to talk to strangers about Charlene and what I do besides work here, which is nothing, getting back on track to living has been a slow process but one I want to get right.

2017

Frederick

March 2017

ONE DAY AT WORK I'M NOT FEELING TOO GOOD, MY HEART IS SKIPPING AND MY stomach is rolling, they say I need to see the cardiologist after a referral from the doctor that removed the tumors on my head last year, I didn't ask if they were cancerous and can't read the report, so I still don't know. Doesn't matter to me either way, this time they say I need a pacemaker and I can't work anymore. I find it odd that I am just existing, trying to get by day by day and they want to prolong this, maybe I have a purpose?

After too many appointments, hospital stays and pretty nurses, the day of the installation is here. The pacemaker is in and I made it through the operation. I don't understand technology at all and now I am monitored from afar every day. What people don't understand is that during many of these procedures you are awake enough to feel, pains that are remembered years later.

I scattered Gabby's ashes before my surgery, not knowing what may happen to me while under the knife. Since I can't read road signs, doctors instructions or anything else I have all these sayings to help me get through; "under the knife, behind the wheel, over the bridge (where I can't go anymore), up the hill, by the bank". I seem to frequent the same restaurants, the ones with pictures on the menus, have never eaten any foreign food because I don't know what's in it, I just say I don't like it to avoid further embarrassment for me and the person offering. If I need to go somewhere now there is always a trial run since Gabby isn't with me to help direct the way, she was good with maps, now I must go and compare address numbers with the ones written on the rectangular appointment cards.

You know one thing I always liked were people, every age of people, all colors, we are entirely different and alike at the same time, if I approach them happily, they are happy. I am not a menacing man, but short and generally pleasant in brief encounters. I drove to Cle Elum last weekend and had pie with different faces, but I know, besides the truckers, who the usual's are. You see I don't have one place but frequent many since I have all day, every day. The same people seem to return to their usual hangouts, that's how I met my friends at the Corner Café. When I walk in and smell the burnt coffee and grease, see the torn up red diner booths and scratched tables, that's when I know I am home and accepted. Sitting there all day is comforting, sometimes all I do is observe, eat a pancake and drink coffee. People here probably know I am lost but they don't know much about me, just that Gabby is not there anymore. I go there when I don't have much gas money because it is close to home if you can call where I live home. We all greet each other with "how ya doing?" but usually no one answers, we just nod and smile, occasionally someone tells big news good or bad. We all have the same form of relationship; we know each other enough, whatever we chose to share would be accepted. I accept every one of them has a story, but it is not mine to know so I make one up for each person, makes my visits more fun.

In my head, the waitress Sally lives in her mom's basement that has old olive colored shag carpet, with coffee cans filled with coins from tips, the washing machine whirrs as she tries to sleep and the old furnace hums and smells like natural gas. She doesn't pay rent, so all the tips are hers, her only expenses are those long brown cigarettes she smokes and her clothing. She probably drives the beat-up gray Buick in the parking lot that is parked way in back like it's hiding.

The cook Dale is a young guy but looks like he has been through some stuff. He has a scar that runs from under the left side of his chin to his right ear, looks like he might have found some trouble somewhere or been the problem himself. I heard his grandpa owns the barbershop I use, I bet he lives in the back and cleans the barbershop for rent, he seems too shady to have a real life outside of here. All I know about him is that he is a good cook.

I have heard the owners of the Corner Café live in the country and have horses. I bet they have a mansion and life is grand for them. I am thankful they have given us all a place to be ourselves and hope they are happy.

I hear that the Corner Café will be closing next week. This is devastating news to me since it is where I sat and cut Gabby's food for her last. All the things and places we had in our shared life are changing, gone or closing. All of us regulars are invited to one last meal there, instead of my usual pancake I got a cheeseburger and fries because that is what Gabby would have eaten, I even cut it up like she would have preferred and ordered extra pickles on the side.

Gabby and I have a secret; we were together for thirty-six years but thirty years in we got divorced. Not because we didn't want to be together but because we needed more resources for her health and together, we didn't qualify. No one knew of this crazy event, we had to go to a different county, so it wasn't in the local newspaper. That was devastating to both of us, in our heads we were married all along. About three weeks before she passed, maybe it wasn't right, she didn't recognize me all the time, but we got married again. We had a friend who was able to perform marriages come into the hospital room, no one knew what was going on. I had carnations and even a three-layer chocolate cake. Gabby was all dressed in her special maroon nightgown with the red roses embroidered on it. So, when she left this earth, we were one, husband and wife just like we were forever meant to be. That has been such an enormous secret it feels like a weight has been lifted off my chest to have released it.

After the Corner Café closed in December, I didn't know where to go. Some afternoons there had been lunch with Holly, but she was extremely busy, and I didn't know her at all after being out of her life the majority of it. I think I had only seen her a dozen or so times in our lifetime, I wasn't good at that connection, and I couldn't see past losing Gabby, that was all that was in front of me even though, in reality, it was behind me and I was allowing it to surround me. It was hard to grieve for Gabby and with my new existence at Trillium's house when I couldn't relate to anyone or even work, I didn't know how to move on, it was like a part was missing that everyone else had. The only thing I could control was where I went when I could afford the gas money, I made trips everywhere that Gabby and I had previously gone. I would pretend she was with me, but I was tired and sick, she was gone, our car, café, apartment was all gone too, what was left was me. That was when I started driving through the City Square Cemetery, one day I parked and went for a walk, I couldn't read the names but could figure out the dates always looking for ones that had significance to me, some close to my birthday or an anniversary, sometimes I would even move the flowers from grave to grave. Most days I would end up there, seemed like my car was on autopilot, I had found a place of peace, after walking I would nap in the new car, comfortable in a sense even I didn't understand. In some way it made me feel closer to Gabby, I had no idea that someone had been watching me, one day I was approached by a ground's keeper named Bob. I always wondered if he had seen me move the flowers, I never took them just spread the happiness, I guess, it's become kind of a game sometimes moving the same flowers multiple times. I think I like Bob, seems like he may understand people, his eyes seem all-knowing. I hope he didn't see me do the other thing before my surgery.

Detective Munser

April 2017

SOME OF OUR GUYS ESPECIALLY THE ONES WITH FAMILIES WERE ON VACATION with spring break and all, it was sometime in mid-April. I didn't generally respond to homicides but got called out in the wee hours of the morning to cover a crime scene in West Seattle. I took a minute to drink my coffee and dress for the day since there would be no returning to my home anytime soon. I made sure I grabbed my winter coat on the way out, the winds can bring the cold saltwater across Alki Avenue at this time of year. I said good-bye to my only responsibility, a house plant I had found with a stick in it that had the name "Margo" attached. I made my way across the darkened street to my car and headed south on I-5 to the West Seattle Freeway. The views are spectacular up here, especially at this time of night without rush hour traffic when I can take the time to look at Harbor Island and the ships. I need something to be thankful for because of what I'm heading towards, who knows what this may entail or who I may be questioning in an hour or six later.

As I approach the secured scene there are already officers that I know in attendance, we seem to meet up at unfortunate cases like this, we nod at the sad remembrance of other crime scenes and know we will add this to our list. There wasn't a reason to suggest that a crime had been committed except the picture I was presented of the body of a young red-haired girl/lady behind an ice cream shop, she was beautiful. No signs of a physical struggle or tyre marks, nothing. The medics said she appeared to have been there for about four hours, was extremely cold and barely breathing. They rushed her to the hospital where they found a slip of paper in her pocket that was from the ice cream shop. She was either a customer, had made a purchase or an employee handing out an order. It didn't look as if she had been dumped, it looked like she had just laid down, my job was to find out who she was and why was laying behind the eatery on this cold night.

After waking the shop owner and giving a description of the young lady we knew her name, Iris Mortelli. They offered to look in her file to locate an emergency contact, I declined, figuring I could get that from her driver's license that was located in her back pocket versus waiting for the owner to go to the store and retrieve it. A call I hated to make, to her family, certainly at such an early hour and to someone many miles away. Before dialing I picture their day getting underway, the aroma of coffee or toast that will be lodged into their brain now and forever as bad news, I can't wait, I ask for Vernon Mortelli, he said, "this is him, how may I help you?" I was calling to give horrific news and he was asking how he could help me, this made me regret not having someone else do this part of police work. I explained all I knew and asked if there was someone local for Iris, he told me about Daniel but didn't have a number had only met him twice, a nice young man he said.

After arranging an emergency flight and obtaining a taxi they arrived at the hospital in Seattle, hours later. Mr Mortelli told his wife about needing to get ahold of Daniel, she had his number, Iris had called her from it when her phone had been dead a few weeks ago while they were on the road. Mr Mortelli called Daniel, but no answer, they gave the number to Detective Munser. Daniel arrived within minutes of getting the call, the detective talked to him but wasn't sure if he was a suspect or not, there weren't any clues anywhere. Daniel said he hadn't seen Iris since the day before which was normal for them, also stated no one had any problems with her including him. After days of research the only clue they had was from Stuart, another employee who had seen Iris drive out of the employee parking onto the street in her VW Bug while he sat at the curb out front waiting for her to leave safely, said she pulled out and waved. There were some holes in this story, Stuart and Daniel, where were Iris' possessions? Her new turquoise gemmed cell phone, a slew of bracelets, car, backpack, laptop and whatever else a busy young lady stores in her car, probably towels, clothing, shoes, cooler, games, volleyball and books. Not one piece of anything was left at the scene, if Stuart were involved, he would have had to hide the car or have an accomplice. His alibi panned out, he went straight home to his parents after work, arrived fourteen minutes after clocking out, their alarm history verified that. Daniel was another story; we didn't know anything about him, no alibi, said he was sleeping at his apartment. We checked the traffic cameras and saw Iris' VW get on the West Seattle Freeway heading to Beacon Hill around 11:00 pm then no traffic cam sighting until about 3:30 am headed southbound I-5 to Tacoma, there wasn't a shot where we could see the driver's face, only overhead pictures, but it was Iris' green VW for sure. Someone parked the car and got out downtown on Pacific Avenue, didn't take anything from the car, ascended a flight of stairs up one block and disappeared. We never saw a face but went to retrieve the car and it was gone, there was nothing on the cam to see it disappear. We only knew this case had to be solved because Iris was lying in a hospital bed for no apparent reason, there wasn't a motive to this crime just a young lady with family in limbo, life and death being the question of them all.

Daniel

May 2017

HELLO, I AM DANIEL METTENBURG, CURRENTLY, I AM TWENTY-FOUR YEARS OLD and wish I weren't in this book. People my age shouldn't have to think about anything like this, you see it happen on the news but don't think it will happen to you, this time it is personal, closer than real life. I don't want to be connected to this story in any way but because of the sequence of events that occurred almost three years ago I am placed here beyond everything that I hoped in my being. I have memorized every moment of this story, it is etched in my mind, I don't even know how to process this situation and move forward, the concept of that is not in my grasp. One moment I want to scream, the next break things, the next cry a million tears and then the next emotion is no emotion at all, just needing sleep and being numb but the cycle starts over again as I don't have any previous experience with this. None of the cycles happen they are just residing my head; I have always been in full control of my emotions since I was a small child. You see I am a former foster child, taken away from my mother Sylvia Watson at five years old, one day like many others, she left me in our pathetic little apartment, behind the yarn store. There was a small weathered staircase that was slippery due to the worn off roofing shingles when it rained or iced up, if anyone were on it the rickety planks would make an eerie sound almost like a groan, like it was too much for the staircase to bear the weight. I had been alone for a couple of days which was normal for me, the nightlight was on, I heard some people on the stairs and thought it was my mom coming in from God knows where. I was excited not to be alone even though with mom home you never knew what could happen or who she would bring traipsing in with her acting like they owned the place. I looked out through the broken slat in the old wooden blind, next thing I know the police have the building surrounded and they want me to come out with my hands up, I was just a little guy scared out of my wits. When I bravely came out and down the stairs, they didn't believe me that no one else was up there, they kept telling me it was ok to tell the truth, but I already had. You see a man was on the stairs drinking whiskey and they saw me in the window and thought the guy was a lookout for someone robbing the yarn shop because our apartment wasn't really an apartment, it was just a storage space and it was the back way into the store. Well they took me away and no one ever found mom, I have no idea who Mr Mettenburg, my supposed father is, he most likely doesn't know about me either. I didn't finish high school because I couldn't be homeless and graduate once the foster care checks stopped my roof and meals ended. Joe and Sylvia, my foster parents came to me one night, Joe was a skinny guy with an eye that twitched when he was nervous, he was twitching so I knew something was up that didn't look good for me. They said they needed to open my room for a paying child, Sylvia in her usual uniform of a dirty housecoat and slippers said I had been a good boy and they wished me well, being someone's paycheck always left you a bit on the edge. You never knew when the road would end or, should I say, the roof would disappear. I left as they asked, spent some time with the other runaways and people downtown for a few days. I wish I had been more prepared for this, my main goal was to graduate but that seemed a distant memory now. I knew I needed a real job and didn't want to make being homeless a profession as some people did. I met Eddie one night, he was in his fifties but looked like he was about eighty, he told me there were people who had been out on the streets a dozen years or more. He talked like it was a badge of honor to stay homeless, it is a tough line of work but not for me, I loved my roof.

Mr. Filbert had seen me around for a few days, he asked if I was interested in employment, he was nice enough to let me clean his shop and stay for my wage. Told me not to let anyone know I was living there as he could get a visit from the authorities. I eventually started a fulltime job with Mr. Filbert and that is how this all began, I think. Maybe it began back when the police surrounded my house in 2001?

I was working one hot summer day, August 4th, 2016 to be exact at Filbert Auto Glass and the most beautiful lady came in. She had long red hair, green eyes and the biggest embarrassed smile I had ever seen, she also had about twenty bracelets in all primary colors and was a lot to take in, her being seemed to take up the whole parking lot or at least all of my mind. She needed a wind shield, her story spilled out like it was pushed, she said they had been playing hacky sack with her college friends and one of the guys landed on the windshield, was worried about her parents having to pay for it or their insurance rates going up, they had been scraping everything together to send her to college. She was working part time at an ice cream store by the beach to pay the rent, I sold her the windshield at cost and installed it for free upon Mr. Filbert's suggestion.

I found out Iris Mortelli was twenty-three years old, from Armstrong, Iowa and studying marine biology in Seattle. She loved the beach as she didn't grow up around one. Volleyball and bonfires were her passion. She wasn't always available to see me in the nine months we knew each other. She studied and worked hard, her parents came out for Christmas and met me, I was over three years younger than Iris and they were concerned about their daughters wellbeing and my intentions, but by spring break, we were still seeing each other and even drove all the way to Iowa. I got half a day off and we left on a Friday afternoon, it was St. Patrick's Day, we joked because her car was green, took us a couple days each way. She would sleep and I would drive I woke up in a new land. I had lived in Seattle my whole life, never even ventured outside the city limits, that must have been my comfort zone, something I could control. This Iowa thing and all the miles in between was totally new for me, wide open spaces, everything was there just smaller and less of it. The lakes were so small they didn't have names, the golf course had bigger ponds than the lakes, it was also the friendliest place I had been, everyone knew everyone. Iris' parents Vernon and Cookie were some of the kindest people I had met in my whole life. I couldn't imagine growing up in this town, in a house with parents that loved you enough to help you fulfill your dream, even loved you enough to give the sacrifice of you leaving.

A couple weeks after Spring break and we were back in the swing of work for me and school / work for Iris. We were supposed to see each other the next day because she was working a double shift at Scoop It Frozen Creamery today. We sometimes saw each other every other day, some days it was just to share a basket of fish and chips for dinner on Alki beach as I was getting off work and she was just getting ready to start her shift, I swear we knew some of the seagulls from the way they swooped down to ask for French fries.

After a long day at work, I had just fallen asleep in my recliner, I received a call from a number I didn't recognize early the next morning. It was local, I decided to see if they would leave a message as no one ever called me on a normal day. After checking my voicemail, it was Iris' dad Mr. Mortelli, he said I should make my way to the hospital quickly, they had just arrived from Iowa, that was the entire message. I still have it; it is my one main connection besides this city, her braided black bracelet, and my memories of Iris. She had been getting off work and been robbed behind the ice cream shop. Robbed of her car and nothing important in it, the only thing of importance was Iris. The reason the employees were supposed to leave in pairs and never alone was for utmost security, but Iris had parked in the employee parking and Stuart was out on the street, it was hours before they found her laying in the parking lot behind the shop. Her green VW Beetle, the twelve dollars that she made in tips, her life, spirit, soul, mind, all of her being and my sanity were gone. I was empty, nothing was supposed to happen like this, we were young, not in trouble but making our way the best we knew how. She was twenty-four years old, was supposed to use what she had learned in school and graduate. I had the ticket for the ceremony in my pocket that was a sure thing, not this phone call, a call that needs to be erased from the story of our lives.

Iris' parents were good to me, they treated me like one of their own, when the various doctors came in with somber faces and tried to tell us of the nonprogress, they always let me be there and hear the report firsthand. The first doctor said Iris had a lot of brain injury and there wasn't much hope, but time would tell, maybe a few days and the reports might look different, all we could do was wait, so we did. Her parents told me they were happy she had met me and felt she was safer being with me in such a big city, that they had been terrified of her leaving their cocoon of life in Iowa but had to let her go and fulfill her passion. I always wonder if anyone feels I should have been there that night, that's the thought that runs through my head on a nonstop reel, what if, what if, what if?

After seventeen more days, May 3rd at 7:29pm, they unplugged all life sustaining equipment. It was so quiet you don't realize how noisy all the life support machines are until they are off, realizing this was the silence before the real end, the one we had not been prepared for but had been sitting here at this hospital with only hope. We all stood there watching the monitor and seeing the heartbeat but no brain activity, we all hoped and prayed, we each spent a few minutes saying all that was in our hearts and minds to Iris and waited. On May 4th, 2017 at 5:04am Iris passed away with me on the bed next to her, her mom and dad in fold out plastic recliners across the room. The sudden noise of the flat line startled us into where we are today, where I am today, there is no turning back from this point in the story.

Iris

~fl~

May 20/7

GOOD MORNING, I GUESS I HAVE ALWAYS BEEN A MORNING PERSON, DADDY USED to wake me up at the crack of dawn to ride the tractor with him, that was our special time. We used to play a game to see if I could keep from spilling his water while he drove over the rows of fragrant plowed earth, he grew so much produce the local stores would buy from him, they depended on our family for certain products every year. I am Iris Mortelli, summertime was my favorite time of year, we would go on dad's boat to all the events on Lake Okoboji, the 4th of July celebrations were the best with the barge and all the people. I think our whole days out on the water were what stirred up my curiosity and led me to marine biology. I loved the idea of preserving and protecting the waterways, I wanted to do my part in helping different communities in their struggles with pollution and erosion, I also would include courses in aquatic biology in my studies. After visiting the National Mississippi River Museum and Aquarium for my junior year field trip I knew that was what I for sure wanted to have as a career. Our school would organize clean up days for our water ways, dad and I always helped with those.

I was accepted into a special program in Seattle, WA, then to tell my parents that I was leaving, surprisingly, they took the news well, as they always wanted the best for me, I knew they would worry. I had to work a year to cover some of the costs but in the summer 2014 we loaded dad's truck with most of my earthly belongings and had Sweet Pea my 1974 neon green VW Beetle on a trailer behind us. I am sure my parents were worried, but they never blinked an eye or shed a tear, they always said we are here for you and know you will do well so that was the only option for me, they were counting on me. I had a job lined up at Scoop It Frozen Creamery, an ice cream shop on the beach and a rented room close to campus that works for a place to sleep. As far as school went, we were on the beaches around the Puget Sound and on Lake Washington more than in a classroom, many of our scheduled lectures were online so I could be anywhere. It was a rigorous schedule but it was so much fun, we would go from school to volleyball and bonfires in minutes all in one location. Washington was different than Iowa, no huge snowstorms and the summers were not as scorching. I went home a few times but didn't want to lose much time at work as I didn't want to depend on my parents and their tight farming budget.

Then, in my junior year I met Daniel. There was something steady about him, adding him to my life and schedule was challenging due to my obligations but well worth it, he was possibly the best person I had ever met outside my family. I was twenty-three and he was nineteen almost twenty but going on 40, he was so calm and let me stew in my embarrassment of a broken windshield. He also had a kind spirit and helped me out by installing the windshield on his own time.

Daniel knew Seattle well; I didn't even know that he'd never left the city until we were in Iowa on my spring break. I guess I didn't show him our lake while we were there, but he was used to huge lakes like Lake Washington, he had friends with boats and knew how to water ski quite well, would show me tricks that he called by his own names; plane dog, jump rover, over saddle. I'm sure he made those names up but he was good at them.

Daniel didn't tell me much about himself until between Christmas and New Year when my parents had just flown back home, and I was missing them terribly. His whole story came out, it was a shock to hear everything that had happened to him and he was still okay, I was impressed that it didn't show on him, he fit right in everywhere and I would have never known. I am glad I met Daniel but am not so sure it was good for him especially how it all ended and changed his life course. Of course, we never know what may happen in life minute by minute, one second you could get the best news or the worst delivered. I know Daniel and I loved each other deeply, it was in that huge old hospital on the hill overlooking downtown that I realized what we had felt was like years of knowing each other, possibly decades like we were on the same rhythm but I couldn't move, my ears could hear and my body could feel, there just wasn't a way to respond. I was too young to realize the depth of any relationship until my last few days on earth. I'm sure nobody really knew if I could hear them, I could, and I believed them, but I couldn't seem to come back from where I was deep within a dimension. Maybe the fear of failure was overpowering or the fear of success and the man who robbed me gave me a way out, he definitely gave me some time to pause and make decisions.

I never even saw him, I remember unsteady footsteps, even if I woke up I wouldn't be able to give them clues. He yelled at me, I started to turn around and he grabbed my neck so I couldn't see him, I asked him something I don't remember, but he hit me on the head. My last thought was being cold and then I was warm with light and unfamiliar noises. Then I heard familiar voices, dad was telling Daniel they were glad he had been with me all this time. I know Daniel felt responsible for not being with me, but our store had a strict policy that no one should ever leave alone. I guess when Stuart saw me drive out, he went on his way home himself after a long day. What he didn't realize is that the person with the hoodie driving wasn't me, I feel bad for Stuart, but it wasn't his fault either. It was just something that happened, I wish I could tell Stuart to not blame himself but that is beyond my capabilities now.

They decided on May 3rd to unplug me. I am not sure if there is truth to this, but I felt there was an option to at least control the length of time I was there without all the tubes. It was May 4th at 4:30 am, all was quiet, I could hear dad's steady breathing and slight snore, mom occasionally made a faint noise but what mattered most to me was that it was quiet and

Daniel was on the bed with his arm draped over my waist. They had all been here nonstop for a little over two weeks if I am right, I still have a sense of time, talking, eating, crying and begging me to come back. I know they were exhausted and frustrated, am sure they felt helpless. Daniel read my graduation invitation a few times, he was so proud of me and excited to go to the ceremony. I will miss all my near and dear people, but I don't know how to find the hole back to the spot I was in before. I love you all and will see you on the other side. Be safe, be well, rest and heal 5:04am May 4th_____

2018

Detective Munser

August 2018

It had been a long year, actually over a year without any leads on Iris' case, at the end of a hot summer with plenty of activity on the beach, I got a call from fellow Agent Flagstaff. He was working with a federal agency as it was a federal employee that had found a guy with some strange possessions, he had been reminded of Iris' bracelets and called me. I drove to the west precinct where they had the suspect, Vincent, detained. He had been sleeping between the sidewalk and street, appeared dead, a mail man who we dubbed "Ratchet man", with a bad hip and a jerky walk had seen Vincent and called 911, the EMT had remembered the bracelets and told the detective of his suspicions. After interviewing Vincent, he stated he was asleep in the dumpster corral hoping for a meal and saw Iris laying there, thinking she was dead, he removed the bracelets, right off her arm. He did hear her car leave but said that was normal, he slept there almost every night, usually two cars leave at once, he waited for the second one and it never came. He exited the big green dumpster containment, peaked around the corner and the parking lot was empty. The ice cream shop was last to close, he stayed there so he could check the dumpsters at all the restaurants along the beachfront walkway after most people had gone to their safe, warm homes, he hoped never to be seen by anyone ever in his quest for food. He said he just fell asleep on the sidewalk today, maybe had partaken in too much of something, sometimes that happened with him, felt lucky he wasn't run over. He didn't match the stocky build of the person on camera we had leaving the car, said he would continue to stay living where he had been staying for over three years. Seemed sad as he peeled off the bracelets one by one, acknowledging the colors, blue, turquoise, black, like he had formed a relationship with the jewelry, said he had never had anything so special and he was sorry he had stolen them from the sweet dead girl who sometimes brought him ice cream, chocolate his favorite, he will miss her. This is not our suspect but another step in the investigation. Meeting Vincent was a pleasure as my usual suspects are not remorseful or as transparent as him. There is much to be thankful for in a day, even meeting Ratchet Man knowing he is pounding the streets too just in a different way, another public servant. My occupation is solo most of the time so I am grateful when I meet people who are an asset to the community, I would say both men are.

Luther

December 2018

WELL HERE I AM, LUTHER WASHINGTON I WAS NAMED AFTER MY MAMA'S DADDY, Grandfather Luther Maxwell Washington. I came from a long line of Luther Washington's, we all had different middle names, it was a family tradition for the first son to be named Luther and the middle name used was the maiden name of the mother, well my mama was something else, she named me Luther Apollo Washington. She was a wild one and a dreamer, had been learning everything she could about the Apollo Theater in Harlem, said she was heading there someday soon. She thought that was probably where my daddy had gone off to and was going to find him, we lived in Austell, Georgia. There might have been 1000 people in our town if you count the ones who had already left for bigger destinations, everyone had room to move around and be themselves. I think I was a businessman from the day I was born and was left to my own thoughts most of the time, momma never paid me any attention unless I was on the wrong side of her. Once I had worked and bartered to get a bicycle, I rode all over town and collected any bottle I could find and turned them in for the deposit. Mama worked as a maid for different folks, she seemed to like it and her and her pretty friends that would be out most of the night. We lived with grandma Clara on Robin Road (mostly I lived with Grandma Clara) after daddy took off and Grandpa Luther passed on, we were there to help her mama said. I was sad when Grandma Clara took ill and passed on, things got different real fast.

Mama said we had to leave Austell and live in Atlanta with her cousin Marcella. Austell was the only place I had ever known, and I had never been across the county line for anything in all my nine years. We packed up what we could in grandma's Plymouth Savoy with the shiny fins, I would pretend we were flying, the wind whipping around the seat to me in the back, we headed out for our new place. It was amusing to see this many people all at once, fast and noisy, I had never seen so many cars, roads or commotion. We stayed in a small guest cottage behind the main house on Robin Hood Road, which was easy to remember since we had just left Robin Road. It was nicer than Grandma Clara's house with the big expanse of yard and long driveway. Marcella was sweet to me; she would often leave me treats under the aluminum white tin cake cover with swirly blue flowers that she had on the back porch. I suspect it was her old cake cover but the treats inside were fabulous. I don't think she cooked but had enough money to share the treats with me, I knew someday I needed to be able to have enough money to share too. Marcella taught me about working hard, "don't listen anyone's negative remarks," she would say, "stay on your mission." That is what I did and what got me so far in life, thank you Marcella for guiding my way!

I think this is where I gained momentum. Outside of school I had most of the time to myself, I collected so many bottles that I needed a basket for my blue Schwinn Ballooner bicycle that I bought for two dollars at a garage sale. I found an old wire basket frame for the front by an alley and a milk crate for the back that I had to tie on with some rope from Marcella, I was going into business. One day, while I was out and had an unusually large load of bottles my bicycle had a flat and I met Mr. Stickle of Stickle's Tire Company. He fixed my flat for free and asked if I would like to learn about tires, he said "son there is big money in tires". He taught me all he knew, now I can tell you all there was to know about a tire, a few years later Washington Tire Company bought out Mr. Stickle and offered me a job at Mr. Stickles recommendation, they said they were going nationwide in no time at all. Mr. Stickle was the starting point of my foundation, if it weren't for him who knows what I would be doing, maybe still peddling bottles for a deposit. I managed that store I called "Stickle's" until I was twenty-four years old and they asked me if I wanted to move to Seattle, WA and manage my own store. I saw no reason not to go except Simone whom I had met a short time ago, she was my deciding factor. Mama had since taken off for New York and I had been at the cottage alone helping Marcella for the past few years. I talked this idea over with Marcella and she encouraged me to be on my way if that is what my destiny was, said she would miss me.

I met Simone one day when she brought her car in for tires, what a fine young lady, said she worked at the bank, she also agreed to have supper with me. I suppose she thought I owned the store since the name of the tire shop and my last name are the same, she also thought I owned the nice house that was Marcella's after asking where I lived. Before I could accept the job in Seattle, I had to let Simone know the truth, ask her to marry me and see if she would go with me on my life's journey, she said yes and yes. She was looking to move somewhere new and a branch of her bank was also in Seattle. So, on July 7, 1977 (7/7/77) my beautiful Simone Edwards and myself, Luther Washington, were married in Atlanta, GA in the old Baptist church downtown, it was a small wedding, a few of our friends were there and Marcella. For wedding presents Marcella gave us a new car and Simone's family gave us a large check, one bigger than I had ever seen. We had decided to make the trip across the country for our honeymoon, the USA was ours that year, almost coast to coast, 2600 miles of freedom in our new life, no job, no worries, no stress, just me and my new wife getting to know each other for a whole month. Neither of us had been west of Atlanta, everyday there was different scenery to see; The Grand Canyon was something else, who could even fathom something so deep and with animals that were like zoo creatures running wild, crossing mountains with beauty so intense you would start singing *America the Beautiful*. We were happy now and excited for new adventures ahead.

I was more than proud of who I had become with my wife and the Washington Tire Company. We started just Simone and I in a one-bedroom apartment in a four story walk up, with walls so thin you could hear the neighbors fart. We knew we had to move by the end of our one-year lease. Then came the babies, looking back so much had happened, we bought the elegant two-story house with a large picture window, a basement and garage so our children would live in a safe and stable community not far from my work. I think we were the only black family in the neighborhood when we moved in, we knew most of the neighbors from the tire store, race was never a trouble for me, maybe it was my confidence and ability to help that allowed me to sail through life. There were the usual family, everyday troubles but nothing we couldn't handle, it seemed either Simone or I were equipped for whatever came up.

But there was one moment that had me stumped; in 2007 after thirty years of driving cars a customer brought in a new smaller import, one like I had never seen before, it was a black, shiny, contoured model, fancy and sleek. They wanted nicer tires than the factory ones, that happens all the time and they never want the factory tires back, they dropped off the car and said they would return. They forgot to leave the keys, I laughed so hard when I found out there wasn't a key, it had a push button start. I think that was the funniest moment of my career. Pretty soon those push button cars were popping up everywhere, and they all had remote openers. It always made me feel like I had control of something when I could jump in a vehicle and bring it around for tires, I couldn't count how many cars I have driven. The time that one didn't start with a key made me consider what else I may not have control of, I know one thing I did that no one knew about. I would save all the new factory tires for the people who really needed them, that was my gift of safety to Seattle and the struggling people, safety of children and who knows who else. A tire is an important tool, I consider myself lucky to be able to pass on the blessing of what was given to me, I think it's what kept my business going. I will let my lovely wife Simone take over from here, she probably has something to say about our story and is an awesome storyteller.

Simone

HELLO EVERYONE, I AM SIMONE EDWARDS-WASHINGTON, I WAS BORN AND raised in Rock Hill, SC. My father owned acres and acres of treed farmland; he rented some out to other local farmers but mostly we farmed peaches. Those trees kept me entertained and goal driven, in the summer we would all be out there with the hired hands to make sure the peaches were being boxed and transported right. Autumn is when we would repair, plant and prune trees, sometimes we would run across green snakes as we were pruning the water shoots. Father taught us that in the winter we should make plans for the next year so when spring came around, we would already know what was to be done, he had a system that occupied us all every day of the year, father was a planner, he was never left unaware of the next step. They also provided me with a nice house, the best clothing and training, my father, Thomas Edwards, was a real businessman. My mother, Evelyn, ran the house and sewed, she belonged to every quilting bee in York County and beyond. We had quilted table runners, quilts for our beds, potholders, lined curtains with quilted edges, just like every other household belonging to the quilting group. They would save their scraps and make quilts for babies, the needy, birthdays, for auctions and raffles, that's what they lived for, beauty in fabric.

After graduation I was accepted into Emory University in Atlanta, Georgia in 1974. It was a beautiful place and there were so many people, I liked the big open space that I was used to and the dormitory. My first-year classes were challenging but since I was so used to a strict schedule, I made it through in a breeze. I found it refreshing to have new school colors after the black garnet of high school, almost like a new chapter to open in blue and gold.

One day, not too long after, I had started my last year at Emory and my car started making a strange noise like "wat a tat tat". It seemed to drive okay but the noise got louder as I went faster. I looked over and there was Washington Tire Company as I stopped with my noise subsiding a nice-looking gentleman came out to help, he introduced himself as Luther Washington and was extremely polite. I explained the noise, he didn't try to sell me tires, didn't even laugh when I was telling him about the wat a tat tat noise, he even asked if he could look at my car before touching it. I knew he was a professional and not just some joker at a garage. He wasn't all greasy and didn't leave handprints all over my car like so many places do. He looked under my pretty yellow Mercury Comet and discovered my speedometer cable had come loose, he located a suitable fastener in his shop and didn't even charge me. I knew where I would go next time I had a problem with my car. He said he doesn't normally fix cars but was glad he could help this time as he knew his way around them a bit.

A few days later, during my shift at the bank I saw Luther again, he was surprised to see me, said he had been thinking of me and asked me if I would go to dinner with him. Our first date was at the Crossroads Restaurant by where Peachtree and West Peachtree came together, this must have been a sign for me, he didn't know where I came from or anything about the farm. All Luther knew was that I lived in the city and went to college, he told me a little bit about himself, he lived on Robin Hood Road, I knew that wasn't too far from where my dorm was. He didn't say too much else about himself, I thought maybe he was shy but wondered how he could afford to live in such a nice place. We hit it off well and saw each other almost every night for a few months straight.

One-night, about a year after we had met, Luther called and was acting strangely, he asked if we could go back to the Crossroads Restaurant, we hadn't been there since our first date. He said he had something important to talk with me about. I was concerned that he may have gotten wind about the new promotion from the bank that was offered to me in Seattle. Since he had that business, I didn't know who he knew at the bank or who may talk to him. I was still contemplating the position and being so far away from my family.

Luther picked me up and was quiet the whole way, I knew something was wrong, we were headed to Peachtree right where we started, and I thought we would end here too even though I wasn't sure why, I was starting to grow really fond of Luther and his gentle ways. We had just pulled up to the curb, I was having trouble keeping myself together when Luther turned the music down and blurted out that his house was his cousins and he lived in a cottage in the back, the place where he worked did not belong to him but a tire company with the same name as his and they were opening up a shop in Seattle, WA and he wanted to know if I would marry him and go with him. I was astounded, I thought he had found out about my promotion and was going to tell me to stay or go without him. I said where he lived was never a thought as long as he wasn't already taken by another woman. Then I told him about my promotion and said yes to his proposal of marriage, we were beyond excited, and he felt bad for not having a ring. He thought I would think less of him not owning the house or tire business and walk away so he hadn't bought one, he was thinking we would be breaking up not moving on.

The next weekend I took Luther to meet my parents, Luther drove us there in his Oldsmobile Cutlass and we told them our news. They were happy for us and said they had news that fit with ours. They were selling the farm and moving to Montana, had been worried about telling me since I was seeming to be settled in Atlanta. We did buy matching rings the next day, agate rings that were multi-faceted all the way around, both in jade, just sizes apart.

We were married at the church downtown on July 7, 1977 and left Atlanta the start of Labor Day weekend just over a month later. By the following Monday we would be halfway across the country, just the two of us. We were so in love.

Once we were in Seattle I worked at the bank for a while then we had four children in a row. Just like that, one day none and it seemed the next day, four. Luther loved me, the children and the tire store. They offered him a franchise and it was his, he ran it like a professional.

Now our oldest son Drake is a pilot, Clara, named after Luther's grand-ma is a physical therapist in Long Beach at the Navy base, Thomas, our third, opened a motor cycle shop in Seattle and restores vintage motorcy-cles and our youngest lives here in Seattle too, Lucille works in an EEG lab studying sleep disorders. I wonder how she gets sleep since she is up all-night monitoring others as they sleep. We couldn't be any prouder of our four children.

It's December 31st, 2018 looking back I think everything fell into place when Luther started at the Washington Tire Company in Seattle at the right time of the year when everyone was needing their tires for winter. It was easy to get business in Washington with a name like that, the company was smart to start their first franchise here and they will probably never realize how lucky they were to have my Luther. I didn't really like the way the bank here was run and the news of our first child was a relief to not work past my delivery date. Doors always seemed to open and close at the right time for the Washington family, I think it was a genetic confidence and elegance, all our children were able to follow their dreams with scholarships, open doors, and talent. Somehow, they arrived at the path they had chosen.

One winter Luther was feeling tired, by spring he went to the doctor and was told he had high blood pressure. Probably from not doing too much exercise at work since he mostly did paperwork by this point. The doctor said he needed to watch his diet and exercise. He had always liked music, so he bought some big wireless headphones and a shiny track suit and started walking, he was enjoying the earth blooming and music. In Autumn he went back to get checked and his blood pressure was lower. He went out and bought warmer workout clothes and reflective leather high tops as the daylight grew shorter, he said he felt like he was in high school, he looked like he was a boxer, would dance around our kitchen throwing punches and making me laugh, that was my Luther. The weather was unusually warm for December, in the high 40's, Luther decided to take a walk and try out his new gear, he had been wearing the shoes around the house breaking them in for days. The next sequence of events was so unexpected I still can't comprehend them.

On December 27, 2018 one week after his sixty seventh birthday while he was out walking there was a knock at the door. As I approached the new door we had just installed with the faceted arch shaped window, it looked like a police car outside, there were two Seattle Police officers on my doorstep. I saw the blue uniforms and heard the words coming out of their mouth and entering my ears that didn't want to understand anything they said. They told me Luther was walking and someone swerved on the sidewalk, he managed to avoid that car but being scared had ran into the road to avoid one collision and was struck by a truck, he had died instantly and there was nothing he or anyone else could have done differently. That was three days ago, he was alive right here being funny for me. Now all four of our children were back to work and the house was quiet again, almost too quiet. I sit at our kitchen table that we have been at every day for forty years; Luther is gone, four days have passed since then. I haven't spent a New Year's Eve alone in forty-one years.

Simone

December 28-30, 2018

IT IS THE QUIET OF THE MORNING, THE NEXT DAY, BUT NOT YET TWENTY-FOUR hours since you've been gone, left this earth and my life, your life, the one you were supposed to live, now we are at until "death do us part". In my pocket is the tissue that collected the tears I cried for you; it will stay there for as long as I feel is right, I can't pull it out for fear of it crumbling as I have, I loved you just as you were, past tense verbs already coming out of my mind. I sit at our huge, oak table that has held many joys and heartaches with our big family. What mattered to you is null and void, not because I don't care but that is how death is, we all have our own set of troubles to deal with, I am left with mine, here and now. Most troubles don't even have voices connected to them, either we ignore them, and they enlarge or take steps to prevent what is capable of being prevented. There are things that have no cure or prevention, things that just happen like your death, it was your day to be done. As hard as that is to comprehend, I honestly believe we all have a predestined number of minutes, you used yours to the fullest Luther. These are not thoughts I had prior to this moment but a reality all the same. Your dreams, fears, plans, what was on your calendar, appointments scheduled, not happening for you, but my tasks are greater with your exit from our world. Now I feel too much and nothing at all, you were here yesterday getting ready to have breakfast, it is all a circular thought pattern. Will the circle enlarge as the days go by without you in them, more tasks in territories I have no experience? There are grueling questions and events to be completed, I am not sure if you took the easy way out after it was all said and done, and I am here to stay for the hard part. You didn't even know it would happen, one moment here, the next on the other side where we had discussed many times, the other side of earthly death. Death is a fine line between absence and presence, you are here and not at all in the same breath. I almost believe, at this moment, that you are more present than absent as the details of your death are combed over meticulously with thought and honor. We had us, I had my world, you had yours. We were a couple together, parents together, apart we had our lives but that was all built on us as a unit. I see how much of an important presence you were to this city, the Emerald City, you always liked that name, I would say "Evergreen State" and you would respond with "no, Emerald City, my city." You loved this city and the people in it, you used to say, "almost everyone needs tires." I think you were right about that; I had never put much thought into how significant your business was and how far it reached into each community. Now I see just days after your passing, the service not even scheduled yet and the notes, cards and calls what a staple you were that helped many people, people I have never heard of helped provide food for our table with their purchase of a set of tires. Luther Apollo Washington as I go through the tasks of your sudden death, people have reached out with flowers, food, tears, smiles, awe, laughter, anger, letters, and every other raw emotion. Some have sent money to pay their debt for their 235 75 R 15's that you so graciously sold them on credit. One lady who maneuvered a beat up white Granada with a leather top, that should have been off the road years ago but still ran somehow, said she had been worried about transporting her babies on the bald treads when she stopped in to have a leak fixed. She said Luther went in the back, came out and asked if she minded if he put some used tires on her car, she explained she didn't have money but Luther told her that her babies were worth more than gold and there would be no payment, those tires were new, she now had more tire than car left. She asked me how to pay that debt, I told her to give elsewhere to help someone along their way. I heard these stories repeatedly, how did all this news travel to me as fast as it did? It helps the tasks at hand, it is like the world knows and is connected by a secret society of tires.

2019

Simone

January 2019

I WAS AT THE CEMETERY A FEW DAYS AFTER LUTHER HAD BEEN BURIED WITH NO idea of what to do with myself. Remembering a few days prior and the funeral, something no one knew I had done, hours before the funeral I couldn't sleep, I had to escape our home. I drove to the cemetery knowing your body was still there above the earth, where just days before, our family had sat and shopped for a casket from a catalog, we had picked out the hammered metal one like the coffee table you wanted that didn't match out décor. While driving through I saw a blue and white truck with a small crane, as it turned the corner the early morning sun reflected off the metal, after watching where it would go I discovered it wasn't the metal of the truck but of your casket. They parked by the hole they had dug just a few hours before, a man jumps in, disappears and shovels some dirt around, they don't know I am watching from my car still wearing my pajamas. The men take into consideration the height of the trees, discuss them and slowly lower the casket as they call it, I say slowly lower Luther to a resting place for the family to attend the celebration of life just a few short hours from now. As I observe further, they roll out the fake grass, an electric golf cart brings chairs, two men jump out, one sweeps the grass the other sets the chairs behind him. This is all preparation for you my dear Luther. They all leave, and I go sit by you for an hour or so knowing you are not in the box but by my side. I can never talk of this to anyone, this is a scene from the brokenness, possibly a part of this I want to be selfish with, your body's last moments on this side of the dug-up earth.

In the long winter evenings Luther and I usually played board games or a few hands of competitive cards after supper. Last night it hit me, the games that we had played for years and had connected over wouldn't happen any longer, as your life tries to get back to normal you discover the missing pieces and what really was the glue. No matter what had happened each day we had our time to be us and talk while we shuffled cards or moved pieces or pegs around a board, I am not sure either one of us enjoyed the games but we loved each other and knew it took effort on both our parts to keep that daily connection alive. There were years that we tried to fit us in around work, chores to tend to, four children who wanted to be the center of life and the intentionality of us, we were there, moving pieces around a board or shuffling cards keeping the bond intact. On many nights we would sit with our cards dealt at the oak table just holding them, talking, making a connection after a day apart, errands run, homework done, tires sold, taxes filed.

Before last night there had been arrangements to be made, family to tend to, all that food to be boxed up, dishes washed and put aside for everyone who has been so kind as to bring their form of nourishment, with their names on their dishes I am glad they will not expect anything in return, I am numb inside and haven't thought much about eating. My thoughts on that subject were driven by Luther and our love of certain food we shared, now he is gone, I have only thought about getting rid of the food. After calling around I decided to take the untouched food to the women's shelter, that is where I met Gloria Wilson. Luther was well known from his tire shop, the funeral and after event had so many people, I didn't know half of them, they just showed up at our house. They just kept bringing in food, someone had organized a list of who each dish belonged to and their phone number. I wondered how I would be able to call and see them all later as I looked at the stacks of dishes on our oval table. They were beautiful stacks, from each home of different patterns and colors, not like I am used to a matching set, these were brought with love to my home showing their part in sharing the loss and grief of Luther. The aroma of so many different foods mingled and rose from the ceramic dishes, it reminded me of all our meals and years, Luther and I had partaken in together, at home, potlucks and with friends. There was so much of it, you would think I still had my four children at home to feed for a month or more. I froze some of it for later and for when the local children stop in so they think I am well enough to cook and can report back to the others that I am doing well. I don't know when or if that will happen, but I have my wits about me enough to know someone will be checking on me, so I better at least pretend I have it together, otherwise they will worry and be bothersome to this adjustment period in my life, my comfort is of the utmost importance now. I realize they would only be trying to help in their way, so they didn't have to worry but I need to get through this in my own way.

A week or so later, a lady named Gloria called and asked when it would be a good time for her to stop, retrieve the dishes and the list so she could return them to everyone. That was a task I had forgotten about; I was getting used to staring at the stacks of dishes, pans, casserole bowls and ceramic cake plates, I had even used a couple.

When Gloria arrived, I was surprised by who she was, this was the lady I had so graciously taken the food to at the shelter. We had a cup of coffee, loaded the dishes, she asked if I would care to go with her to distribute them. We got into her yellow, peppy little sports car, I was surprised this was what she drove and that the dishes all fit in her trunk. Gloria was smooth, professionally explaining to each person she only had a minute and had to run onto the next stop. We had dinner that night, she gave me her card in hopes that I may volunteer someday and said to stay in touch. She explained all the work that everyone put in at the shelter and how it had been such a blessing to her as it was to the ladies that benefitted from the services. I may have to call Gloria someday when I start my life back up.

Daniel

January 2019

It has been over a year and a half that since she has been gone, almost exactly double the length of time Iris and I knew each other; I still can't stop going to the cemetery. I feel like I need to go as I'm the only family Iris has here, I am not even family but feel we had a deeper bond than if we had been blood, I seem to be drawn to her grave frequently. I feel that the Mortelli's knew that and it is why Iris was buried here. Mr. and Mrs. Mortelli have stopped in a couple times in the past year, maybe they can't face it daily, so they have put this death in a compartment they also were certain this is where Iris was happy. Their version of confronting this is to get on a steel tube and fly here to look at the grave, call me, mourn, we all have our versions of how something like this goes but it happens as it unfolds, there can be no planning except possibly and airline ticket. One thing I was adamant about, and even paid for, was a brass vase attached to the headstone which has now turned shades of green and brown and blends right into the earth as Iris has done. I felt I didn't buy enough flowers during our nine months together so I would buy them now, this was something I could control, flowers were not what I thought of when I was with Iris, she was a flower. If I were out for a test drive I would always stop in as the cemetery was close to work and I don't have a vehicle of my own.

Scissors and a small shovel are something I always carried to make sure the grave site was manicured. That was an idea I got from a lady I saw further down the same row. Kind of scared me at first, someone with a shovel in the graveyard, then I saw what she was doing, maybe it was etiquette to tend the grave of a loved one.

I saw her on a crisp morning in January 2019, she must have noticed I was watching her, she was undoubtedly watching me too, there was no one in this usual park like setting except the two of us that I could see, I realized my watching her was making her nervous. She said hello and told me about trimming up the newly planted grass around the headstone. Humorously stated it was a good thing her husband couldn't see this side of his grave because he would be rolling around under the ground. Luther had to have the most perfect lawn on the block, he spent hours in the yard, when they finished burying him the grass was all wrong. She was hoping it would grow back being as it was so cold; she didn't know about grass maybe the snow would push it down. She apologized for interrupting me, talking so much and confided never in her life had she cared about the lawn, dandelions, weeds, moss all were welcoming to her. She introduced herself as Simone, Simone Washington, just like the state, said her precious Luther had just passed and she wasn't sure what to do with herself. Sharing this moment with Simone was the first time besides Iris's parents that I had felt a connection because of loss. She apologized again and went about her business, I turned and looked back, she was bent over busy with the grass I could smell the dirt as it had been freshly dug, winter was here again I could feel the cold in my bones as the wind traipsed through the cemetery. Next time I come here I want to check out that headstone if she isn't there. I probably come here too much but it helps me and is harmless to the rest of the world, it was comforting to meet Simone today.

Come to think of it I don't have any connections anywhere, I don't feel like making friends anymore. Iris' friends were from the university and fine while Iris was there, besides they have probably graduated and moved on to other waters. It seems I have grown old with the death of Iris, like I am an old man, probably because death is normally an older subject, you don't expect it to happen at a young age. The person I have known the longest is

Mr. Filbert, he had retired a while back, stops in now and then. I pretend he comes to see me, but deep down I know that's not true. He knows I'm alone and lets me work as much as I want, also knows I am genuinely there to help him keep the place in order. Another thing he knows about is Iris; he is the person who suggested I volunteer my labor and gave the discount on her windshield. I think he liked her too, he must have had love in his life somewhere. I have not heard about a Mrs. Filbert as a matter of fact after all these years I don't know much about Mr. Filbert, not even his first name or where he lives.

Simone

February 2019

It has been just over a month since Luther has left this earth, been taken from me or is not here, whatever phrase fits the moment or circumstance. There are the endless days and others filled with a slew of phone calls unraveling his life from this earth. Credit cards, bank accounts, business licenses, friends and the list feels like it is multiplying, the more I unravel the bigger the ball of yarn is. This may sound harsh, but I am thankful that if this was going to happen it happened at the end of the year so next year there would be no wages or anything to explain to the IRS, creditors, bankers, or anyone else. They all have the same spiel; I'm sure they deal with this daily since there are so many people that pass on; they say sorry for your loss then ask their questions... "do I have a plan?" I have dealt with as many as I can think of, except getting the auto ship tires to not be delivered, if mail comes with his name and mine or just his, Luther A. Washington I put it in a stack and spend a day, weekly, so they can adjust their computer, check a different box, ask how it will be paid, do I want to cancel? How am I going to pay? Would I like to continue the service? On one call I said sarcastically, of course, "I would love to receive 25 gallon bottles of windshield wiper fluid monthly." But then I decline their offer politely. I know this is their job and they must ask but I am tired of it, my new system is, on Tuesday I look through the mountains of mail, if it comes after that it will wait until next week. This is my time of loss, my system for dealing with it; they will not be directing how that goes.

I am not sure if I am doing okay since this is my first time losing a husband. Some days I sit and stare, others busy with tasks, the children all take turns calling to check on me, I know they talk amongst themselves, so the calls come on a schedule. It's not that they don't want to talk to me but they would only call when their heart was in it prior to this, there used to be such gusto in their voices, they are all dealing with this in their own way too, Clara and Drake alone from a far. They send Thomas the most likely of the bunch to check on me, Lucille works nights so she will stop by early mornings or late evenings infrequently, but it is Thomas who comes to eat and tells me of his shop Rip the Road that he is so proud of, tells me of the latest Harley Davidson, Indian or Triumph that he has been working so diligently on and about his customers. He has a knack for the perfection of restoration, some of the things that are painted on the bikes are amazing, seems as if you could walk right into the scene and get lost in the reality and fantasy of it all.

When Thomas shows up, we almost always have dinner, he seems to like to come and relax, maybe it is his way of healing, being where his dad was. We haven't talked much of Luther or me, generally it is topics that are safe; "did you hear about a bridge closure? It sure was cold today, glad you cooked mom", things like that. One night I knew he had something on his mind and I came to find out he had been the chosen one to talk to me. They all thought the house was too big and I should move on to something that didn't need maintenance, or taxes so high. They had many reasons why I should move, I assured him I would think about it but knew I wasn't moving to a two-bedroom condo anytime soon, told him he could report back that I would not make any major decisions for a year, that kept them at bay for a while, I know they are only caring but is it so they don't have to worry? What would I do with Luther's yard tools, his car stuff, his scraped-up headphones that the police returned to me after his death, these were the pieces of his life that I was entrusted with. It all kept coming to that moment, the before and after moment, so precise. Now it is after the fact and everyone wants me to act differently, live somewhere else, eat like I am feeding Luther, go to the places I would go before but this is not the same life I was part of. It was changed for me. I need to adjust to it as it happens, create a new system, that won't be tomorrow and I will not make decisions like selling the five-bedroom house anytime soon, I rather enjoy the memories of my family right here, I created that family right in my body. This is home, this is where I last saw Luther, where I became a mother, learned to be a wife, a cook, console in crises and celebrate in victory, sew, be a woman, decorate a house and juggle a family, I am not going anywhere until I choose to. Thomas will have to report back to the rest of the crew someday that this is my choice, they don't need to know yet. He is the easy going one of the bunch, so laid back and lets things fall into place, don't get me wrong, he is a go getter; like when he wanted that shop there was no hesitation, he just doesn't seem to stress over decisions. To tell you the truth he is probably the best one to have come and asked about my moving because the others would have pushed and not heard what they wanted so they would have tried to be more convincing, they don't want to have to worry about me. They didn't worry before so they can stop now. Thomas can stop by, we can eat some of that food I saved in the freezer, he can see me dressed and eating and report back. In truth I may have a bowl of cereal or a peach for dinner when no one is around but I don't have to cook or think about it for the first time in forty years, so a banana and crackers for breakfast, lunch or dinner is fine with me, I am an adult and can do as I please. When the freezer food runs out, I will cook or suggest take out, but for now, that freezer food will last quite a while, thanks to the kind folks Luther knew.

Simone

April 2019

IT WAS A BEAUTIFUL SPRING DAY, THE FLOWERS WERE JUST BEGINNING TO BLOOM, there was a park with a hill by our house that had a taller than a normal cherry tree, after the powerful wind storm we had it looked like the hill had a pink carpet installed over night. This reminded me that I should probably go check on that grass around Luther's grave. It had been a couple months since I had been there, it was too cold to go and hang out before today.

I stopped at the park on the way and scooped up some blossom petals from around the edge so as not to disturb the perfect way the wind had blown them, to take over to Luther's grave. I don't know if he would like them or not since he liked the perfect lawn but I liked them so that is what will happen now. Winter was a hard time to lose someone, the dark and dreary days all strung into one long season. I prefer to be out in the sunshine, so this is my day that the wind blew the clouds away. I laugh and listen to our favorite CD, the one he listened to as he would walk the city and observe the goings on, as I drive across town with a bag that is covered in pink petals memories fill the car and my mind.

This year since I only have me I needed something to be grounded and have purpose, I will start noticing colors, when they arrive, all winter there was gray, brown, white, and blue with an occasional hint of red holly berries and of course our vast array of evergreens that are present in every season in the Pacific Northwest. I think after a death and a colorless season I need to notice something more to start feeling again. Maybe journaling about the colors and their arrival will bring excitement to me, I need to smile and not just exist. Luther was the person at the center of my life, also surrounded it, woven in here and there and being he was so suddenly gone it has taken a few days, maybe months as I see the calendar with the Christmas ornament page has not been changed from last year for me to get out of this fog. I am still here missing, grieving, and sorting my life with Luther but will get to this thing called life one day at a time, sometimes one hour or minute at a time. Maybe I will start with the pink petals and see what else is blooming, take notes and write about them. I used to draw and paint, I could write stories of my healing process if there is a way to heal from this, I will take Luther with me as I start since he was my biggest fan. He always carried my doodles in his wallet, I wonder if anyone saw them when they found him out on the road. Maybe I should look in his wallet and start by drawing the things in there that he held dear to him only paint them larger on canvas. Plans of healing come precisely at the right moment, this doesn't mean I am healed or will be anytime soon maybe ever, but it does mean I have life in me, life to create and plan.

The cemetery was quite surprising, many graves with Easter lilies, I don't know why I hadn't thought about bringing one or anything else for that matter. Luther and I had a unique relationship as all marriages are so this part of it will start with pink petals, whispers of gentle truth. As I stand there seeing the rolling hills and Luther's lawn around his grave settled in, I hear a male voice. Not too loud but like someone trying to talk in a whisper, I see a man in jeans, the color all older men wear, bent over a grave with a vase adding white carnations and carefully stuffing red roses in between them, he is talking about all his years at the factory, this explains his loudness, he has probably lost his hearing and his wife. He is telling her after all these years he has never taken a cent from her but now that she is gone, he thanks her for leaving him the money for his new black Toyota Tacoma with all the options. He has brought her flowers to thank her and show her the truck. I felt a connection to this man just feeling we have both entered a stage of grief, knowing it is a personal compartment, wondering how long it has been for him to decide on the new truck.

After returning to my car I decide to go get some canvasses, paint and an easel, I think the house is large enough to have an art room. After shopping I go out to eat at our favorite restaurant, I order my meal for there and Luther's enchiladas to go, knowing I will eat them tomorrow just like we always arranged, Luther did not eat left over take out. I am proud of myself for getting out, recalling memories, making new decisions and plans for the house, maybe I will paint a picture for every room. I will start with one that symbolizes the love Luther and I had from the drawings in his wallet that will proudly hang in our bedroom.

Bob

May 2019

A WHILE BACK I MET A DETECTIVE HERE WHO WAS INVESTIGATING A YOUNG
lady's murder. That was a tragic story I don't know the ending except she
is here and a young man with a tremendous number of cars comes to be
with her often, I generally see him a few times a week. The detective was
only just here once asking about her. My job has never taken me close to
the young gentleman; I always seem to be up the hill when he drives by. A
few years ago, they installed cameras all over here, I can access the footage
through my phone and have been wanting a closer look at the young man
with many cars. He could be a suspect in the murder of the young lady,
it has been a couple years that he has been coming here. I still have the
detective's card, maybe I will call and see if her case has been solved, if I
can find the card I will call tonight and leave a message.

I had seen the young man again, this time driving a rattle can painted
neon green Honda with a black fender that flapped in the wind, that thing
might not have had a muffler. Not sure if he was respectable or just didn't
want to bring attention to himself but on the way out a shiny newer Honda
tried to race him, and he motioned for the other car to go ahead. It makes
my job easier to be able to access the cameras and follow people who may

cause trouble in here, deal drugs or other illegal activities. People think because it is a graveyard they won't be seen.

There is the card Detective Jeffery Munser, Seattle Gang Unit, all these titles that raise questions in my head. What did the investigation for the young lady have to do with the gang unit? Maybe she was caught in a drive by? It doesn't seem, from the looks of the young man, that he is gang related but what do I really know? He even wears a uniform of some sort, has shorter hair, seems mopey or withdrawn and always comes alone. I have left a message for Munser to call me, with hopes this case is closed and the multi-vehicle man is just drawn to the grave. Well legally closed, of course for the young man and her family it will never be closed. It's disturbing to know some of these bodies are here and the killer has not been connected to the crime, maybe never will be.

Detective Munser called back, he stated that the case of Iris Mortelli had not been solved, I don't know why I had never gone over to look at the headstone to see her name, just like in life everyone here has a name. I could still see the detective in my head as he spoke over the phone, like his picture was taken there and installed in my memory. He is a tall, bulky man with curly hair almost black, seemed like he was on the fly when he was here, like the world was his box and he could operate business at any location, under any circumstance, his hood was his desk, the car his office, walking about his phone and radios summonsing information. Detectives must have a heavy case load, if they could slow down a bit maybe the people being interviewed could think long enough to answer. The detective said they were still searching for leads but honestly that case was many murders ago and there weren't any new open leads. Unless there was a witness, a connection to another crime or the suspect who was willing to confess there wouldn't be much hope, he told me of Vincent and the bracelets, the hope and dead end that was. I proceeded to tell him about the gentleman with many cars, he said he would have to dig the file out and asked if I would get any license plates if I saw him again, I agreed hoping now to help with this case.

Detective Munser

June 2019

KNOWING THAT BOB BARTON WOULD HAVE NEVER CALLED ME UNLESS THERE WAS a deep suspicion in him about this young man, I thought I ought to take a closer look. From the description, the person he call about was most likely Daniel, checking through the file, which seemed thick in the reality of the case, having no leads, Daniel Mettenburg still had the same cell phone number and place of employment. Those were not characteristics of an unstable person or someone wishing to hide something. As far as I know he doesn't have any ties in this city so if he was guilty, he could have left, and no one would have noticed. He wasn't being watched, technically no one was being watched in the Mortelli case, there were no leads, none. There was no one to point a finger at, her father had called frequently in the beginning but rarely anymore. A case far from most of my other cases, a young lady, with tremendous potential just getting off work, not even a bullet, no casings involved, without the car there weren't any fingerprints, no one had made contact with her it was an object of contact that had been taken from the scene, erased from our site.

Daniel Mettenburg answered my questions without faltering, but I sensed an irritation in his voice, the answers seemed matter of fact and rehearsed, it could be that some were the same questions, others new and he now knows someone is watching him closely to know of his visits to the cemetery and car swaps. His demeanor was standoffish, if he is guilty, he will probably flee or if he is innocent, he will keep his normal routine, although I don't know what that is, to see if it is different. There is something about that young man that alerts my radar, being a detective for this long has taught me to trust my instinct, I am not sure about him yet.

Daniel

June 2019

My life would be mentally easier if Iris' killer weren't still out there, how can her whole car disappear? There haven't been and leads at all, are they looking into this? They say they are, I can't keep calling the detective and expecting him to know anything, so I haven't called in forever and now they call me, isn't it their job to figure this out? Last week, early morning, like he had been out working all night while I was sleeping, he called me and had a few more questions but they were ones I had already been asked, except the four that seemed quite odd, did I visit Iris' grave? He had to have known I did because of the second question. Why did I drive to the cemetery multiple vehicles, my answer seemed to satisfy him, I am positive he will check out my story? The third and fourth questions were personal I felt since I don't discuss my feelings with anyone, as a matter of fact, I don't talk to anyone about anything except their windshield, the detective asked why I went so much and was there anything else I could think to tell him. I know these are all questions that he needed to ask, and they are also related to me being a suspect. It had never occurred to me that I would be a suspect in Iris' death but during the unexpected phone call with all the questioning being done, it made me wonder if they had any new leads or there weren't any so they were just going to try and pin this on me, the one person who loved Iris, would the polygraph register my answers untruthful due to the guilt I felt for not being there the night she was murdered? I have only had one in depth experience with the police and that was the night I was five years old, they automatically thought I was lying about being alone that night, I have tried to steer clear of all police activity since then and have done a good job of staying above the law. In the original process of investigating Iris' murder, it was her parents the investigators talked to mostly or so it appeared, anyway, they were with me during all questioning, so it was like we were all being asked the same question. Some they knew the answers and others I would fill in, other questions we had never thought about, possibly friends from school or coworkers could possibly answer, we weren't even sure of most of their names. As of this point in time the right answers have not surfaced, now I felt like they were checking me out again and would watch my movements, do they think I have her car? I, without a doubt, have never had to defend myself physically, am not sure if I could, have never had a serious argument with anyone, especially Iris, because I avoid all people at all times to avoid conflict or emotion, so I know beyond a shadow of a doubt Iris' killer is out there and this makes me angry thinking they may try to turn the spotlight on me, hoping my anger doesn't make me look guilty.

Detective Munser

June 2019

LITTLE DOES THE DEPARTMENT KNOW I AM A PUBLISHED AUTHOR OF LYRICS UNDER the pseudonym of Mun Det J of many songs that are played in the clubs all over the Puget Sound region and world. Some of the bands have made it big and are on tour with my words rattling around in their heads and out of their mouths, trying to get them into other people's minds or on the satellite radio that is so popular these days. They ride in vans and buses, small bands that started in garages and end up hitting it big with their trash rock and rap. The words of mine sloshing around in their heads as they roll down the road, somebodies' children out living the dream one town at a time while I stay in my city protecting it the best I can, my fate has been chosen.

Because of that scene at the junk pile back in 2015 and the insanely aggressive music they were playing I started writing again and became Mun Det J. My job takes me to places that only music that slicing could go, it is a filter to undo the thoughts and images that roll from my mind having to see the things I do on a regular basis. I am not sure I could do what I do if there wasn't an outlet, my landlady has no idea of my hobby or slowly budding career as I can wear headphones while I pick away at the electric guitar on my deck overlooking where Salmon Bay and Lake Union collide or in my living room with the old brown shag carpet and plaid 1970's sofa wearing my flamed swimming trunks, flipflops and old flannel shirt, looking like a rock star from Seattle. All the furniture looks like it did when I moved in as I sit in my recliner or at my desk, it is all in good shape and was part of the lease so many years ago. The style of the room and the beginning of the major music scene reasonably go together. In the house some days I perform as I used to in the Green Pyramids, leather pants and boots, ripped up shirt, spiked hair and chains, drinking plain coffee, before the many options of coffee exploded on our city. I am not sure if I am planning on growing up ever, but I am an asset to the City of Seattle; solving crimes and who knows how many people hear my songs, my words that reverberate through the speaker and come out as punctuation, the punctuation of life as it is seen from the street, there are probably other Officers that have teenagers who play my music in their houses, that cracks me up to have another harmless identity. We all have a secret; it is my job to find the secrets of others but no one's job to unearth mine.

Sea Cruise Via Sidewalk
Getting' off the liner floated into town
Wearing floppy, velvet floppy hats
Walking all gangster style fixin' to empty the clip
Clip a money they are dumpin' dodging rats
Sailing in like big cats, pumas on the run
Looking for action pumpin' up the streets
At 3 am still be out. Lookin' at action
Intercepted crossfire
Of a discreet clip they stumble across at my beat.

Should be rockin' on the liner
Drinkin' up the free bottles gin and beer in the cup
It is on your mind
Never even made it back, in a bad position
Many facets to the story

This is not Baltimore showing up your money roll
Not a smart maneuver
Failed to run for cover
Need an earth mover …

The story ends for you goes on for me
I just started my gig, you be done,
Lookin' at the excess
Floppy velvet hat at the curb, blood run
She a pretty one, dressed up for the town
In the rain, your girl be a mess
Now she lookin' at you lookin' like a clown
Wonderin' if I will ask her to confess

The streets be brutal in the night
Strong is not the need
Wisdom at its best
Shoulda, shoulda, shoulda so they say
Not out playing life on speed
Dead is done, done for me
As you look on, whoever you are
Solve the crime, grieve the loss
But for sure gone
Mun Det J 2015 ©

Detective Munser

July 2019

IT WAS A HOT DAY TOWARDS THE END OF JULY, THE AROMA OF SALT WATER WAS pushed up the rolling hills of downtown to the precinct being led by the hot wind, not a cool breeze on the horizon only invisible steam rolling under cars and being shifted from the movement of people. Seattle was amped up for their festivities, those hydroplane races and air shows with all the heat and water make a city dance with excitement, people do things during the associated events that they would never dream of doing at any other time, people who were professionals in our community, who were the anchors that make the city operate were letting loose during these events. I had just started my shift and got a call from Metevior, he said he had made an arrest and the person only wanted to talk to me, this wasn't a gang related crime, the arrest was for a simple scalping of tickets that went wrong. He had some tickets for box seats at the parade and it was supposed to be a simple transaction, then another person, the only description is a striped jacket and red hair with a knife who tries to kill the ticket scalper, these weren't even the best tickets, sixth row up and at the beginning of the parade where things are trying to mesh together, not flowing nicely yet.

I showed up, earlier in the day, this was an unusual time for me to be doing business, most of my shift load happens after dark, I am not used to the heat of the day especially when it is 10:00 am and already over 85 degrees. The pavement seemed to be rejecting the rays of sun and it's heat that bounced around from object to object with too much energy to land and be absorbed. The wind had ceased as if upon command to allow the heat to rule and radiate off the city of concrete and brick.

This guy is not a gang member or anyone I know, had never even had a traffic ticket before and wanted to keep this off his record, this sounded like a joke I thought while standing there looking at him. His name was Joseph Martin, he said he had bought the tickets from a friend's dad who would be out of town and he couldn't use them because he had to work that day, never wanted to miss a shift, he had almost gotten killed and didn't want any trouble for trying to sell them. I don't think he realized he hadn't committed a crime and that he was the victim, he was shaking and wanted water, wouldn't or couldn't give us the name of the man with the knife and striped coat, didn't want to tell us how he met the person, but said he wanted to spill some information in exchange for a lighter sentence, this guy had been watching too much late-night crime television. He had been looking for an economical car last year, a friend told him about a VW Beetle in Tacoma that was for sale, he had a bad feeling about the people when he arrived so he didn't buy it, didn't know Tacoma well but knew it was off Bridgeport close to the Narrows Bridge on the part that was named Jackson and the reason he could remember the name of the street. He went on about why they would name the street Bridgeport and right before the bridge change its name, didn't make any sense to him, he said he wanted logic in city planning, this guy was a peculiar one but turning out to be useful, more valuable than I had planned at the beginning.

After an hour of questioning he agreed to make the trip to Tacoma with us if he wasn't seen by the people where the car was located. It was a good friend of his who told him about the car, who didn't know about any murder either, later he had done some research and heard about Iris' murder. It had always been in his heart to do the right thing, but he had feared crossing his friend and this was a murder, he had never had any dealings with any crime before. You could tell he was out of his normal environment as he sat in the back of the police SUV, he was slump down as if he had been defeated, wondering what his fate would be. When we got close, he led us around a couple blocks and through alley ways, located the alley where the car had been, before recognizing the faded yellow garage with dark green trim peeling from the frame weather worn. Metevior and I drove Joseph to a sandwich shop a mile or so away, dropped him off with some cash and returned to the house. An elderly woman answered the door happy for a visit from someone, even us, said it was Derek's car, her grandson and she would let them in to see it. Stated he acquired the car about two years ago, but it had never run as far as she knew, she opened the garage door with her cane and there was Iris' car, all the contents seemed to be inside. Mrs. Carter, who was quite elderly, was shocked to hear this news and called Derek; he didn't answer but sent a text saying he was in class, she fills us in on his study of criminal justice at the local community college, but she promised he would get ahold of them that evening. We called a tow truck and had the car towed to our impound lot in Seattle, picked up Joseph, who we are sure didn't eat in the whole two hours he had waited, asked him about Derek who he stated he had never heard of, drove him back to his home in Seattle and thanked him, assuring him that he wasn't in any trouble saying we would be in touch and advised him not to leave the area, he wasn't who we were worried about. This will be a big break for Iris, her family and Daniel.

After finishing the interview and meeting the detectives to tell them what I specifically need from the Mortelli's VW I call Mr. Mortelli, break the news to him that is actually no news yet, this could be a break or nothing, just a car. My next step is to see if Daniel can help us out with Joseph Martin or Derick Carter, he states he has never heard of either person and just wants answers, they are answers I can't give since they just aren't there, I was hoping Daniel knew something. Big breaks like locating the VW bring more work and sometimes no more answers.

Derek did call late that evening; said he was scared to call that is why it took so long, he had never been in trouble before and had been sold the car for cheap then it just stopped running the first week he owned it, so without much money he just put it in the garage. He was extremely nervous which made him look guilty. He said he bought it off a guy from school about two years ago, who doesn't attend anymore, the guy was creepy, had black hair with a hairline that went half way back on his scalp, always wore black polyester pants, a black long sleeved button down shirt, black knee length trench coat that flew out as he walked and black boots that used to be shiny military style, said he was going to be a private detective, looked suspicious to say the least. After a long conversation and some more leads we told him to stay local, accessible and that we would be in touch. So far, it seemed all the people connected to this were just innocent victims that got caught up in the wrong moments, seems like that happens more often than not, now to locate the odd man in black. That would be another day, see what forensics pulls off the car, it sounds like it has changed hands many times since the traffic cams caught it leaving Seattle in 2017. According to the community college admissions office the person we are looking for is Everett Sunshine, he had dropped out without a proper withdrawal of courses Fall quarter 2017, that makes him a bit more suspect.

Simone

October 2019

NINE MONTHS AND MORE DAYS HAVE PASSED SINCE LUTHER HAS BEEN GONE. IN my mind I think in present tense because my memory doesn't leave there, the memories stay the same, sometimes I turn to share them with Luther because he is in the memory and the only person who can relate to it like I am at that moment. Then forget he isn't next to me physically, I share the memory out loud anyway, no one is here to know I do it, it has become habit to let Luther know where I am going or when I'll be back. Luther was and is my companion, best friend, we shared a life and heritage, raised children. I am grateful for both of us that we didn't end up in this spot due to a lingering disease or a condition that took over our lives. One of my favorite memories is when Thomas and Clara would stand outside as you would drive off to work, they'd yell. "bye daddy have a good day at work." I always wondered when they were old enough to realize what that meant. In reality it was deeper knowing they had true grasp of it, genuine, and would be here awaiting your arrival, wanting to know what you had done that day, you would patiently sit and give them animated details of your day as they would laugh and bond with you. This brought me as much joy as it brought them and you, just watching the people we created being entertained by us, knowing they would grow up and it wouldn't always be this simple.

I have learned in your death that I can be stronger that I knew, how much I miss your roaring laugh that our house absorbed, your warm smile, our unspoken humor, the peace you brought when I would worry or be anxious. What you left behind is the evidence of life that you meant something and everything, your life Luther Apollo Washington, my memory recycles it daily, you are at peace not having to do the books and sell the tires but somehow I don't think that is what you envisioned for our life or yours, I must accept with a heart in denial that your minutes ran out, that you gave it your all.

One thing I am grateful for is that Thomas, out of all the children, is the one to report back and the close one, he has your manner about him only where you were loud, he is calm. He can come in, sit and eat a meal leaning back in the chair, with one leg resting on the other, looking so casual and looking like you at the same time, he brings peace and is comfortable wherever he goes like I am sure he does in business and the reports of me. Death is multi-layered, I see it from this side and learn what I feel, and you are on the other side visiting with the ones who went before. Marcella will be happy to see you and Grandma Clara who had passed before I was even in the picture, I am sure. It is different for all of us on this side, left behind so suddenly, I am not sure how all of our children are, as they returned shortly after your service to their desired locations, they call, but you never know what that really means, is it out of duty or do they miss me? Do they not call because it's too hard since I can't pass the phone over to you after you have waited patiently for my chatter and excitement to end for a short word with one of them? That was our style for every phone call, they knew when both of us would be home. After our conversations we would mesh facts and discover we hadn't learned much about their life, it was good to hear their voice, you raise a child and the government says they are eighteen and can go. I know it must happen somehow but I have always wondered why the one-day separation of child to adult, the child ready to be free, the parent programmed to care, guide and worry about their well-being. Letting go of a child is a process but I had to let go of us physically in an instant and preserve what you stood up for at the same time.

I remember the year Marcella passed away and left you inheritance, she wasn't someone I knew well, had only met a couple of times, sweet is the word that comes to mind. Years prior she had married a predominant figure in Atlanta and lived well, had come from a middle-class family but her husband over the years taught her how to act being rich and black, you always told me she taught you how to preserve your heritage and dignity with honesty and hard work. Halloween was one of your favorite times of the year, you would dress up in elaborate costumes every year. The year she passed you dressed up as yourself, a black man, just like you are, wore your normal clothing. I was surprised when you came out of our room looking normal, you said it was in Marcella's memory a special person and a special time of year for you colliding in your mind. With you dressed like you I really took a look like I hadn't before, you wore your gray brand name tennis shoes, your favorite t-shirt with the tree on it, the one you mowed the lawn in, a brown worn belt and blue jeans. You handed out candy looking like Luther but only I knew it meant something to you and your heritage, your tribute to Marcella was the barest statement of honesty you could make, it was brilliant and subtle at the same time. Marcella said there was no need to prove yourself, make a mess pushing yourself forward, standing out with your honesty and actions will be proof enough to those who need to see it. She told you to act like you own the place and be fair, that will get you where you need to go. Your thoughts were funny about cars, you would drive one for a while and then get another without attachment, never anything new or fancy, that year you bought a used little hatchback with your inheritance, I was surprised at your thriftiness. Another piece of advice from Marcella was to only buy what you need unless you really want something. That little hatchback still sits in the garage, I will go drive it next time I am out, maybe I will learn more about you Luther.

I sit in the garage in my car, comfortable but know I need to get into the other car, Luther's hatchback. I get out of mine slowly almost unwillingly, unsure of my intentional actions, take the bunch of leaves and tools, open the door to the hatchback and get in, placing the leaves on the passenger seat I see his green work jacket laying there with his name embroidered in red, it has been there since he passed and I had no idea. I don't suppose he needs it now, but I do, I will hang it in the hallway just like you always did. I pick it up, check the pockets, he was always meticulous, so I wasn't surprised when I found only one piece of paper in it with the name "Frederick" and phone number. I don't know who Frederick is but maybe I will call him, someday when it feels right.

I drive across town to the cemetery, the wrought iron gates are wide open welcoming me saying come in and pay a visit, the lawn manicured as usual, flags, pumpkins and sunflowers spotted around the grounds. It feels unfamiliar to be driving his car, somehow not right to visit his place of rest with it, I pull up as close as I can get, the wind is whipping across the field of graves, leaves are dancing up the hill swirling, a couple cars scattered about and people are present, I get out with my own leaves, the ones I brought for Luther, I think I bring strange items and wonder if anyone one else visits the grave to see them as he was so well known. These leaves are from my heart to his, he loved this time of year, the smells of hot cider, pumpkin pie verses sweet potato pie that we always cooked and agreed they were both equally superior with real whipping cream and a touch of cinnamon.

I stand a bit, it is good to be outside, I enjoy the dance of leaves, lost in thought, realizing I had put the coat on when I got out of the car, like it was mine, I am suddenly warm, hearing his name coming back to this world and leaving the one we now share, the one I created when he left.

It is a short man who had called his name from afar, as he gets closer, he stops and apologizes for his mistake and turns to go with his unsteady gait. I say, "please stop." He turns back to face me apologizing again for his error, I ask him how he knew Luther, he said the tire shop, they had been admiring the new hatchback last he saw him. They both loved simple cars, ones you could work on, told me Luther was going to sell him tires next time he came in, he had offered credit but the man didn't want to owe anyone, plus he was hoping to buy a car he has seen on Aurora at a lot, said he almost had enough money. I don't think he realized where he was, we were standing over Luther's grave and the man asked how Luther was doing, I pointed at the grave unable to speak, a tear ran down each side of the man's face instantly, then many, so many he was over taken I had the feeling it wasn't just about Luther but the burden he carried with him everywhere he went, this was news to him and Luther held a special place in his heart. He gained his composure as best he could, explained he couldn't read so he didn't know what the sign on the door of the tire shop said, he had gone back a couple times, turned to leave with words of sympathy, me knowing he was carrying a heavy load himself, he got back in his beat up car with the teddy bear in the front seat, turned one more time and said his name was Frederick. I said please be any other name, he looked at me like I was crazy of course death does that to a person and coincidence, I pull his phone number out of Luther's pocket, Frederick was shocked, smiling with relief at the connection we now had. I asked him if he had some time today, he did and agreed to follow me not knowing where we were going, just trusting me and our connection, we were going to the DMV to transfer the title of the hatchback into Frederick's name, I would then drive it to his house and take a cab home, Luther you knew exactly the exact steps to take today.

Detective Munser

December 23, 2019

CHRISTMAS TIME IS ALWAYS DIFFICULT FOR ME BEING ALONE. IT'S SOMETHING I should be used to, I know I am not the only one and am drawn to City Square Cemetery, there are a number of graves here connected to my cases, some solved some not, it seems as if it is peaceful, nonetheless. There are moments of silence inside the curved gates, I look through the cedar trees swaying in the slight breeze, across the expanse of still frosted lawn two deer walk in the distance so gracefully as if they were gliding on air, gentle creatures, always ready for a leap, they touch each other as a form of communication almost like they didn't belong in this world but had been dropped in as a prop. This brings me an unnatural feeling of zero stress, one I am not familiar with and am unsure of how to react if at all, but it creeps in over me on this foggy, cold morning, peace beyond measure. I bring my gaze from the deer to the pond which is even calmer, not a ripple of movement, like the world is on pause at this moment, outside of these gates I can hear the traffic but it is not here in my bubble of peace. The next second the silence is broken by the wings of the blue heron's sudden flap, flight is what breaks my spell of silence, life resumed, birds take flight everywhere, like they were waiting for permission, robins red breasts remind me of Tucker my childhood dog. I remember him, so proud one Christmas morning getting a bandana and dog treats in his stocking, he pranced around in his red bandana proud to be alive and part of the family, a family I miss.

I have been up all night which is quite normal for me, solving a crime in the daytime isn't always possible, you need to be out and up when the people who committed the crime or their group is out on the streets. Following a lead may take days, a crime scene is a tedious task, especially outside, in the dark or in the rain, you don't know what was there before the crime was committed, determining the age of a cigarette butt is necessary but seems wrong when you are seeking a killer and their family is present. Last night was particularly hard, a young lady twenty-five years of age, Esmerelda Martin was returning to her family's apartment complex from the corner store with some sweet treats for them and was gunned down as she pulled back into the parking lot. She'd been in town less than twenty-four hours, no reason that we could find for her murder, she was from Bakersfield, CA, visiting for the holidays. Probably had an entire life waiting for her return not put on pause as originally planned but now canceled for the remainder of time, what happened and why? It's the why that can drive a person crazy. Family members call and beg me to solve cases, it is my intention to solve every case that is assigned to me, I know how hard it is on the family when the answers are not there, every rock has been turned, every person questioned, every bit of footage watched, all we can do is wait, hoping someone slips up or wants to provide us with information later. When a family doesn't have answers it makes the crime real every day, sometimes bigger, when they meet for holidays and the laugh is missed or another quirky trait, a tradition that involved the missing one, a birthday passes, cake eaten without the recipient celebrating the life that is supposed to be, or the anniversary of their death arrives. We acknowledge our loved ones who have passed how we individually celebrate them; it is a personal choice how we relive the memories. Life and death are not in our hands but are presented to us daily in one form or the other, whether long or slow they are both inevitable.

When I arrived last night in the cold, an old, short security guard and tall, young officer were guarding the scene, both equally weird, white clouds were forming around their faces as the crowd was getting more agitated and they were trying to preserve all evidence, even though there wasn't really any. No one saw anything, the usual story, the only tire marks were from Esmerelda's borrowed car, the shot had been made from the street, her last earthly breath was taken as she was laying on the pavement slightly under the small sedan but next to the passenger door in the assigned parking spot #24 for her family's unit. She had been retrieving the candy cane ice cream, a tradition of celebration for the season that went way back in the Martin family and now has a tragic reminder, candy canes and death, so far the only connection in this case. There was one person, Uncle Ray Martin as he introduced himself, I got a strange set of vibes off of that man, hair combed perfectly for so late in the day, everyone else was in relaxed clothing, but even though he lived there he was still in his dress shirt, jeans and dress shoes, his walk clicking as he approached and departed with his over eager urgency to meet me to tell his story.

2020

Daniel

February 2020

Filbert Auto Glass had been my place of employment for almost six years, the place had come a long way, getting paid for being in a place that I enjoyed was always a pleasure, there was something about the comfort of putting on a crisp clean uniform every morning, I had never minded working six days a week and Mr. Filbert knew he could count on me, he was as tall as a skyscraper, rail thin, always wore coveralls, the kind with the vertical stripes and an arm span that could reach across a windshield.

It was a bitter cold day in February somewhere around Valentine's day, I remember because I had been thinking of getting some flowers for Iris to set in her special vase, I always left one of the bunch at home for me in the old jelly jar, a tradition I had started from the beginning of this. Out the window I see a silver Lincoln pull in with a windshield that looked fine, the first thing I always check, a man wearing a gray tweed suit, shiny tie flapping in the wind and a brown overcoat with shoes to match. He stood in the doorway to the shop, said he was looking for Daniel Mettenburg, stated his name was Cecil Collins, attorney at law. I knew I wasn't in trouble and figured it may have to do with my mother who I hadn't seen in more years that I could remember trying to calculate that time span as he paused waiting for my response. As we stood there in the cold looking at each other, I invited him into the waiting area, he took off his coat, pulled a file out of his worn black leather briefcase, on the tab it said "Filbert". After confirming I was indeed Daniel, he said was there to read the will of Mr. Filbert and wondered if I would like to make an appointment to come into his office or would I have time now. I didn't even know Mr. Filbert was gone, my second dealing with death, trying to remember the last time he had stopped in, now I was extremely worried about my future and employment at Filbert Auto Glass.

As I listened I wasn't sure I was hearing right, I asked him to proceed, Mr. Lawrence Filbert had left me the business, his 1991 Mercury Sable, 1960 Ford F 100, his 3-bedroom house just around the corner and three bank accounts. One was for the business, the other, his personal one and the third contained the life insurance policy from his wife Ester who had passed away a few days prior to me showing up the first time. It was mine in its entirety if I agreed to not sell any of it in a specified timeframe. All I had to do was sign on the line in front of me and it was mine. I was in shock at my dear friend Mr. Filbert passing, he was the closest to a stable family that I had ever known. I had never owned a car, let alone a house and this man was offering me the pen to accept, just needed me to reciprocate in ink. I had never imagined ink could solidify this much for me, a couple signatures he coaxed.

It seemed like too much to take in in fifteen minutes let alone a day. Mr. Collins handed me the keys to everything; titles, bank books and wished me a farewell. I sat there in that same spot on the classic black waiting room chairs for a quite a while before closing for lunch too scared to walk to the address on the paperwork to look at the house and get the car, not sure this was real yet. I waited until my second break, closed the shop and walked a couple blocks to see my new home and vehicles. I wanted to call Iris to tell her, I wish that impulse would go away, it's annoying to come back to reality, a reminder of her death and now another.

In all these years it had never occurred to me where Mr. Filbert lived or what his first name was, now I see he lived near his business. I entered the house which felt wrong, it was Mr. Filberts other life, I only knew him at work. The house was tidy inside and all the furniture, carpet, television, and appliances looked brand new. The refrigerator had a gift card in it for $200.00 to Safeway and a note.

Daniel,
You have blessed me with your honesty and steadfast work ethic. I hope you can bless someone someday as I have you.

The truck doesn't look like much, but I had the engine overhauled please use it to move into your new house.

Lawrence

It occurs to me that since Iris has been gone, I have not rested, really rested. I've been on edge every moment, wanting answers and wishing I had prevented her terrible last moments, my guilt overrides any logical thoughts. I sit on the sofa in Mr. Filberts house that is now mine, lean over and cry myself to sleep thinking this is what bittersweet means, to have it all and have nothing.

Detective Munser

March 2020

D<small>URING THE</small> COVID 19 <small>PANDEMIC DOWNTOWN WAS RELATIVELY QUIET.</small> I would drive through after going to headquarters and only the people out are the ones that aren't supposed to be, but they are then unmonitored folks, most offices and businesses are closed except the essentials, grocers, hospitals, day care centers, warehouses, pot shops. It is an eerie feeling when you drive through and the homeless are walking around like zombies because there isn't any danger or consequences for committing a crime and they can do as they please freely day or night. This has affected everyone in a different manner, some are making extra money, others are making none waiting on unemployment or a new profession or idea. Everyone is on the edge walking around with their rolodex of emotions pulling out an index card at the drop of a hat, tempers flared like fire. The jails have been emptied of nonviolent offenders, I heard things like, a couple guys broke into a bread store and they were written a ticket and let go, no new arrests, it seems no one is allowed to do their job as it is described, how would you work with a mask anyway, this is the perfect year of hiding your face, video footage from the eyes up. These lyrics were written one night during that time because I was used to seeing scads of people in the downtown core at night and was wondering what they were doing and where they were going, knowing they can't all resist the draw of the streets, I am sure one of them will be calling for assistance soon. I had an idea that many wanted to go back downtown, where the action is and sometimes trouble finds them, or they find it.

City of Distance During C -19
Downtown, downtown all around in my head every thought
Where'd I start to go Downtown in my mind? They say not
Every night the lights traipse around in my head
Knowin' the buildings and streets belong to me
Absorb the sights, every window a whole life
take in the lights, see the pretty ladies
All dressed up for the night. High heels rollin' down the sidewalk
In my mind I have a plan, steal the show, rule the night

Downtown in my head stay, stay in they say
No food except to curb, all the clubs be closed
Lights strobe in my head
Everywhere this is not in my mind trying to give it clout
Every screen flashin' do this don't do that
Wash, stock up, don't hoard,
Stay away 6 feet from who?
Do I need a pool noodle belt to go out?

Too much advice in all this seriousness
Allow your dreams to ignite
Truth will excel in the mindfulness
This time is yours waste it not, think, walk, write
Create bring it from within
Bring it around tonight
Downtown
#MunDetJ ©

Gloria

April 2020

DURING THIS TIME OF COVID-19, I AM NOT SURE WHEN THE LOCKDOWNS ARE and no one obeys them anyway. As I am part of the vulnerable group due to my advancing age, I am staying at home most of the time except my drives to the lakes where the gates are closed, and the beaches have warning signs to stay out. It seems only yesterday that Ethan was a small boy and would come with me to these parks and beaches, we would play all morning and he would nap on the way home.

Prior to this my time at the shelter was becoming less and less involved. I am 90 years old, fit as can be, but felt a couple years ago it was time to train someone else for my role. The stories have gotten more distraught as the years went on; I don't even know how long I have worked there but it has been a few decades. There have been some wonderful success stories, it has been my joy. Almost like I own the company, I still have an email account and can video conference with the staff and Carl III, some of my former clients know this is how to contact me of their triumphs and trials. Those ladies and staff have been a blessing to me all these years, at the end of this year they don't know it yet, but I will be stepping down, one hundred percent out to go and be me. Someone else can answer my emails and phone calls. I have given the shelter many years, tears, joy and sorrow, pretty much all of me. Now it is time to rest in my nest (since there is a quarantine) watch the city lights from a bird's eye view and enjoy my days on my hill that I have lived on for what seems like forever.

After observing the stay at home order for such a long period of time, organizing my life in the place where I have lived for what seems for an eternity, and being only able to get minimal essential supplies delivered, I think I arrived at the bottom of myself where the cesspool whirls with laughter and irritation. Thoughts of Carl Sr my husband, why he left and all the festering that has caused over the years. Not just for me but I am sure for him too, things like this go both ways he left for his reasons, all these years if I can admit that now, I've had irritation in my spirit at his presence, no matter what the occasion, he never had an explanation, just left and went on with his life, showed his face at every turn except where it was needed, didn't share in the grief when Carl Jr moved away, that is our son, didn't help with Ethan when Lorena had suddenly taken off, our only great grandson. He had plenty of time and resources in these moments and many other situations that life has thrown up but he just showed up at the dinners with his smile that I used to like, it is what drew me to him. He also brought his famous Bonsai Baked Beans and a slew of containers for his take home food. Who does that? Is there no remorse? These are our friends and family of decades and he brings beans, a smile and expects to leave with another meal? I am sure I irritate him too with my ways; he just looks at me like I am a fixture in the mix with no true acknowledgement of my existence, I always wonder what he is thinking, does he remember us at all, the beginning of us? He used to have thoughts in his head, maybe he has become one of those empty-headed people I heard about. They walk along with no thoughts and then see a dog, say there is a dog, then go back to being empty headed until another object of their liking or dislike enters their field of sight, I can't believe he is like that, we used to always share dialog running through our heads all day long. Probably like now he doesn't have any, is most likely sitting on his balcony watching traffic or lack thereof in this pandemic that may have gotten me to start thinking deep down, thinking of the petty sludge. Things like he has never addressed why he left me or us, just did and now lives with that, like it has always been that way, there is evidence to prove it has not. He has always taken the easy way out which is the hardest in the long run, seems like he would see that by now, of course if you don't think about things and have an empty head it wouldn't bother you.

I am at a place where it is time for me to not feel this way anymore, there really is no reason to gather, being as old as we are, most of our friends are buried or put away somewhere, Carl III and Ethan could come and see me and Carl Sr could make his plans separately, we could go out to dinner or a nice lunch would even be better, there is really no need to involve my time with Carl Sr any longer, he has lived elsewhere for more years that we were together. I don't hate him, just don't really need to see him only on the occasions that are meant to be the most joyous days of my life, he doesn't have anything to do with my joy. I think he has taken up quite enough of my space since he wanted his, it is time for me to move from this union that no longer exists. Also, those famous baked beans of his, I saw him hiding behind the trunk lid of his new classy two door car, emptying them from a can into a thrift store casserole dish and putting bacon bits on the top right in Carl III's driveway, Ethan almost caught him last year. They are the same brand of beans I introduced him to at the women's shelter yearly BBQ on Mercer Island Lid Park, the year before he left, the ones you can buy in a big can at the restaurant supply grocery chain, it's the little secrets like that that cause the irritation, he is not cool. Is he smiling because he loves to be with everyone, because he has his secret beans or because he is happy? He always complained about social gatherings, would raise a stink before we went, I never let him drive because he would always be mad about going and drive erratically on the way home, would head home after all in a snit and sit with his arms folded like he had been tortured and now acts like king of the show with his beans and used stained containers. He probably takes them all over the city, so he doesn't have to cook, just buys beans in the economy size, bacon bits and shows up with that smile. It is thoughts like this that make it so I know I need not to continue with the holiday's as we previously have, this quarantine has led me to live with all these thoughts and I am ready to release them. I am sure Carl Sr has his issues with me too unless he is indeed empty headed, I can just hear and imagine what he thinks of me. How my life almost stayed the same without him, maybe thinks it doesn't matter to me that he left, I still live in the same place overlooking the city, my wonderful place, he wanted to leave so he needed to find a new place not me. I still, in a remote fashion, work at the same place, probably eat the same foods, do the same things, go the same places. He probably likes or pretends he is living with all the new friends he has made over the years, maybe he just didn't like socializing with me. My thoughts are that he didn't want any responsibility ever, but it was the thing to do back when we got married, probably never had but after getting into having a family, then a grandchild he had had enough. To tell the truth he was probably done a few years in if it took that long, he did a good cover up for many years I suspect. I wish him well with his Bonsai Baked Beans and freedom, I free myself by not enduring those sentimental moments that were supposed to be mine and Carl Sr's but are mine and will continue to be mine to cherish as I wish with no resentment, this holiday season should be different for all of us. I know I am thankful for this quarantine; it has affected many in a negative way but for me it has been positive, I feel this time has been used wisely.

Daniel

April 2020

I HAVE VACATED MY APARTMENT, MOVED EVERYTHING I OWNED IN ONE LOAD AND donated the rest in another with Mr. Filbert's truck and have been sleeping in Lawrence Filbert's house that has had my name on the deed for nearly two months, it still feels awkward. I discovered the pickup doesn't have a stock motor in it, there was an invoice for a perfectly balanced 292 Y block V-8 installed January 16, 2020, the gas petal is one of those old 70's model feet. Having only dealt with windshields and not actually having my own real car this truck is a treat, it almost purrs, I didn't know you could balance a motor. The ladies look at me as I float by, but they just appear like eyes staring to me, invading my space, it has been just short of three years being next to Iris. Somedays I do okay, but mostly, I wonder how to make it to the next and really live, not just let each day go by emotionless but I don't know what that means to live like that.

During this expanse of time there has been a substantial amount of thought on how everything happened. Have been more emotions surfaced than I knew were possible, generally I keep them intact and don't have a need for them. I was listed as a dear friend in the obituary but I was much more than that, I was Iris' lover, supposed to be her protector, windshield installer, dinner mate, the one who took the sand off her legs, feet and back after a day on the beach. I was really everything and nothing, no one in truth knows the whole story except for us and we were so young I am not sure we knew exactly the depth of this. All I know is I was more than a dear friend, sometimes Mr. Mortelli calls to say he will be arriving in Seattle out of courtesy, I wish that I wasn't connected to that part, I don't know what to say to a him and Cookie who have lost their daughter. Do they think of her and this great loss daily as I do or is it something they store up and pocket for their trips here? I know it is the loss of their daughter, but I have enough grief of my own and sharing moments, silence, thoughts or a dinner with the Mortelli's will not change why we pretend to know each other, it is just one common bond, Iris. What do they think of me when they visit, do they wish they could come to Seattle and not see me, why do they call? These are not questions that can be asked of them, being rude is not who I am, I am used to containing the grief alone and sharing it seems unfair to me as I face it daily, maybe they do too we haven't talked of that since I ask no questions of them.

Lately, there have been more visits to the cemetery since I have a steady car and am not borrowing a customer's ride. I always prayed nothing would happen to the borrowed cars while I was going to the cemetery, too much to explain in my sideward adventures. The Sable is in perfect shape, Mr. Filbert never had to drive far since he only lived around the corner, I may have put more miles on it in the past month than he did on an average month. It seems I go not because Iris is there, I know she isn't but it helps me preserve the memory of her, how her bathing suit straps always slid past her t-shirt, her hair would never stay in a pony tail but fly on all sides of her head and the sun would shine through and reflect like her head was a sphere of fire, her car was always full of clothing and blankets. Iris was a lady on the move, she worked with the movement of the water and everything that moved in it, she was a natural person to change, stagnation was not her method, now she is stuck in time on this side. I feel torn between moving on and staying connected to Iris, I don't know how to do either, neither one feels healthy for me, not being stable as a child has made it hard for me to let go, running the business, owning a home and automobiles has taken some of my time recently. Women talk to me at work and I suppose make advances, but I choose not to see or act on them. Who knew having money would feel so strange and be hard to get used to? My life is routine to the core, but everything feels peculiar, knowing my schedule and calmness I can anticipate the next step, but for what I wonder? I run the business just as before, Mr. Filbert would be happy that I have kept his life intact.

June

~

May 2020

LET ME INTRODUCE MYSELF I AM JUNE FRIDLEY... I REMEMBER THE DAY JUST LIKE it was a blink of an eye back. Charles and I had met on July 3rd, 1956, he was in one of those olive-green jeeps the military used, and I was wearing my oldest gingham yellow dress with the patched pockets and had on my comfortable saddle shoes. The second I laid eyes on him everything and everyone else faded away, even the fireworks stand we had arrived at with the red, white and blue scalloped banners hanging from the awning and our friends disappeared from our sight, it all just faded away, we later called them the faders, happened everywhere for us.

I knew beyond a doubt that he was the one. Exactly one year later we were married, July 3rd, 1957 less than a month after my high school graduation I was Mrs. Charles Fridley. The whole USA was celebrating with us. It was a beautiful day in the park, and we would leave for Turner Air Force Base in Georgia in about two months. I was young and naïve, had so many ideas about a new home, what I could cook with all the peaches I had heard about, my new life with Charles and felt I knew it all from the Home Ec classes in high school, I had never cooked a whole meal prior to being married, I hoped Charles would be a good sport in my learning.

After we returned from our honeymoon and opened the few wedding presents, there weren't a lot of physical gifts as our friends and family knew would be moving and had a long drive ahead of us. There were quite a few cards, as we opened the rest there were mostly money and gift certificates that could be saved for later for things like dishes and TV trays, when we were settled. One gift was unforgettable but seemed so out of the realm of our new life, it was a prepaid certificate for a double plot at City Square Cemetery, caskets and headstones included, gifted from Mr. White the city park gardener. We didn't know him well but had visited during our picnics and he had helped us with our wedding arrangements in the park. I think he was as excited about our wedding as we were, helped us pick colors of pink and green to match the park. He included a note that said "*this may seem strange, but you will need this someday and I wouldn't want you to worry at a time like that. Have a blessed life between the dash*" Lovingly, Mr. White.

The day before we left, after packing, we stopped at our favorite restaurant and decided to go see the cemetery, it was beautiful, like a park, tiered, and well-manicured, American flags flying everywhere. The leaves were green and fluttery, flowers were blooming and there were people all about, the place was alive. We had never been to a cemetery before with the thought that we may actually pass away someday, life had just begun for us. We registered our certificate and left for our life's journey, oh, what a journey it was, we travelled all over the world. It was always a challenge to learn how to live lightly and be carefree. You know how it is when you see things that you want or to give your husband for a special occasion.

Charles

May 2020

HELLO, IT IS CAPTAIN CHARLES FRIDLEY.... THAT IS HOW I ALWAYS INTRODUCE myself even though I am long retired from the Air Force. The day I married June was the best day of my life, the thought was beyond words that she said she was willing to travel the world with me. Of course, with her father being in the Army she was used to not having roots too deep or entwined anywhere, she could get packed up and be ready with a couple hours' notice, one of her specialties.

The day at the cemetery seemed like the burial package could be an investment, something to sell later, I didn't think the we would ever be back in Washington, I must admit it was a nice place, funny how we ran into Mr. White there, I think our life really started at that cemetery. Looking back that is when the reality of how important each moment is, this fact seemed to lay on us even though we didn't know it then. After our visit with the staff we left to return some books from the library before leaving town the next morning. June had a couple books set out to read along the way that were our own. She started reading to me as we were heading back to sleep on the floor of our first apartment, as a married couple. It was so small we could barely fit a bed in there, I think she read to me every day that we were together. Reading had never been something I enjoyed doing for entertainment, but I loved to hear the stories, I was able to rest and see the pictures as she read, towards the end of my time that was my favorite part of every day. After coaxing me to eat a bite or two she would read, I think that was why I ate I so loved to hear her voice and speech patterns.

Time went by quickly, one day we were young and headed out to see the country and the next, we were gray headed and had seen the world, after my retirement there was plenty of time on our hands and we couldn't seem to stop traveling. One thing we had never done was show each other the homes of our first memories. Mine was in Duluth, MN. June and I traveled to my old house on North Lake Avenue the house still seemed tall and stately after all these years, a bit weathered from the harsh winds coming off the lake. We didn't have much but dad who worked on the docks found the house while walking home from work one day. He saved everything he could while we lived in a small apartment where my brother Samuel and I shared a room and then dad surprised us with the house. I remember running the neighborhood, it was half a mile to Lake Superior, but my mother, Lily, ran the house and us boys like a well-oiled machine. We knew the rule, we had to play on the block where we lived. By the weekend we were ready to see the water and ships closer than from our upstairs bedroom windows where we would guess what was on each ship, my favorite were the red ships, they stood out in the water, our parents would take me and my brother, Samuel, to see the ships as they came in. Sometimes dad would even drive us down in a snowstorm and buy fried fish and chips for dinner, these memories lodged in my head brought me back like I was a young boy again. We thought we were on top of the world, a house, bicycles, a car and each other, dad and mom gave us a good foundation. That night June and I had dinner at a little café by where my dad used to work, they had pictures on the wall of the fishermen, one had a photo with many men in it, I found his name in the caption, Floyd Fridley. I couldn't stop talking and am sure I talked June's ear off that night, it is funny how memories, smells and food unite us into who we are. I think that was some of the best fish I have ever eaten, it was good to be home to the smell of my lake, Lake Superior.

The next day we headed towards the first place June remembers living. Since neither of us had been before we took a few days and visited Iowa and Nebraska on our way to Cheyenne, WY. June was so excited it was the first house she remembered, quite possibly the only one her family lived in that was not on a military base. There it was, on Morrie Avenue, it seemed so small from the road, but it was recently vacated and there happened to be a real estate agent who let us look around. It was a comfortable 4-bedroom and quite spacious, you could see the little girl June had been when she turned from the hallway into to her childhood bedroom. She remembered sitting on the kitchen counter while her mom, Janice, made lemon cookies, those were her father's favorite. She told me all about Thomas, her dad, how he was in the Army, but she never knew what he did, he would leave with the other Army men and be in his dress greens, she would always be able to pick him out from the others when he returned because he was so short in the crowd next to them, said she remembered the year she grew as tall as her dad. He used one of the bedrooms for an office and the other was her mom's space she used like an office too sorting out her life. Being taught to be organized was a challenge growing up, but a skill June mastered in her travels.

The second year they lived on Morrie Avenue June started kindergarten in a brand-new school called Hebard Public School. Some days, her dad would drive her, and they would pass Holliday Park, on the way he would say "the next sunny day we can stop to play". After first grade they moved onto many other schools and places, seven schools in eleven years. Sometimes she would see friends from other schools as they would get transferred to the same place. Military life was a challenge but exciting for the family to see new places.

When I grew up, we only had two homes the small apartment and the house by the lake, June was already a professional at being a nomad. I am seventy-two now, have traveled for almost fifty-five years of my time on earth and have seen most of what I would like to see, we don't have any children, we are thinking of buying a small ranch house close to where we met and finally settling down. We heard that there was a new hospital built on the Army base and have decided on a retirement community with a pool and many activities, we want to keep active. I think I would like to play shuffleboard and learn to use a canoe. June says she will try something new like synchronized swimming or calligraphy, she has always liked to keep life fresh and learn new hobbies.

Health wise, I know we had been blessed, never more than a routine doctor visit in all our years. It was ten years almost to the day since we bought our place that I started having symptoms of discomfort and being extremely fatigued. I never knew there were so many more doors and machines in the hospital, clinic, doctor's office, labs, radiology and the list goes on. Doctors' visits, scans with contrast, without contrast, blood draws, x rays, biopsy then the news. It's not good the doctor reports to us, as we sit across his mahogany desk with a glass top, but we have some time, he relays like a speech he has been forced to deliver to other occupants of these gray leather chairs, maybe a year or more. It was then November 17th, 2017. We decided together that we wanted to get all our affairs in order and have as much fun as we could for as long as we could, we visited the City Square Cemetery on the way home for the first time in sixty-one years. It seemed strange the first time we were here was a lifetime ago, maybe a million miles ago, young and free neither of us were ever wild. As we went to see the space that we had been gifted so long ago, the reality of my life ending was unspoken but sitting between us in the car. Entering the building to make decisions was the biggest step, after picking out the particulars and planning my entire event, it seemed as if this was for someone else, we went to see where Mr. White had waved to us from many years ago. There was his headstone, James E. White and it said on his gravestone *"have a blessed life between the dash."* Next to him was Stephanie R. White, he had been visiting his wife when we saw him last. We were so young it didn't occur to us why he was there, he had recently lost his wife Suzanne just prior to our marriage. What a wise man he was to have given us the gift of the plots, when you get news like this it is easier when some steps are already taken care of.

That second time we visited the cemetery was the last occasion June and I went there together alive. On our travels we listened to books on tape and June still read to me when we were stopped. There were a few books we went back and reread as neither of us could remember the ending, getting old is funny like that. We traveled short distances for a while, spent nights in cabins by the ocean being lulled to sleep by the saltwater breeze, the sound of the waves, sea grass swaying and colliding in noise and foghorns. One time we went to a valley between the mountains, a place we had never been to before to see the vast fields of wildflowers, there was a shuffle in the tall grass, and as I sat on the porch a moose walked by our rented cabin. Moose are incredibly large, majestic creatures; I had never thought about or realized how colossal something like that was until it was right next to me, less than a yardstick away. It walked by like I wasn't there; it was so large physically but mentally and spiritually it stuck inside of me and moved me like nothing else ever had, I was wondering if I would see moose in Heaven, Heaven had been on my mind frequently. This moose owned the forest and knew precisely it's route, destination, and mission, me, wondering what that was but knowing I couldn't follow. That was our last major trip, I started needing more sleep and we went for short drives usually along the waterfront since it was close. Seems like during our entire marriage we have made a life by a body of salt water. Sometimes you forget the water is there, while driving around on errands and then you turn a corner and see a glimpse of the most beautiful scenery, it draws you in, the next thing you know you are driving closer to get a better view, binoculars have been standard gear in the console of our car for years. You know there are seals, whales and fish and the ships carry God knows what from there to here and back again but it is the water that draws you, every time we have searched the sea, we have discovered something new.

It was the middle of May, June and I knew that our ride on planet Earth together was almost over, I was skin and bone, you could see the weariness on June's face, body and movements. She was determined to keep up a normal life for me, on Memorial Day, May 25th , she went grocery shopping and got burgers, potato salad, BBQ chips, baked beans and a big flag and brought them into the dining room where my mechanical bed was and we celebrated one last time, the patriotic holiday that held so much meaning to both of us. I woke June up at 5:23 am on May 30th and at 5:27 am with June by my side I left this Earth. She will have to tell the rest of the story.

Charles

May 2020

I GUESS I DO HAVE MORE TO SAY AND ANOTHER MEMORY. BECAUSE WE WERE married on July 3rd, we always celebrated our anniversary privately. It seemed that we never told anyone when our anniversary was as we were in different parts of the world almost yearly, it was more ours if no one knew, but we had traditions. On July 3rd we always had a Thanksgiving meal, a list of what we were thankful for in each other and watermelon for dessert. It was our special tradition even if it was too hot, we managed to figure out the cooking with a crockpot or doing take out. Sometimes it was chicken and not turkey, but we felt it was important to thank each other for being there and getting through another year together, it was a tradition every year we looked forward to Thanksgiving in July, like it was our leaping off point to navigate another year united. I had a little notepad and wrote what I was thankful for during the year, June would sit the night before and write hers out, we had such different temperaments and styles but that is what made us bond, she was able to find humor in me and I in her. If I would start at the right she would start at the left, I think we taught each other patience and showed the other that everyone is uniquely patterned.

Every year on the 4th we went to a gigantic firework show, like I said earlier, we have always lived by salt water. On our tenth anniversary we were lucky enough to be in Long Beach, CA during the 4th of July festivities, it was one of the first years they had a boat cruise to see the fireworks. We had dinner on board and June had snuck on a container of watermelon for our private celebration. Kind of like a special cake, I remember one time looking out into our yard, she had toted the biggest watermelon I have ever seen all the way from the garage. That night as we sat on the boat rocking, we watched the fireworks, viewing the sparkling lights of downtown Los Angeles and promising each other again we would be together always. We were lucky to have found each other at the fireworks stand and with each firework we watch we knew how lucky we were, squeezing each other's hand. It was almost as if the 4th of July smells, foods, noise and bursts of lights were our bonding, these traditions are what held us together and lasted for another year, we would compare the shows and food, also try to go somewhere different for every show. It was when we took our vacation for us to celebrate us, the fireworks and festivities were a bonus. Small town were the best with their parades of homemade floats, farm animals, children with decorated bicycles and homemade clowns.

It seems that there are many variables and "what if's" in life. What if we hadn't both gone to the fireworks stand that day but one of us went another day or time? That stand wouldn't have been there if the old muffler shop hadn't gone out of business just a few weeks before. You must wonder what propelled two people to decide to go right at that moment, the heat was sweltering, the prices were sky high on the eve of the 4th, neither of us really had a passion for the holiday and it was wrenchingly humid no one should have been out in that mess. June said she didn't want to go that is why she was dressed in such an old dress, but her friends insisted. The dress wasn't what I had been looking at, I also had friends that pulled me along for the ride, the 4th of July wasn't my thing, since I had outgrown sparklers the smell and sight of fireworks just didn't draw me in. My friends Greg and Stanley were gung-ho on getting whatever would make the most noise and lights, Stanley had small house off base so we would go to his place for a barbeque and to light the gigantic fireworks they purchased off in the street. All I could think about that night, the next day and the rest of my life was the sweet girl I had met at the stand who had, for some reason, given me her phone number. This was back in the day when phone numbers started with words. I always found that not right when the phone dial was mostly numbers and you only used two letters anyway. June's number started with Broadway 2; she would always be the star of the stage in my show.

Gloria

May 2020

WITH ALL THIS TIME INSIDE MY MIND HAS BEEN GOING IN CIRCLES, IT ALMOST seems like I can't stop it from traveling at high speeds, memories recent and distant. I am used to being out and socializing, even helping people is nearly impossible from where I am. During this time, I started noticing the different brick formations that are visible from where I reside and the various ways it was laid. I had no idea there is so much public information, I now know the years that the adjacent buildings were built and have learned how important the brick laying trade was to a city. I suppose it is a blessing I wasn't downtown when the riots took place. We were lucky that nothing happened to the shelter or Carl III, he is good about keeping me informed and called as soon as he was on his way home, the short commute he has. He assured me that Ethan and he were safely tucked into their building until this chaos subsides. This reminds me of a poem I once saw in one of my favorite poetry books titled *War*.

War

War is in foreign lands
War is on our street
It is not on other sands
It is not something we have beat

The child who goes to sleep
Every night with voices violent
For this child it is too deep
He prays for it to be silent

War is not just other places
It is in our homes next door
The world is having races
The children oh so poor

War is not just violence it's drugs
It's ignorance and oppression
Sometimes it's thugs
We need to stop this obsession

Love can cure it all
Knowledge is the key
But not if we the people stall
What do we as a nation want to be?

©*2004* **M. V. Meadows**

I hope you don't get me wrong, it is with gratitude of life that I have been staying in, some days I organize but have gotten rid of most of my possessions. We spend fifty years collecting and whatever time we are allotted after that we are giving our collections away. I am most grateful for Ethan and Carl III at this point in my life, with them still out in the community I am unable to visit except for when they bring my supplies. My handy grocery trolley and I ride the elevator down to meet them on the street, have short sidewalk visits and collect my bags, accepting what they think I should have. I believe this collapsible wagon has been the second-best investment I have made since living here, it makes it so I am capable in normal times to purchase heavier items and not need assistance, it is important to everyone that I stay independent, no need for questions of if I should leave my home.

Carl Sr and I purchased a unit in this building on Belmont Ave E. but moved up to the penthouse after it became available. The views are spectacular, from my vantage point I can see the Space Needle, downtown with its twinkling attire, Elliot Bay, Puget Sound, the Olympic Mountains in all their changing glory, Lake Union and its endless supply of boats, Queen Anne and Fremont and, of course, the bridge with all the traffic and I have enjoyed every minute of each of them, but I need to get out on the street, at least walk among the people, observe their attire and demeanors, see their arms swing as they walk, look at the differences, I have been in for far too long.

I don't have a mask as I wasn't thinking of leaving here until just now, at this instant my breaking point. This is the only time since being quarantined that I have proposed going out, I have a purple bandana that will have to work because I am leaving, going out. All my life there has never been another time of staying in that I remember. Now should I stay in, maybe I am getting stir crazy, as they say, should I go out? I am on the 11th floor and will probably run into someone if I cross my own threshold. There I go again, over thinking, this has never been a trait of mine, this has just started since the stay at home order, I have always made a decision and went with it, that has to be the case at the moment.

I remember my keys and pass card on the way out, almost forgot them while trying to get my bandana in place, ride the elevator and manage to not see anyone, I have made it to the sidewalk and was not prepared for this, my world, my city running around like bandits, so many varieties of masks, where did they all come from? Here I stand an old lady in my version of mask, I am used to large crowds of people going by with visions in their head of the mission they are about to perform, not people mulling about with half their face covered, not having work to report to but simply meandering.

As I head south on Belmont and take the slightly inclined ramp into Tashkent Park with my cane and 90-year-old shuffle I am mesmerized by the beauty of the towering rhododendron, such deep varying shades of white, frantic bees buzzing unrestricted by human life, almost as if their life depended on that moment only, the large tree releasing a sweet pungent aroma. I don't think that if it weren't for my days, weeks, months inside that I would have ever been here on foot much less entering this park. What a tremendous awakening of my senses suddenly, it is almost as if I haven't lived before or possibly this is just a quieter level of existence. I see a statue and placard; I am positive this place is beautiful in the autumn months with the towering trees, I wish I had brought a lunch to eat while I was here. My thoughts upon leaving home today were to get fresh air not a whole new perspective on life, I read the placard and discover this park is connected to a sister city, why didn't I know that before? I live close enough for a 90-year-old to walk. I am feeling my age now, needing rest I venture further into the park and sit on the benches under the pergola, after resting a long while just enjoying my only day out during the virus, I decide to head back home and get some lunch as it is well past my usual eating time that seems precise during this pandemic. I heard a noise and turned back the way I had come, a beautiful blue jay flew by with such ease and gust of light wind sent the sound of a familiar voice my way, it was Carl Sr with someone, I had never gotten a glimpse of any of his friends prior to this, it felt like I was spying on them being so deep in conversation that they felt like the only two people in the world, it certainly wasn't purposeful on my part as I had just been sitting there prior to their arrival. He sure was looking older but so was I, my thoughts ran, is this a person who goes to his house, socializes with Carl Sr, has eaten his famous Bonsai Baked Beans, filled his to go containers? What happened next made me sit down again without even thinking about it. I know what the expression "that had me floored" means now. Carl Sr reached over and touched that man's face and they kissed ever so lightly on the lips, smiled and parted ways. Over the years I have known many people with a grand array of family orientations in my line of work which whatever works for them I am one hundred percent accepting, it has nothing to do with my services, except this was my Carl Sr and it explained entirely everything about what had happened with us. I don't know if I would ever be able to tell him what I saw but now I know, I think I will take another way home so as not to walk through the picture. Today had been a gift, my outing and long-awaited answers to what went wrong, a weight lifted from me that always nagged at my mind, now knowing the truth as it lay.

Detective Munser

May 30, 2020

WHAT A BEAUTIFUL DAY TO SIT ON MY DECK AND LISTEN TO TRAFFIC, A DAY TO just sit, finally a day off, the city will have to get along without me. People cannot be obeying the stay at home order, that is not something I enforce, I am a person of authority but seem to run behind the scenes, possibly by choice. There is no way all those cars are on essential trips; I am glad I can relax this morning. My case load is in order at the moment, of course I could work twenty-four hours a day all year long and never solve all the city's deep mysteries or even the ones I am assigned, I do my best to follow the leads but some crimes don't get solved. The smell of the city drifts by with the warm wind, evaporating water, diesel fumes, exhaust, flowers, pavement, dirt and dust and I fall in love all over again with where I live, my square of earth, the city of Seattle and state of Washington imprinted. My feet are propped up in the new, multicolored blue flip flops for this season, finally a day to be home, it has been warm enough for this not too hot, the total unwind. It is the quietest it has been for me in a month or more.

It was about one o'clock, right after my nice lunch, when I had just drifted off for a much-needed nap and my service phone rings, I almost didn't answer it, now I wish I hadn't. The call was from Officer Johnson who I hadn't been in contact with normally but knew his name from reports that had been on some cases we both had a connection to. He said all personnel was required to come in and report, there were not any other instructions, so much for my rest as I leave my flip flops inside the door, I tell them I will be back. I ease into respectable clothing and real shoes, exit my house, merge into traffic thinking this is an essential trip which is a new phrase and get close to downtown, there are rioters everywhere. I am not sure there is a path to headquarters, luckily I know secret squirrel routes and make it without delay, there are explosions, fires, bullhorns, people everywhere, broken windows spilling on the sidewalks the color of sea glass beauty in itself, people running from stores with all they can carry. It is utter chaos, I am instructed to man a window three stories up, with a video camera and radio. By the time I arrive at my post the retailers as far as I can see have been pillaged, people going in and exiting without anything because it is all gone, it is a war zone, police cruisers have been set on fire, the fire department can't respond or get anywhere near the scenes, people are being herded to who knows where. Yesterday it was COVID-19 pandemic, today no one seems to have any separation or concern. These criminal acts of destruction and escalated violence have created health and safety issues for first responders and civilians caught unaware of this event who may have just been at work, I hope no one dies tonight, people can get trampled in a mess like this, life is something not to take for granted.

Videotaping this from afar has given me an advantage to other crimes that have occurred prior, I am seeing some familiar faces and can observe who they are associating with, this information may help with future installments of my job. I have seen a few of the Cobalt Tribe and Emerald Jetters although they have been close in proximity no usual gang activity has been reported, that is not what this is about. I am hearing on the local news that this started as a peaceful protest of prayer and pastors in the downtown core, use of weapons is prohibited by law enforcement and the National Guard have been called on to help look at these people. Fireworks are going off, I am hoping not inside stores, people live over them, hold their lives over them, I can't see far or hear at all from my location but there is a stream of people, some with masks, they are all chanting and yelling different phrases, maybe I can decipher it once I replay the video with the sensor to pick up dialog that I want to call film but in reality it is digital. This is like a movie but is right here in front of me, I can't wrap my head around all the destruction, this is my beautiful city that I am required to protect and now I watch it be destroyed.

 I was relaxing in my flip flops an hour ago, now am in an office I have never used observing crime but paid not to stop it. I am aware Seattle has had prior issues with protests and have worked them on the streets, I, of all people, know that the behavior of others and what they justify is a secret known only to them and why they did what they did, some are just peacefully walking with signs, it is not all people that have caused this chaos, there is more than one group messed together hiding amongst the other with different motives. Some people will lie to the end, even as they are convicted with evidence of pictures and DNA, I am all for the innocence of a person and realize the many factors that are involved in some crimes, truth above all else is a strange thing. There are facts such as the person I just caught on camera wearing a black hoodie, bandana facemask and mirrored sunglasses who threw a bottle directly at another protesters head. There is no doubt this person is here for trouble and not to protest, after seeing him I start to take note of these people that are under five percent of the crowd. Why doesn't the group of rioters see them, don't they care? Maybe they blend into the crowd too much because they only attack a couple times a block then retreat to being a peaceful protestor, there are groups that are protesting but not these ones they are making trouble, dividing the groups. I continue to attempt verification of the imposter protesters, their actions are what drew me to them from my fortunate vantage point but they must be organized too, there it is this one has a yellow earbuds coming out of his hoodie, I don't want to broadcast this news until I am sure, as the hour goes by I locate several more who basically look like the other people out there but these bottle and rock throwers all have the yellow earbuds. I radio the person in charge directly on the street so they can at least make sense of one aspect of this protest and know who to watch out for even if it is a slight coincidence.

When the SWAT team arrives, there is an escalation of violence, the presence of uniforms is not helping this rebellion of force. In another city I hear a fire department was set on fire, here it looks like the crowd may be dispersing by the way they are milling about. Our city is in shambles Pike, Pine, 5th, Olive, too many streets and locations to name. From my vantage point three stories above the sidewalks I wonder where the homeless are? There are no shopping carts or people carrying bags in the crowd, where are the people who were working? I have no idea how we can recover as a city, who can we trust, will businesses be able to afford insurance to be here, will downtown be a ghost town, will I want to stay and work in this destruction? Heartfelt questions without answers, only the future of many cities will be told in later days and months. I am not confident after all the high emotions and new rules to everything that have been put in place in 2020. If I wish to transfer from this window to the disheveled city that I have loved and proudly served for twenty six years. I am one of the good guys, the one people call for in times of trouble, I have spent countless money of my own on ponchos, blankets, stuffed animals, books and cases of water that I transport around this city in my trunk to crime scenes that people weren't prepared to be a part of but end up participating anyway, so I bring a small form of comfort to these people caught up in the nasty messes of society that are a reality for me and now for them, life forever changed.

After exiting this building that I have breached the glass doors of many times prior to today, and been changed every time but nothing like this, telling myself that it is for the benefit of the city all the changes need to be a reality in me, that it is up to me to help the unsuspecting people that the truth is different currently. What they saw on television has now happened to them firsthand and I keep telling myself over and over, possibly I can make a difference Detective Jeffery Munser is able to assist. Today I don't feel that in my spirit, of being able to help anyone not even myself, maybe my well has run dry, possibly I think it is time to go and not come back, the people chant for the police to die, I have never done anything but help humanity and my city, the one I love. It could be a different story where I turn around and leave my badge, that won't be today even with the city demolished as I knew it, a landmark taken down, a staple of the land and a piece of community glue demolished, forever gone, the tree with the bent broken top trampled toppled over. I know deep in my heart there are murders to be solved, I still have a caseload to close and more will be added undoubtedly, people can't seem to help themselves from killing others, like proving a point somehow, this has happened from the beginning of time.

The yellow earbuds will have to be enough to give me hope today, I am thankful for the keen training of my eyes that has been instilled during my work for Seattle. Head hanging, heartbroken, I drive through my city not with authority but with honor that it has taken the beating and disrespect, and, in my heart, I know it will survive.

#Seattle Strong
#DJMunser
#MunDetJ

Detective Munser

June 2020

Summer is in my blood, a time of year to be vigilant and busy, the weather was warming up a couple of days even over eighty degrees, that means more people out and more gangs ramping up trying to push their territory lines. Whatever it means for gangs it means the same for the department, if they are on alert, so are we, they just know ahead of us. I still haven't talked to anyone about my observance of the yellow earbud instigators, there may not even be a theory to that, just might be a cheap brand or popular one. Every day since I have been looking for someone anywhere to be wearing them or selling them, so far, I haven't found anyone. I round the corner off Freemont Way onto Allen Place and there is my first lead. I have seen this character around for the last few years, not just here but downtown come to think of it. Always wearing some type of soda pop pants or pajamas hanging around a convenience store.

I roll around town in plain clothes and push the line on what I can wear, they like us to wear what I call "suit gear", but I dress down to blend in most of the time, t-shirts and jeans mostly, I also let my hair grow as long as I can before they start riding me about being respectable, people talk to me easier without the suit and classic cop look, the suit jacket is in the trunk as required. Maybe it helps with the musical side of me to have some hair movement while I rock out and write. I circle back around, which is no easy task from there under Aurora and back again, he is still there, as I walk in he asks for a spare dollar, no dollars are spare but I have a gut feeling I need to know him better. I give him two dollars and proceed in the store for something unknown and decide on some smokes, I don't use any tobacco products, but it helps on the street in getting information, I buy a different brand every time, usually the one on sale, the people I hand them out to probably think I smoke cheap cigarettes. I am at the counter paying and Soda Pop Pants comes in for a couple scratch tickets, he talks to me a bit about winning over a grand from one a couple weeks ago in the ghetto. As I am wondering which ghetto he is referring to and what connection he has to who, pure profit he says as he buys more with my two dollars. I secretly hope he doesn't win with my money and buy the next ten tickets after him, I didn't win either but when he went to pull his huge red headphones up that matched his pants I get a small glimpse of the yellow cords to the earbuds connected to his cell phone. The first I had seen since the protesters throwing bottles, I need to look for this guy in my footage, he would stand out, most of the protesters were fairly thin he was not, I am not sure he could even get a hoodie on with the ponytail being his only hair that he wears so high on his head sticking straight up.

You always find interesting people at convenience stores, most are there to grab a gallon of milk, a snack or pack of smokes but then those who stagger in to feed their addiction or addictions, the ones who are lucky enough to have enough quarters for laundry or maybe enough money for clothes to wash, everyone has to wear something but they don't have to pay for it. Tonight, I will go home and watch the footage for clues and yellow earbuds, this is the mission that has kept me going for a few days.

The night is still young, it is unseasonably warm, summer has laid itself down here earlier than usual. I can always tell with the smell of evaporation and exhaust, they seem to filter between the houses and buildings, some days stagnant and others just a hint of diesel will waft through the crack between my house and the neighbor's square of reality. Sometimes I wonder how people with unlimited choices can reside in such close proximity to each other, share walls, parking spaces, driveways, it gets nasty some days and that is why I am needed. What bothers one may send another into murder and may not phase another, I see all the playing factors in the unwanted scenes that I am dispatched to, it depends on temperature, temperament, territory, how much someone needs to live there, what someone thought you saw even if you didn't, where you exist, who you know, who you don't and what color your choose to wear.

The taped scenes are forever etched in my mind, I only saw a few blocks from my vantage point but need to make a connection from Soda Pop Pants to the crowd, he is my only lead right now, and hope to see him around again. After rewinding and watching the video four times my eyes are crossed, I have seen six people go by with the yellow ear buds all throwing bottles or rocks, they must carry their particular ammo with them and communicate with their phones on locations, it appears they are evenly spaced apart. Their strategy is precise, undercover, fitting right in, looking just like the rest of the crowd, skirting the edge, when it gets noisy or violent, they aim at their target, throw and ease out of the crowd to stay out of harm's way with an unfair advantage being as they are the ones who started the ruckus. Out of the six identified, there is one face I recognize, Bernard Hoadley, he was a suspect in another case a few moons back, someone I couldn't forget, his hair unruly, always wears mismatched shoes, says this is to throw off people when they give his description. Most people remember him by that one unusual trait and have dubbed him "Flame", he likes to be the leader and have mules do his dirty work, just like the rest of the business people of the street. I will see what part of town he stays in; I don't have enough to go on for a case now, but this is building.

June

July 2020

SPRINGTIME WAS WHEN CHARLES PASSED AND NOW IT IS TWO MONTHS INTO SUM-
mer a whole other season, I see how this happens, time moves on for the
living, no matter what. I haven't done much except be here and watch the
lights on the water and the moon pass the Space Needle nightly, I don't
know much about super moons but I have been enjoying them as Sandy
sits and purrs while we stay up past midnight when they add new time slots
to order groceries on the app, that I am grateful for now. I can get groceries
and not see anyone except the man loading after I hit the trunk button, I
don't feel much like eating but have gotten Sandy some cardboard flats
to lay and scratch on and specialty canned food. You may order fifteen
things and get ten. I think she likes this arrangement other than Charles
not being here, I am home most days all day. At this point I am glad we
didn't opt to get a place in a retirement community but chose this beautiful,
over the top, new construction standalone house with the perfect view for
our anniversary. Charles and I were used to being alone in our travels, it
would seem strange at such a devastating time in my life like this to have
people stopping by unannounced who knew us both and felt they had to
come around and check on me all the time. I enjoy my own company and

when I need people, I go out sometimes I just need to see them from afar like in the cemetery, just to know there are others out there too, I believe it is in my temperament to be even and am self-occupied, surely don't need people telling me how they felt during their loss of anyone, this is me and my Charles, Sandy will help me through this.

Thinking back on our sixty-three years we traveled light because we frequently relocated but when we stopped our lengthy journey and settled down, I think some things could have changed. Our traditions were special and that was why we picked the house we did and not in a retirement community as planned. Our first question to the realtor was "can we see the fireworks from our front yard?" This is the second year you will see the fireworks from the top side and me on the bottom. We knew the multi-level modern house on Prospect Street was the one, it was way over the budget we had planned but with all the money we had saved over the years without children and not buying each other gifts for birthdays, holidays and anniversaries we had a great deal saved. When we moved in, we had the same number of boxes as when we made our second move, the only things we ever really purchase were clothes and necessities. The Air Force would send a moving company every time they wanted us to go somewhere else. It was like a game to us, they would hand Charles paperwork, he would bring it home and I would ask "where are we going?" We were experienced, had a set of melamine dishes with ivy on the border, green bowls and coffee cups, an old percolator, plastic drinking cups and a place setting of four silverware. I don't think we owned anything breakable except the light bulbs, we would wrap them in our towels and fish them out upon arrival. It was a surprising experience to see our familiar everyday items follow us to so many different locations all over the world, there were duplexes, houses, small apartments on and off base, I loved the security of living on base.

Once Charles was promoted, we lived in larger houses on base, it felt like we were living in grand style but never bought new houseware just had a larger footprint to live in. Our one large, brown sofa was deep enough to fit us both laying down, we also had a dresser, coffee table, set of aluminum TV trays with acorns and leaves, two wooden folding chairs and a bed. When Charles retired, we donated it all to the base thrift store where I had worked all over the world, it was still in fine condition and filled our new home with furniture that fit the modern style of our new home. I had always wanted a kitchen table; my mom said a house isn't a home without one, we found the perfect one, it had leaves but I don't think we will need those, it could seat twelve the salesman said, we only got six chairs. He also sold us another brown sofa, a couple of recliners, a round, metal, sleek looking coffee table, a bedroom set with a big decorative headboard, desk for Charles' writing, a couple more chairs and a corner bookshelf, even after all that the house still looked empty.

It was at the point of buying the house that we started collecting things, looking back on it I wish I had bought a couple gifts for Charles. Before the house when I had various jobs on base, I would think about buying him something but knew it would be burdensome on our moves and routine packing. After we were settled, I still didn't feel the need to buy gifts for our special occasions but now that Charles is gone, I see I could have surprised him with a new set of golf clubs. He ran into his old friend Stanley from the fireworks stand who asked him to go golfing, they went once a week until he couldn't anymore, he just used Stanley's old set. Charles was a simple man and appeared to be fine with the old clubs and bag, I think it was Stanley's company that drew him to golfing.

One blustery day we were sitting in the kitchen enjoying the view of the Space Needle and the storm we heard a scratching noise. That is how we found Sandy; a pet was something we had never had due to our extensive travels. She was extremely thin, ribs sticking out her sides like they didn't belong to her, poor girls fur was tan, matted, and dirty, we opened the door, she came in and laid down next to Charles' foot, I suppose cats find their people, she sure found us or Charles anyway. There were flyers hung, we ran an advertisement for a found cat in the local paper, left a message at the Humane Society and no answer from anyone claiming our girl. It looked like we had a cat, we named her Sandy after all the sand traps Charles found in golfing. She followed him everywhere, I think she especially liked being in the garage with him while he cleaned his clubs. If Charles was gone, she would lay in her fluffy sheepskin bed by the window waiting for him, when he arrived, she meowed, howled and turned in circles, you would think she was a dog, I am not sure she even acknowledged my existence while Charles was around. The only human food she ate was green beans, but she would be willing to tell you when it was time for treats or if her bowl was half empty. I am glad she is around now for the company; I think she finally likes me. You know that cat never went back outside after we let her in.

Charles also liked to write stories, maybe I could have bought him a fancy computer, pens, paper, anything. I am not sure why, after his death, there was this need to purchase things for him, he always seemed content to buy a plain notebook at the drug store, a cheap dollar pen and would write for hours. After he passed away I even went as far as to buy a nice pen one you can put refills in and a manly looking notebook with a sailboat on the leather cover from the office supply store and set it on the desk. We had talked about buying a sailboat many times, possibly this is a way for me to still have a connection to him. I know we are still connected some nights as I sit in the house and read, I know he is in the office writing and Sandy will get up and follow my thoughts to be with Charles. She will look at me with the greenest eyes saying don't miss this Charles is here, we both know it, half the time I wake up in the middle of the night on the new futon that I purchased just for the office. It is slowly becoming my bedroom, my pillow, favorite fuzzy blanket with the snowflakes and Sandy are all there, so is Charles. Of course, I have to live life so people don't think I have entirely quit being normal, I just don't know how to act solo in this big house with a cat who has always paid no attention to me prior to this. I am eighty-one years old and have never lived on my own, there were days and months Charles was away, but I went from my parents to married life, I will have to find a hobby or a job to pass some time. Maybe I could arrange and sell flowers at Blossom Up around the corner, there are years of retail experience on my resume from our travels. When I stop in for flowers to take to the cemetery, I ask for something simple with no wrapper since they always seem so busy, this got me to looking at the other arrangements at the grave sites, so many styles, colors and types of flowers. I know a bit about flowers from painting, I took some classes and we painted all the different birth flowers. I used to have a frame and would change the picture monthly to match the flower, I wonder if I still have it? Maybe when I go in tomorrow, I will inquire about employment, there is plenty of money, I am trying to fill my time with activity and people so pay isn't the major concern, I wonder what they will think of this old lady wanting to work for them.

A few days later I finally got the courage to go into Blossom Up and was fully meaning to place an application for employment, but the gal was so busy, it was a small space that looked like a jungle from outside and the line was out the door. The décor is light and purposeful at the same time, I had never thought about how many occasions require flowers. Some people buy them every week for their table, others frequently for a loved one and then some just buy an Easter Lily, birthday traditional flower or poinsettia, yearly. I decided to wait in line, study the shop and make my purchase. Looking out from inside this store it appears you are hidden away in a magical garden with flowers and leaves of plants that I have never seen anywhere before, fairies, prisms, waterfalls, gnomes and various ceramic animals peak out unexpectedly from behind a gigantic leaf of an overgrown beauty, if I worked here I would know the name of the plant that produced that gigantic leaf. I am surer of my decision to work here beyond anything else at this point in my life, I make my purchase of pink peonies for Charles' grave and another fluffy bunch for my table at home and head out after getting the flower mistress' name, Roshelle, the bearer of flora, smiles, fragrance and peace.

Pulling into the garage with the two bunches of peonies, I enter the house with my bunch and Sandy sees the frilly cup sized blossoms and puts her whole face inside on one claiming it as her own. This reminds me of the time Charles, and I were touring Italy and we found wild deep pink peonies growing by Mount Vettore. Charles had recently been stationed at Aviano Air Force Base, Italy. We weren't even unpacked yet, Charles was still on leave to get settled, our few crates and boxes had not caught up with us so on a whim, as nearly all our vacations were, we took the high speed train, exited near Umbria and rented a 1953 Fiat Ghia Supersonic to see the mountains. Charles always had a list of cars that he would like to see and drive, it was a pleasure for him to have been able to rent one of these for the weekend, just to see his smile at such excellence of modern machinery.

While hiking up the ever-trodden trails, with the sun closer than expected, the sparse landscape of trees and grasses it was a surprise to see the wild peonies. We stayed in an old, stone hotel recommended by locals, after the serving of a simple meal of pasta with such deep flavors that could take you into the very roots of the region, the wine was served and in the adjacent court yard of paved bricks the local people and tourist danced all night with the scent of fresh mountain air and calaminta, while the envelope of night opened unto a newly discovered land for us. This was one of many nights spent in foreign lands for Charles and me, even upon returning to our homeland in USA it seemed like new territory after such long absences and landing in new bases. We would stay somewhere abroad or on home shores, be there so long it felt we were forced to act like it was home but be uprooted and   placed in completely different location across the globe to become familiar with. All this reminiscing I almost forgot I was going to take the flowers to Charles. Wednesday afternoon, where has this week gone, this year for that matter?

I place the flowers on Charles' grave and stand a spell, take in the expanse of lawn and space, talk to him of my earlier memories of our travels, I am glad I came today. Marriage is a private union; one you rely on each other for strength, with Charles and I we were a solo set picked up and placed among the nations together. I know the traditions we had, and I still observe are what made us bind with strength. Like last month Flag Day and our decoration was still celebrated by me and Sandy and her new flag collar. June 14, 1777 the American Continental Army was formed so I celebrate my dad and June 14, 1916 Woodrow Wilson declared Flag Day, these and many more are the traditions that bound as a couple. I look for Bob to thank him for helping with my chair last visit, but today he is nowhere in sight. Hopefully, next time I will see him, an asset to City Square Cemetery no doubt, I wonder what his story is and how he started working here.

Detective Munser

July 2020

I AM CALLED IN AGAIN, AT A MOMENT'S NOTICE, THE DESTRUCTION IS HAPPENING again. People for different reasons, demands and conflicts are out, hesitant to show their faces but willing to wear the mask they protest on social media about. Leaders of cities that are hired to see the best interest and protect are wanting to allow people to destroy, lives, businesses, monuments, requesting no one help, hinder or stop the violence. Where does this leave me and my job description that a copy of sits in human resources and in my file at home?

June

August 2020

THERE WERE MANY PIECES OF MY LIFE WITH CHARLES THAT WEREN'T EVEN thought of at the time of his death or until today and in the recent past really. Maybe my mind has taken a break from the sorrow and today I have been allowed to acknowledge the frustration of part of Charles' medical treatment, he endured chemo and whatever else they did in that laboratory. It bothered me to no end, like I was betraying him by dropping him off at the door, some days he was so weak we had to call a nurse and wait until one was available to pick him up in a wheelchair, like that was something I, his wife, was not capable of. This virus came at a bad time or Charles picked the wrong time to be sick and pass away, maybe he had inside information on what was to happen during and after the virus. I would have sat by his side each moment during each treatment, but I wasn't allowed in even though I didn't have any of the list of symptoms they were checking at their entry points to the secret rooms for private service, it was like he belonged to a bad club, my mind wandered while he was in there and I waited outside. Just to keep myself sane during the process since I had to be strong, I would repeatedly think, they are giving Charles the royal treatment, he is a king? No one was immune to the ways this happened, that ridiculous COVID-19 affected so many people in different ways, brought us down to reality. I am sure it affected a tremendous number of others in worse ways than us, we were just going through the worst part of our lives at this time. It just made me feel inadequate, Charles and I had always been there for each other, always. During our whole marriage we were the only people there for each other in whatever slice of the world we happened to be living in. Now it has come to this, I drop him off, wait outside as I can't run errands or go in anywhere because we are vulnerable to the virus and Charles even more so. If I get it then he gets it, things would go much faster than they already are, this seems out of control, at the hardest points in our lives is when we want to do the most and sometimes our hands are tied. I know now it is a good thing we didn't have children, it would break Charles' heart to not be able to see them, especially at the end of his life, how would we visit over the computer? I just couldn't be there for the treatment, that was only one part of this; others had their loved ones admitted and couldn't see them at all, I would feel monumental relief the second my phone would ding with Charles' text saying, "I am on my way out to you." I would know at that moment he would be back to Blue entrusting me to drive him home or wherever he wanted, that was my side of chemo, not a side I experienced medically but a side I went through and I am the one left here to live with it, in order to heal I need to accept and process the facts of my feelings then and now. Cancer may be personal and one sided but with each person going through it there are family members reaching into their souls praying, pleading, wiping up the mess, trying to get to know the last bits of someone, being angry, feeling helpless, crying, being strong and brave when your insides are crumbling, dealing with endless paperwork and unfair systems, new protocols, new mixes of medication, all this to do what you can to keep your loved one alive. Someone who cannot do any of this, not because they didn't have the will but the strength was gone, they were worn and used and tired, too tired to even sit, their voice feeble from the strength it takes to talk, their eyes going blank, you know they are in there by the recognition they provide, you know the fight is real and when cancer has taken over.

It took so much extra effort in those last months to get supplies, groceries, and prescriptions, things we took for granted in the years prior to this.

Time, I thought I should spend with Charles was spent learning a new app, we had used the cell phone before but as our families were gone except for Samuel Charles' brother we used a cordless land line; we only used the cell phone on our travels or if there should be an emergency while we were out. Learning how to purchase groceries on an app, do drive up or pick up which I wasn't aware I had to go in for and couldn't due to the virus and risk, we couldn't get this thing or that product, I wanted to scream, it seemed no one got the severity of this for people who are vulnerable, people like Charles and me. This was all a learning curve and frustration added to my schedule, maybe it wouldn't have been so frustrating if the world didn't have a whole new set of rules instantly laid on us. All I wanted to do was be with Charles, read our books, make sure he ate something, took his medicine and went to the appointments they so kindly wrote on the little business card every time he left, for them it was business, for Charles and I it was life. It was like they were playing catch and release and there was no control on our part. Be here, do this, call if this happens, watch for that, because of the virus, do this don't do that, stay in, come here, rest. We had never had much dealing with the medical field so seeing how it works and them telling us all the time "we don't normally do it this way but..." it wasn't normal for us either, it was all new. I feel tremendously fortunate and am beyond grateful to the medical staff and every person who was there to help, answer questions, administer medication, give direction and compassion during this time that was different for them too. I appreciate each and every one in the entire process but as I look back I see I was holding onto frustration, watching Charles go through the process he went through without any options was hard but at a time like this it was harder on both of us, we were married and connected.

June

September 2020

WELL, WE ARE FINALLY ABLE TO GO OUT, I DON'T KNOW IF WE WEAR MASKS OR not, that keeps changing as does our Phase number. I just kept myself in Phase 1 from the moment the virus hit and seemed to be suspended in time.

This is my first day out where I will go in a real store, probably one that has everything, so I only risk my health once, oh ya and also stop at Blossom Up and see about employment, I will never know if they need me unless I actually stop in and ask. I take my groceries home and new woolen mustard colored socks that looked fun, tell Sandy I shall return and head out for my big interview. I am thinking like this is an ambush, in my mind I already have the job and Rochelle has only seen me on the front side of the counter. Truthfully, I don't know if she needs anyone or can afford to hire me.

I enter the shop and she greets me like always, I ask her about employment, she says she has been thinking of hiring someone part time with the holiday season coming up and asks of my experience, I tell her of my fifty years' experience and many positions all over the world. She asks when I could work and if know about flowers. I tell her between ten and twenty hours a week and I know a little about flowers. She gives me the application, asks if I can show up tomorrow at 10:00 am for when the delivery arrives and says it's ok if you don't know flowers the names are on the boxes when they come in. I complete the paperwork to prove I am legal to work and answer the rest of her questions, ones like "What would you do different here?" questions that took me by surprise.

This was easier than I thought, maybe I waited until just the right time, it felt right. I was there at 10:00 am, handed in the copies of my credentials and in return Rochelle handed me an apron that had Blossom Up and a big flower embroidered on it. While Rochelle was busy with the truck, I checked a couple people out and made suggestions for them. I even found a few stray flowers laying around and made a small bouquet that sold before Rochelle was back, I just sold it for the price like the others. I had always felt comfortable with people and a cash register, now I have flowers to add to that list, Sandy will have to get used to me being out of the house for parts of the day.

I started helping make center pieces out of the beautiful sunflowers, white roses, candles, cinnamon sticks and dried corn. Some even in pumpkins, if they didn't sell and were ready to expire, I could take them home or to the cemetery as I seem to be drawn to. I put a big arrangement on several graves when I could, it feels better to share the beauty than throw it away.

One day, while at work I get an order for fifty two center pieces for the women's shelter annual fundraiser, she tells me not too big and asks for the nonprofit discount, I place her on hold and Rochelle says to assure Gloria all is just like last year. Tells me to ask if she would like her arrangements in pumpkins instead of vases. I get back to the phone and assure Gloria of her price and she says she loves the idea of pumpkins and could get some donated to save on the project, volunteers hollow them out and to just bring flowers, any hardware and show them how to keep them in the pumpkins .

About three weeks later, on the morning of the event, Rochelle wants to know if I would be willing to make this delivery, we usually have a service deliver for us but this is special and needs instruction, I ask where and we load up, they said they would have someone on the other end to get the boxes out of my car so no worries about carrying the flowers. Drive across town to an area I have never been to, very industrial area, I pull into a parking lot as my GPS suggested, not sure what I expected as I knew I was going to a shelter for the first time in my life but wow. The sign said "Charlene's Place", two ladies unloaded the boxes, I came in, they thanked me and in walked Gloria, she was my age; I wasn't the only one out there with white hair on the time clock. She gave me a tour of the place, inside and out, told me the story about Charlene and Bob, his efforts in keeping the place up to par like it is his own house, here or at one of the other locations every weekend, said Bob worked during the week at City Square Cemetery where Charlene is buried, I tell Gloria of my Charles and how he is buried there too, just this last May.

On my ride back to the shop to turn in the envelope with the check, I start feeling like a real person again. I am gaining purpose and have immensely enjoyed meeting Gloria, hearing of the work that is done there for the community and of Bob's commitment to the nonprofits mission. I believe we meet people, do something different or an event happens that can change us for the better in an instant. I hope to learn more about this city and its goodness through flowers.

Ethan

November 2020

WELL HERE I AM, INCLUDED IN THIS MESS I MADE FOR MY FAMILY BEING YOUNG and supposedly smart I did not think this through, not all the way and was only trying to help. I am Ethan Samuel Wilson, aka E> or EMT or Medic. I was born September 2nd, 2003 so that makes me barely seventeen years old, my other pseudonyms came about a couple years ago. I was a freshman in high school and had been trying to get into a Community College program so I could start on my college degree to be a structural engineer, there was a wait of one more year. All I ever wanted to do was learn about constructing bridges and buildings, which was when I met another group of freshmen who were not going to college but out goofing around as I thought at the time. Always being a smart guy and should have known that hanging out with a guy named Ice because he said he was slick was a bad move. Once I got in and started knowing their ways and secrets it was near impossible to get out, or so I thought, I got out alright, just dead. The truth was I was out before I was dead but no one else knew except me and Pearl, she was Axe's girlfriend and wanted to get far away from this mess, I did too. It was getting old, I felt I had mastered the part that took up the space that was lacking in me. I wanted to be seen and now I was, it had been a game becoming so invisible I could tag something with my E> or EMT in seconds and no one would know. I felt important being called EMT, Ethan More Than or some called me the medic, the tags were located all over town. My family had no idea that I had a whole other life with Ice and the crew. I was trusted so much to be on my own that there wasn't much monitoring from my family, I could ride the bus all over the city and tag they just thought I was at the library studying to keep my grades up, at dinner we would discuss what I did in school, their assumptions of my activities made me feel guilty but it was an obsession. There had always been trouble relating to everyone since no one could grasp how easy and hard it was for me to get through a day of school, it was boring and too easy, sometimes I wished my brain would slow down, no one ever suspected a thing when I was out tagging but it helped me. Ice liked that he could go all over and see where I had been, he thought I was serious about being part of his gang. The police thought it was two gang members since I started using two different tags, that was all I really did with the gang that was destructive. I am sure that the dealings Ice had were much deeper than I was, but I didn't want to know, I was easily excused from their activities due to the strict family I made them think controlled me.

My family and I had a whole lifetime of events planned for me, I bet my great grandma had already made a quilt for my college graduation since she was asking about colors of the university I had chosen, and I wasn't even out of high school, I kept my grades up to honor roll qualifications because I had a full scholarship offered from three universities. We as a family went to visit them all, all the campuses were large like cities inside themselves. I decided on the one nearest to home so I could be by my family, we were all unusually close, I couldn't imagine living away from them. The scholarship thing was funny to me since high school was entirely easy and the rest of my talent was swimming. I was like a fish in water, not a popular kid, I didn't have a line of girls wanting to go to prom with me. I tried to dress respectfully especially after I had started hanging out with Ice. One day, at a bus stop, I was wearing some baggy jeans; a large lady came up to me and said she wished she could lose weight like I had so her pants would be baggy too, after that I kept my pants up where they belonged,

I think the large lady was just tactfully trying to give me a clue without preaching. Right before she walked up, I had added an E> to the city bus stop, I wondered if she had seen me as I stood there listening to her story or events about her niece and a new car, one she was going to see.

I had just started my senior year and had managed to keep my friends and my other life at the same time. I never brought them home because I knew my dad, Carl, would know what they were up to, he was smart like that. I am not sure how he got his street smarts, but he had satellite radar built in for the no good or trouble in something. I suspect he had gotten off track in his day but now works for Insulated Business Corporation in the city, they help people start small businesses, opening up the dreams and ideas. He talks about the possibility of each one's success, the help he can give them and then in turn the help they will provide for the city and other small businesses. It is a true calling for my dad to help these people successfully put their dreams into action, he knows what it takes, can show them a successful model and what resources are available for them. He has a true teaching heart that is probably how I received my style of learning, I am grateful for my dad, his abilities, trust and confidence in me.

Figured I should mention this here somewhere since she is a small part of my life. My mom, Lorena, is not reliable or in the picture very much, dad is rather good about letting me see her unless she is too high or has strange people with her. He has only let her come to our house when she is sober and alone, I am not allowed to see her outside of the house or without him present. It was a freezing morning and I had been out tagging (my obsession) I saw her downtown with a distraught looking creep, glad she didn't see me, I think even she would be disappointed in my activity. As a matter of fact, she looked rather eerie, it has been difficult knowing she has chosen the drug life over me, but, by this point I am used to it, she left when I was two years old. Whatever made her choose that life over me remains hurtful like I am not worth her time. Since then she has only been around on holidays and my birthday, she doesn't seem to forget, just doesn't make it any different year after year, maybe she thinks of me often or tries to put me out of her head. If she sees me or thinks of me it reminds her of the failure that she is, and she never tries to make it right with me.

When I see her this Christmas, I will have to remind her about my high school graduation so she will have plenty of time to get sober for a day or two if she chooses. I am fortunate that my dad stayed and provided for me, he has given us a solid life that is more than a lot of people have.

Tuesday, when I was leaving school, Pearl asked where I would be later. I always stayed away from the other guy's girls, never wanted any of them to think I was trying to make moves or let the fast girls move on me. Pearl said she was in trouble and needed help, she asked if I was willing to meet somewhere no one would see us so I wouldn't be involved, with reluctancy I met her eastbound at the Montlake Freeway Station right on 520. That was the strangest bus stop, just last week I had tagged there, I didn't figure anyone we knew would be heading east on the highway since we all stayed in the city pretty much, so we came in on different busses fifteen minutes apart. I was a bit nervous meeting Pearl; this was against my own rules that had kept me safe thus far, this is where I started to go wrong, defying myself, something that should have ever happened.

She got off that bus and looked at my tag, laughed and then looked me in the eye with a stare like a terrified cat. It was so noisy being under an overpass with the traffic going by at freeway speed, the wind swirling and rain coming down, blowing. Pearl said she had heard they were going to rob a warehouse that gets a shipment of medical supplies on Friday night and they wanted her to drive the truck. She knew and had been involved before in many things they did but felt this one was risky since the whole country had been low on all supplies like these since COVID 19. This was 927 cases of things like masks, hand sanitizer, gowns, face shields, thermometers and she doesn't know what else. She told me they had been running paper products and selling to convenience stores for a large profit, but this was going to make them much more cash than that. They would go in through the ventilation system on the side of the building as soon as it was delivered, there was already a buyer for the whole lot, one shot, a done deal. Pearl was going to act too sick to drive or go out, while they were doing the heist, she was going to catch a train to her aunt's house in Kentucky. She knew she needed out and was asking me for a ride to the train station.

I told Axe and Ice that my mom was in town and we had to go to dinner. I had never participated in any of their antics prior, so this wasn't unusual, what was unusual about this part of the story was that Pearl wasn't there. Axe thought something was up but trusted Pearl, they thought she was sick but being as she knew exactly what the plan was, and it was such a big job, they hoped she wasn't double backing on them. They never suspected me of anything because I didn't know what was happening, I should have kept it that way, but I was always one to help, I thought what was one ride? I got in dad's new SUV and met Pearl on Aurora Ave N, she had one large, green backpack and we headed south to King Street Station. Her train left at 9:42 pm, I sure hoped it was on time, I had promised to have the vehicle back by 10:30 pm. It was rare for me to take the car out at night, but dad knew I was sensible and figured this was important to help my friend, Pearl didn't even tell her mom since she was going to her dad's sisters house and he had passed away a few years back. Her mom and her aunt didn't keep in contact at all, she figured it was best no one knew except me. I dropped Pearl off with her backpack, parked the SUV, then went in to make sure she boarded the train safely, not wanting to leave her hear alone. I waved, as she sat in that window seat and the train swayed at low speeds, like a vacuum it entered the tunnel now gone from my sight, I returned to my dad's shiny new SUV, as I was admiring it, I heard my name, my real one, Ethan, then one shot, a piercing burn and a siren probably not for me.

I believe that sometimes people are given those last moments of life so they can process any unfinished business mentally at least. In my last moments nothing moved on me but my brain was still fully operational but different, like looking on myself and being there at the same time, could have possibly been shock to have a bullet rip through me and my fluids spill as I bruised from hitting the asphalted parking spot. Maybe I should leave a message for someone, you hear people say I feel they were comfortable or died instantly and I bet the last thought was let my _____ know I am at peace. It seemed like an eternity but in reality, only a second or two, he was a good shot.

To tell the truth, I decided on the college I was going to because of already losing my mother at such a young age I certainly didn't want to be far away from dad and the rest of the family, truthfully some of the other campuses were better suited for my taste. I hadn't told anyone yet, but certainly the real root of why I was thinking of going away was because I was so smart and high school had been such a breeze but my fear deep down was what if college wasn't that way? I couldn't be the smartest person in the world, USA, Washington state or even King county. There had to be smarter people than me, what if I failed at college, just because I liked skyscrapers and bridges doesn't mean I could design them. This obsession started at three years old when dad would take me downtown and we would watch the heavy equipment knock down buildings, dig mammoth holes and cranes erect structures that were taller than I could imagine, dad explaining the building would be built on giant rollers. I am only seventeen years old, how am I supposed to know the whole path of my life yet, dad does ok and I wonder if he knew at seventeen what he would become, for sure mom didn't know, she doesn't know now even hour by hour what her circumstances will be, I am positive she didn't want to be an addict and have made the choice of failure in areas that aren't suitable for mainstream society. I wonder if life is easier for mom without the decisions we all make, she eats what she can get her hands on, wears what they hand out, sleeps where the newly found roof is, she never worries about bills, taxes or making decisions about her life any deeper than which food bank or clothing bank to stop at or where to score the next drug in whatever form that is, I know she must wonder if this is the one that will kill her as she thinks about the next hit or person she encounters. Sometimes it was just easier to roll along with their story and dream, it was my dream too, but I had been having doubts days before Pearl called. I wanted to go away to college at least for the first couple years so if I did fail it wouldn't be known to my family and I may have a fair chance to recover.

All the tagging was starting to get to me, it wasn't fun anymore, in the beginning there was a whole city to touch, now I had been all over without anyone knowing, not even my gang friends knew the areas I covered, I was always on the outside of everything. There weren't any other places that seemed appealing to tag, I didn't want to stay and see them everywhere I went. I didn't want to get caught or play acrobatics, get hurt, confront another gang, if I went to another city it would be something I stopped doing because it wasn't my town, I was truthfully, tired of seeing my own personal destruction of the city. I hope they figure out the brilliancy of my glow in the dark black light paint, I am thinking that out of the 767 tags no one has had a black light on it yet, I wonder how since there were no clues as to in what way I was connected gang wise if they will ever make the connection to me. Signing off Ethan / E> / EMT, Medic.

Gloria

November 2020

GOOD AFTERNOON, I AM GLORIA WILSON BORN IN BIRMINGHAM, ALABAMA JUNE 24th, 1929. Seems like a long time ago, there has been revolutions of change and development in my lifetime. My daddy, Cecil, a blond haired, blue eyed corn farmer, my mama, Delta, a tall dark-haired beauty with green eyes, me the oldest who favored mama, my three brothers Jake, Cecil Jr and Dowry all lived in a two room shack outside of Birmingham. It was hot and humid in the summer and freezing in the winter. Mama would cook on the old woodstove in the main room when the stove was hot all us kids would bath in the round metal tub that usually sat on the porch, in the summer we liked to say that tub was our swimming pool. We were so poor we always looked dirty no matter how much we bathed, our clothes were worn and old from working, working in the fields through the seasons. I still laugh at some of the memories I have like Jake wearing Uncle Billy's old checkered socks or sometimes mama would make the boys clothes out of my outgrown cast offs, I didn't do too bad since I was the oldest and the only girl. Sometimes I even got clothes made from mama's old dresses or the sheets if she didn't turn them into curtains, we used every scrap of everything just to get by.

Before my time, daddy almost lost the farm and had to take in odd jobs, he was handy with his tools and got a job in town helping to build a large hotel. I had only seen one story places; daddy said this one had more than ten stories and was right next to another place, they could see in each other's windows, there was even plumbing inside, that was unheard of, said he had used the flush toilet himself right indoors on the eighth floor. He would come home most weekends and tell us stories of the city, one Friday daddy showed up with all his tools and said we needed to pack light; we were heading out in the morning. His boss would pick us up, drop us at the bus depot and we would transfer to a train in Chicago headed for Seattle. Daddy had a job and house all lined up it was 1939. We got on that train and people had fancy clothes nothing like we wore. Mama said act like you are wearing what they are, and no one will notice. On that trip we saw Lake Michigan, large cities, countryside, fields bigger than I ever imagined, the Rocky Mountains and then finally The Puget Sound and Seattle. We took checkered taxi to our new home in Hillman City, it looked just like the other houses, I had never imagined being crowded in like this, we had always had room to run, corn to hide it. Inside our house was nice and we had indoor plumbing with a toilet and tub, an electric stove, even had a yard with a wooden fence marking our small boundaries.

The next day daddy went to work building apartments at Yesler Terrace Housing Development. I was hooked on the city and all it had to offer, I think my brothers and mama were happy too. Living was better, we went to school, people were around, and everyone shared what they could, and daddy was home with stories and food every night. Seems like we were just really settling in when Pearl Harbor hit, back in those days' knowledge was not as quickly available as it is now and news didn't travel like it does currently so being young, I didn't grasp the severity of what had happened. I knew it was bad as my mom would cover the windows for black outs at night, she didn't want to worry us, so she said she was keeping the heat in, but I knew in my heart things were different from the stress lines on my daddy's face when he would come home carrying a story and a newspaper.

Life was simple and went as planned I went to school, graduated in 1947 and attended a secretarial college downtown plus worked part time as a secretary for an optician. I rented a room above a drugstore from one of my friends that was graduating, it was an eye-opening time to be able to support myself and learn to cook on the hotplate we had in our common area and be a young woman in the city. One night I met Carl in 1950 and life flowed as you would think, courting, dances and marriage, nothing with big flair. I kept working and we moved to a small apartment complex on Capitol Hill, we could see the city light in all directions. There were no thoughts of having any babies and never planned for any but in 1961 along came Carl Jr., he grew up as a city boy and adapted well to business, maybe too well since he hit it rich and moved on, I miss my boy, he was a delight and surprise. He married, had Carl III in 1982, got in early on a new adventure, retired in Florida at fifty-two in 2013, two years after my Carl Sr moved to his own place. Maybe he was waiting to see how we would get along apart, Carl III is Ethan's dad who stayed in the city and became interested in social services and my work at the women's shelter. That is where he met Lorena, she had been with us for over a year, was clean and sober, going to school and had a job lined up that paid well as a flagger for a road construction company on federal projects. She looked confident in her reflective vest and construction boots, that may have been what attracted Carl III to her, he was a businessman and she was of the streets, but both were confident in who they were. She had just gotten a small car and cell phone so she could report to the assigned locations when they called in the morning for work, then she would slowly transition out of the shelter to her own housing. I was so proud of her, she did well except she never moved into her own housing, she moved into my grandson's luxurious condo that his dad had left him, and they had Ethan a year or so later. After a couple years of juggling work, being a wife and mother, Lorena started acting out of character but probably like her true self that she couldn't resist. She was out later than normal, failed to pick up Ethan from the babysitter, groceries weren't bought, the lights and water got turned off, Carl III confronted Lorena, she said she had relapsed and would move out immediately, Carl III offered rehab or any other help she needed, she refused, packed and left to be with her drug of choice instead of her newly found life. They say it is easier to keep it together than get it together but that was not the case for Lorena. The drugs seemed to be an overtaking priority, over her being, marriage, son, home, and all that she had worked so hard for, maybe it didn't feel real to her.

This is when I stepped in and helped with Ethan most days, he was such a joy and looked just like my father Cecil, tall with the white blond hair and blue eyes. I thought it was strange how traits and even movements could travel through blood lines of family members that had not ever met. He was so much like my dad that it almost felt like I was a little girl again only I was grown with all these blessings and sorrows; life brings you interesting twists and memories in strange ways. Ethan was an easy boy, he didn't rebel against the school system, mine or his dad's rules or schedule, he didn't even want much, we would buy him things like a bicycle, and he loved it, but it was like he had never thought of wanting one, same with his video gaming system, he played it and would accept new games but never asked for any. Even after his mom left, he seemed fine, pretty much went with the flow, and did what was natural to him, he always told us where he was going, we trusted him to travel the city alone, he never went anywhere except to the library, school, and the waterfront that we knew of. He loved to watch people and see the seagulls glide in the wind, he studied, picked a college close to home and was generally in good spirits. I had expected some sort of trouble just due to him being a teenager, there didn't appear to be a bit of rebellion in him.

I think the night Carl III called to say he was coming over at 1:00 am, I was sure that Lorena was gone, that was a phone call I knew would happen someday, I wanted to be there for Carl III and Ethan. Carl III showed up in a taxi alone which was strange, I thought maybe he had been drinking to calm himself which was out of character for him or was too distraught to drive, Carl III opened his mouth to tell me but couldn't speak. That was when I knew it wasn't Lorena, he had gotten over her years ago and her passing would not break him to the point of no words. He finally got out that it was Ethan, Ethan was gone, had passed away, been taken, shot, that a Detective Jeffery Munser from the Seattle gang unit had left about the time he called me, the detective had sat with him for over an hour to be sure he was fine which he will never be after that moment of notification. He said

Ethan had given a friend a ride to the train station, the police were looking into it, that didn't matter to me what they investigated, because Ethan, my beautiful boy was gone way before his time, this wasn't news I allowed to sink in that night but I knew it was real just didn't want to process it yet, I wanted to be strong for Carl III. As I sat and looked upon Carl III slumped over with his chest almost resting on his legs ,in the recliner, I knew there were no words for being in this situation, only sorrow deeper than I ever thought was possible pouring over us in different ways. This may sound crazy but the mind does unreasonable things at mournful times, I thought I would have to bury my boy Ethan with the quilt I made him so we could be close and in my mind he could continue on since it was made for a passing from high school to college, now we had to face this unbearable passing, I don't know how, this is harder than anything I have been assigned to in my lifetime.

Detective Munser

November 2020

I WAS JUST SETTLING IN FOR THE NIGHT BUT AS USUAL KNEW MY REST WOULD BE brief, I sat in my favorite rocking chair my shoes were untied, my feet on top of them, just needed to rest a quick minute to be ready. The streets had been active all summer and early autumn, was hoping there could be a quiet night sometime soon. This was the first night of my four-night shift that usually turned into a ten-night stretch of details, territory and tears of my clients as I call them, I know they had not signed up for this and I wish they weren't on my caseload but we are connected by an act of someone who wants to be in control.

It was 9:57pm Thursday, November 12th, I had just turned the television off and didn't want to see the any of the news let alone the top story, the drama of the news casters rehearsed as the enunciate pointed words, like they are hoping you will believe their story more with their acting abilities. I was on the streets daily and saw the truth that was not what you see on the nightly news local or national syndicate. I try to avoid TV but once a week I watch a show on the free channels, crazy I have a paid subscription for cable just to get the free channels, there is always a loophole somewhere, I see it in the justice system every day how people get away with almost anything they put their mind to.

I get a call for one bullet in a parking garage, usually at this time of night doesn't even draw attention to anything. I arrived at the scene about 10:10pm, the suspect was young, on the ground with blood to his left side, whoever had shot him had walked right up to him and fired at close range. He still had his wallet and keys to a brown SUV so new there weren't plates on it yet. This was not a robbery, I wondered if the vehicle was stolen or the reason he had been shot, was he trying to leave? Could he have taken it from a gang member? My thoughts wandered to why he had been here and was someone he knew on the train or had they got off and killed him and why? Variables that the train schedule may connect or rule out, I don't see any cameras but that doesn't mean they aren't here. This appeared to be a private matter, targeted, not just another rolling shootout, it was different than most calls. I am not sure why they called me, but I am glad they did, these are the types of calls I want to solve more than anything, he was so young.

Most scenes that I arrive at have many witnesses, but no one saw anything here. Most are done in the open light of the day with children on the playground, people going home from work, others fetching a gallon of milk and a quart of beer from the corner store. They just shoot each other, leave the body and drive on like it's another day. When they join the gang, they are told there is a bullet with their name on it somewhere and it is their mission to avoid it. It could be on their own turf or as they advance across a line not even intending to into a rival's turf. It is a war that no one wins; you take a bullet for what? To sit in a wheelchair if you're lucky or to leave what you have to your fair-weather friends that will just as soon kill you if you cross them. If, at a young age, alone, seeing this life and were honest with yourself you would never make this turn to where you are today. This is not a joy ride gone wrong, a city hunting trip, the boy or girl wearing different colors across the street line has a family just like you. They have a mom, dad, brothers, sisters, aunts, uncles, cousins, grandparents or some combination of the above. You might think you are a bad ass, but I have been there at the second of death for too many people younger than me, they all say, "tell my mom I love her". You may read about it online or hear it on the street, shoot and never be caught or take honors from your crew but this is the link that needs to be seen, the families that are affected by each bullet. Next time your family is together imagine some people just gone, look at the ones who are not gang affiliated, what if they were in the crossfire, who would miss them, what are the connections?

The victim's name was Ethan Samuel Wilson, 17 years old, blonde hair, driver's license says 6'2", 165 pounds. By 11:00 pm the scene is cleared, SUV is towed, he is in a body bag heading to the medical examiner to see if we can retrieve the bullet and make a connection in our database. My job now is to visit this Carl who owns the SUV, presumably Ethan's father. I drive just north of the city center, thinking there have been too many of these calls lately, I wonder what Carl knows and how will he take the news, I ring the building entry system even though I could enter with my police access card and knock on his door, this is not that type of news to deliver in a building like this with a knock, this will give Carl Wilson a moment to process the police are on their way up, it is quite possible there aren't many police calls to this distinctive residence.

I enter the silver and wooden elevator, pushing the button to the six-teenth floor, arrive at the door of Carl's residence too quickly, Carl answers the door immediately knowing something is wrong, he states his son Ethan was due back forty-five minutes ago, has always been reliable and rarely goes out at night. There doesn't appear to be anyone else at the residence, he knows now by my silence that this has to do with Ethan. I tell him the news I never wanted to deliver; he slumps down on a bench in the foyer of their stately town home with sweeping views of the city. From this second forward life will be different, there will always be the before and after line. For the living it is a vertical line but for the ones who have passed it has now laid down and become a horizontal dash, one of which there is no retreat from. After a few standard questions Carl says he needs to leave and realizes he doesn't have a vehicle on our way out, I offer him a ride but he declines, I would assume that he wants to be as far away from me as possible to put some time between us and the reality of his son's death. I wait with him while he stands awkwardly against a tree waiting for his ride. I waited for his safety and to see who he called, I still had no idea if he knew more about this or was just a distraught man. Most people's first instinct is not to leave their home when they get news like this so even the first part of this investigation and Carl has given me a reason to be suspicious. I give him my card before his ride arrives, I had assumed he would call a friend but a taxi appears, the driver yelling the meter is running, Carl looked defeated, slumped over, I ask where he is going, wondering why he hasn't told me, he says to his mom's to deliver the news of Ethan, "she deserves more than this," were his last words to me in the wee hours of the morning of November 13th, already a new day with the prior one pushing it's prompts of priority into my being.

There are an enormous amount of cases that are always being worked, we are a task force of twenty and are up against a city, just as any police force is. As a rule of the streets most people's name or body will come across our desk, sometimes their name comes up because they were in the wrong place and are now dead or have shot someone. Sometimes an innocent bystander even kills a gang member, these stories turn all different ways, this one had a twist I would not have suspected. We thought an unknown gang was in town, a sidestep to an already existing gang, maybe only a couple new members to take over some territory by tagging on turf that wasn't theirs and claiming it but what was different about this was the tags were all over, was it to be confusing and for already existing groups to watch out, to put everyone on edge as it did. It was all done by two members E> and EMT, all over the city, north to Shoreline, south to Burien, east to Bellevue and west in Ballard, there were considerably more of the E>'s. We were watching this for a couple years, it was making quite a statement and wondering what it would spark, some takeovers of buildings or territory and leave a few bodies behind or just another loose wire in the odd mix of cases.

The medical examiner's report of Ethan was delivered a few days later, all it revealed one 9mm bullet and some paint residue under his nails like spray paint, no sign of anything in the toxicology report, not even any alcohol or nicotine. The paint was different than most spray paints, it glowed in the dark with a black light, we had never used a black light in our detective work on a body. No other clues and it seemed as if he had no connections to anything off key. We still didn't know why he was at the train station in the first place, that night I went out and found some of his 700 or more tags and sure enough, it was the same kind of paint Ethan had under his nails, hundreds of cans of paint had to have been used over the past two years, he had to have had a connection to someone to have been targeted. The next day I asked Carl if I could search their storage or townhouse for more paint. I found two more cans of identical paint in the storage with Ethan's bicycle gear, we believe Ethan had bought a can here, a can there, to keep eyes off him. He tagged so much the stores kept it in stock because it was selling, they didn't realize it was mostly one person purchasing it, of course he was all over town.

After the murder Axe, Ice and Pearl were absent from school for more than a week, people said Ethan hung out with that group, which was hard to believe as they were already criminals and Ethan was an honor student. Axe and Ice were easily located on their turf but there was no sign of Pearl. Her mom had been robbed and roughed up a couple nights ago, but she wasn't talking, this could be connected or not. I recognized her from the bar she worked at downtown close to my first beat that Halloween so long ago and a place I frequent in my many calls to the streets, she probably wouldn't remember me being as she had lived in survival mode her whole life.

I have attended too many funerals for the young, sometimes the killer shows up but there are no rules in these gang situations a bunch of killers may show up. They should have respect they already took out one or more, it is devastating for the family of the murdered to find out about the gang affiliation after a death. Some parents are too busy, others no clue, sometimes the behavior of the gang member doesn't change, they lead two separate lives.

It was when Pearl's mom filed a missing person's report at the end of November and we located Pearl's trail, she has since moved onto Ohio and was in trouble there, being in the wrong place at the wrong time, as she said, that was when the info started spilling, she wasn't willing to talk about what had happened in Seattle, Kentucky or Ohio but it would all surface somehow, she would trip up and need a way out. She got someone murdered to stay out of trouble herself and jumped right back in, but she wasn't talking, a zip lip sort of gal, seemed to me she had more firsthand experience than most girls her age, she was in deeper than she let on in her innocence. She said she just wanted out, but I knew there was more to this story, this girl leaves a trail of blood in her wake and doesn't look back, I will be watching her.

Carl III

November 2020

I HAVE ALWAYS ENJOYED RAISING ETHAN, HE HAS ALWAYS BEEN A PLEASURE TO be around and kept me company his whole life and probably didn't know the depth of that. After his mom left, I put all of me into him and when I got the news of his murder parts of me died along with him, my Ethan. He may have needed me for food, shelter and whatever else he never asked for, I would buy him objects that I would think a boy his age would desire, and he would be entertained with it for a short while, but he had ideas in his head that were his own. When he was fifteen or so I bought him a flat screen TV for his room, he says, "dad I don't want to be ungrateful, but can you put that in your room?" If I were to have one, I would need one with a slew of required numbers and letters I had never heard of for gaming. I put that TV in my room and took Ethan to the store to pick out the one he required for his needs. Everything was like this for Ethan, he was polite beyond any teenager and had knowledge above any other person I had met, Ethan knew exactly what he wanted in life or so I had imagined, this time has become confusing for me realizing my son had a separate life than the one I pictured when I left for work every day, a whole other identity.

Now Ethan is gone, in the past, buried, no more of his being here with me, and I have no idea how to wrap my mind around that, I suppose I should track down Lorena if possible, to give her the news. I tried the night the detective visited before the funeral, of course she didn't have minutes on her phone and will try again one more time, she may call someday. For years I paid her bill so she could call Ethan anytime then I realized one day that connected me to drug deals that she or one of her so-called friends made over that phone, so that part of the story ended. Since disconnecting that line, she has never made sure she kept minutes to call or even the same number, or a roof, she is financially precarious in all areas of her life, nothing matters more than drugs or the chase of obtaining them, I can't say I know what drug she uses just know for sure I will not be the person who gives her $5.00 to get a drug that may kill her. The last I saw her she looked about sixty years old and didn't have the means to keep a prepaid phone on, I know the beauty and potential I saw in her being, she quite possibly had the ability to keep this life together for a bit but not the strength or desire to continue it. I do wish she had been here all these years with me and Ethan, I miss the Lorena I knew, it would have simplified life for my boy and myself if she had been there for us, we have always been there for her even in her unreliability. I lean over on my couch as if she is there, someone is there to accept me while I mourn.

I am still in shock, there has been the news of Ethan's death, newspaper articles, talks with the police, a funeral with hundreds of teenagers, everyone knew Ethan, and the extreme quiet afterwards. I have no plans of food, wonder if I should stay living in this place or can mentally stay living here, it is where Ethan resides on this side of his lifeline. His clothes, TV, bicycle, books, sports gear, spray paint, college plans, are all here, my new root beer brown SUV is here. I don't even like that color, but Ethan loved root beer and I thought he would see the irony in it, he always liked underlying jokes and dry humor, would shake his head and smile, me knowing a full-fledged laugh was going on in his head. The idea of the spray paint is mind blowing, the detective says there are tags all over town. Leave it to Ethan to be smart enough to work a gang to be in but not really and make it look like there is another gang in town, knowing him it was probably a challenge for himself to see the city and not get caught. I will have to call the detective and find out where these tags are so I can see where my son has been, I can't believe my son was in parts of town I will hear about.

I sit here in a condo sixteen floors up on Third Ave that was purchased by my dad for his liking many years ago and he kindly gave to me when he relocated to Florida, a place to be desired by many but not really to my liking. I could use him here now; I don't know how to act in this situation, I am a mess, mentally and physically. The view is spectacular, I am not sure I care about much or can feel anything, am not even thinking right anymore. Ethan and I used to watch the ships go by with the telescope and guess what was in the containers, watch the ferry's glide along the Puget Sound or bump along depending on the weather. For most of those almost eighteen years Ethan and I have lived here alone as two guys so the place is decorated industrial minimalistic. We made the third bedroom into a home theatre which has the latest technology thanks to Ethan's knowledge. Now, as my thoughts ramble, I do not believe Ethan ever brought a friend home from school or anywhere, where did all the swarm of children come from at his funeral, how did they find out where and when it was, did their parents know where they were, were they skipping school? I wasn't expecting hundreds of people to show up let alone children. They were outside on the lawn smoking who knows what, when I looked at one group they hid a bottle, they all must have known I was Ethan's dad, not one of them ever said a word to me, they just looked at me with confused sad eyes and looked away at the same time, me not registering on their radar but knowing I was there. How did they know who I was? It wasn't like Ethan would have been showing family photos around school, he was essentially a private person as he didn't have a classic mom and with our residence being higher class than most of his peer's questions could be asked that he wouldn't want to answer. I can't see Ethan explaining why we live in an upscale building, his mom nowhere to be seen and dad works at the shelter in the business incubator with his grandma. That all sounds a bit sketchy, even to me, maybe Ethan's life was too hard to explain, and his tagging was his form of acting out. Wanting answers, I have searched his room without disturbing anything and have found only one clue, it was a brochure to the

University of Vermont. This is not one of the colleges or universities we toured but digging deeper in the desk I find an acceptance letter with his name, Ethan Wilson. Was he running from the gang, from my expectations or himself? No matter what I couldn't have imagined Ethan living so far from me then remember like a punch in the gut, he does live far from me, not just for a semester but forever. Death gives a warped perception to the living, we forget somehow at moments that our loved one is gone and other times we can't forget, every turn brings a memory of them and their absence.

After school most days Ethan would come home, and I would arrive shortly, bringing takeout, sometimes cooking a meal for a day or two, it never mattered to Ethan what we ate, we had an unspoken deal; dinner was our time, he was always there and happy to see me. I would walk in and no matter what he was doing he would stop, walk up the hallway, turn his head to the side in his was like a quirk of his, look at me and say, "welcome home dad, what's for dinner?" Looking back that happened hundreds of times and each time it made my whole day worth working through and entering our residence. If he had been unpredictable this may have been easier if that is possible, but he was always the same to me. I would set the dinner down on the counter or food to prepare and Ethan searched the bags and got out the plates and utensils, he would decide if it would be paper or real plates. How many unspoken sets of behavior did we have? Live a system or groove that worked for us, I need to start watching for that other places and appreciating people because I miss Ethan more than could ever be put into words and can't recall if I told him, certainly not enough. I miss his voice, movement, looking in the bags, his being, himself, quirks, ways and quick wit.

My plan is to try and find every tag my son put into this city. This will at least get me out of here and out where my son has been. Detective Munser must have a map.

With the pandemic that has hit our city this year, things were off all year which threw me on edge. Ethan's death was the pit of it all, when I get on edge, I am not violent or mean but withdraw from society, seems I can't communicate or mesh well. We had been meeting grandma to bring her groceries, I think she has always been stronger than me and taught Ethan those skills too. She is the one person who navigated the funeral and arrangements, we heard things we never thought we would hear at a time we would have never imagined, things like coffins on back order, grave shortages and only a few people at a funeral, think about who you will invite. I didn't invite anyone they; all just showed up, I didn't order a casket but there was one with a beautiful silver finish, I didn't order flowers but there were flowers of blue and white, I didn't pick a grave but there was one between the fountain and flag. Grandma Gloria has always had the ability to take over any tragedy and make it the best she could, it was a skill she had to separate herself from the tragedy and somehow make the path a little smoother with beauty. With all my grieving I believe I have been stagnant in time and have forgotten to connect with her in her grief. We have talked but not much about Ethan or the process of death, what it has done to me or her, she is giving me time, she always seems to know what to do with the respect of others. Maybe she would like to go with me on the mission of finding the tags.

Detective Munser

December 2020

LIKE MANY OF MY CASES, I ATTENDED THE FUNERAL OF THE VICTIM. ETHAN'S DEATH bothered me more than others, the older I get the more I feel, if I had a son how would I want this case to be handled? That is a question I ask with every murder because murder is murder no matter what, even if it is justifiable it is still the loss of life, the facts need to be laid out, every stone turned over. Having to look at and explain to the victim's families is the hardest part, they want answers that aren't there sometimes, there are cases that are never solved, they are not just another case to me but if there aren't any clues or witnesses or people who will speak what can I do? Sometimes an unlikely witness pops up, I took it all on personally, figured I should go to the graveside and see the headstone, maybe someone had left a token of respect or something. It was a cold, early December morning, typical dreary, Seattle day, the leaves were emitting their lasting scent on the ground as the trees finished their final push off for winter survival. This is the reason I stay in Seattle; I love the rain and the gray days, it makes you feel as if you can focus, the clouds make the bright brighter. On cloudy days, my mind isn't saying go out and play even though I wouldn't anyway I prefer the indoors, I write as a stress reliever, I will get into that later Ethan is number one at this point.

When I arrived at the gravesite down the hill, the place was quiet only a Mercury Sable a few rows over, too far to see the model but from what I could tell the person was a young, dark-haired male that looked familiar, maybe everyone looks familiar, so many stories and faces with connection. I hear machinery in the distance hoping if it's another grave it doesn't have to do with me, but of course, the noise could be from the construction site just west of here. They are building a 200-unit apartment complex, more people inevitably more crime, I hate that I am becoming cynical but that is part of the job, knowing and being truthful of the facts. This cemetery is a peaceful place, rolling hills, ponds and a few gardens.

After all the violence committed during the past year, and with everyone being quarantined the city needs to chill but winter is upon us, but not everyone will be inside for the duration of the season, which means some will end up underground and become endless paperwork for me. It doesn't matter to the unruly about the stay in place order, they are out seeking opportunity, opportunity of any kind, even if they create it unexpectedly because they happened upon someone vulnerable. Still too many people home, jobs deleted from society just like they were never there, empty store fronts, mass evictions as if the courts weren't over loaded anyway, criminals released to return right where they were picked up from like their retention wasn't part of the story. Then we have the whole society of homeless people, they have a system of surviving, for a few weeks you see one long enough to give them a name in your head and then they are gone. There was one middle aged man who always had a sandwich and three shopping carts, he spent his days toting them, he would cross all four ways around an intersection an all-day event, one cart at a time I called him Sammich, he slept in parking lots with his head on the curb by the menacing multi windowed courthouse, makes you wonder if something happened to him there that he couldn't disconnect from. Another who you could see arguing with himself consistently, was dubbed the Debater he had a PO Box downtown on 3rd and Union, was checking his mail, a lady walked towards him he opened the box and put his wallet inside stating no woman would steal it from him ever again pulling his key from the lock. There are others that float through, one with a large Army bag I call him the Packer, have seen him in Red Robin enjoying a beer and eating a tall burger. Lately there are a couple new ones, both men, one with a denim skirt that has zippers on both sides, it flows to the curb as he prances around town, he doesn't look feminine in any way, I will give him the title of Maxi D for his long skirt. The other new gentleman has pink and purple spandex and a smile as big as the sky, he shall be called Content by the look on his face, happy to see everyone. It makes you think about where they come from and what their stories are, there are so many the streets need to be swept every morning before the business crew comes in to run a whole other show. I am almost convinced that at dusk the sidewalks open and people you don't see in the daylight come out, then return to their slumbering place before sunrise. The homeless population are the least of my worries in my line of work, I know there are hundreds and they are all connected to a family somewhere, but I don't have much contact unless they commit a crime that appears gang related or have been in the crossfire, which does happen with them being out in vulnerable locations. Sometimes this is how I get information; from someone you aren't sure is reliable, but they wouldn't know what they do if they hadn't been at the crime scene.

Seattle is an interesting place, so vibrant and dreary at the same time, there is just the right amount of friendly and standoffishness in people. It was difficult in my profession to make friends, my shifts changed frequently sometimes in a matter of a second. I could be going to the movies and called in, I just stopped trying to fit into any schedule and kind of enjoyed that, it got into my blood. Almost like being an emergency room doctor, you are just there, and the wounded come about they all have a wound but most of the time no story. The wounded I see are usually on the street but occasionally in a rat-infested hotel five floors up with wallpaper from decades ago and carpet on the stairs worn past its expiration, left in a storage shed or ghetto apartment. They were all busy doing their thing and then I came into the picture, their screen generally shut off, gone from the existence they knew, occasionally one would survive, facts and families to locate. On a personal note I have seen many places I would prefer not to die.

As far as housing goes it was my luck to stumble upon an apartment in an older house on Etruria Street in Freemont, I have been here almost twenty years. While I was still a patrol officer downtown, the city had been hot for a few weeks and dispatch called my partner Metevior and I out on an unknown hang up call. When we arrived, there was a body and a big neon for rent sign with the number in faded marker in the window. I quickly jotted down the number and called homicide, we just guarded the body and waited. The next morning it was all over the news about the murder, I called the number from the faded sign and inquired about the place. Mrs. Johnson was the landlady and asked how I heard about it. She was happy to rent to me especially right after the murder, probably not too many other prospective tenants, we sealed a deal before I even knew what the cost was or what I was renting. Come to find out it was the second-best decision of my life, top floor unit, all utilities paid, with a deck that included a view of the bridges and easily affordable on my tight budget at the time, it has easy access to the city north and south. She has never raised my rent and allows me to do repairs and live my solo life. I don't go out much, but it is nice to get away from my regular areas and feel secluded at home, it's like I am hidden right in site and still in the middle of it all. Gas Works park and the Freemont Troll bring quite a bit of traffic through the area, but daytime is not a time I am out, I have become a night creature myself. If I have slept a whole night through in the past twelve years, I can't recall it, seems Seattle may be a city that doesn't sleep either or at least I don't.

These lyrics are a tribute to my life and the lives of the victims I come across. I'm not sure where they will be placed or sold but they were in my mind tonight and needed to be on paper.

December
The cold air, missing links
I see you in the water
In the plywood covered business
Mass words on the daily blotter
I see you in it all.

On the water, I feel you waving to me
You go with me daily, through the roadblock
I handover my grief and frustration to you
Talk as we transfer location to outlined body chalk
You are deep within my soul and part of me

In the sky, the clouds surround you
Take form inside my mind
Rattle around to make sense where there is none
No answers, not here, not there, not any kind
I am the middle the one who is left

I find you in the woods, deep within the trees
In graffiti, someone's choice of words
Sprawled across the city, so delicately placed
I see you in the flight of the morning bird
I hear you in the wisdom you left behind.

You guide me through the ways
Of paths that are destined
Journeys direction undefined
All for night to find rest in.
#Seattle Strong
#DJMunser
#MunDetJ

Carl III

December 2020

It has been just at six weeks give or take a day since my son Ethan has left this earth, I am prone to use his name now maybe more so than prior to his death, I am sure it solidified in my mind that he was surely here with me at one point and continues to be present, even if that means I recall him to my side. The days have stretched into weeks without me realizing it but knowing this at the same time. My own form of denial, I look at the shiny cap of the city with its dome of moving lights from my homes with a pristine view, the view I always enjoyed, maybe I have never truly lived myself, this is a wonderful place to be but is not my choice of homes, I am grateful for this place and realize not many people could afford to live here.

Five days a week I use the unblemished silver vacuumed and polished elevator to my new root beer SUV, every time wonder how the building stays up with the expanse of the garage, knowing Ethan would know, exit the oversized steel door painted a shade of alley brown and proceed the short distance to the shelter, park in the alley and I help others launch and brainstorm their dream, this is my routine; I am living in this beautiful city and have never truly seen it. Of course, I have been to the park and various attractions when dating Lorena, after Ethan was born and charitable events but I am not a man to notice, places, seasons or artwork. I am sure that Ethan had more internal substance than I have ever had, I must change that perspective, I must change many fragments of my being and patterns of life that I have so lazily fell into to fully understand why I am here, what my purpose is, it must be deeper than this. Every day I crumble inside as I attempt to exit my building knowing this is the last place I saw Ethan and he will not be here asking about dinner or telling me he loves me anymore, I know I can't stay stuck in this scene forever but when I am not here it seems I am in another realm, one I want to escape and return to my own box of thoughts, the only place that feels sufficient to me. It is as if I am empty when gone from home, living outside myself and when I return, I am complete, but I realize that is only me and my process of healing. People talk to me, I still do the same job, drive the same route, look at the Christmas decorations and want to scream, I think that last thought has allowed me to acknowledge the depth of my grief, I am normally a sensible man. I want to think about what to buy Ethan for Christmas not think about what I would put on his grave if anything. I will be unpredictable and late today, it may be crazy but I am going Christmas shopping and buying something for a boy that is every age one through seventeen and drop them off at the shelter while I am at work today, this is something I can control, maybe I can't buy for Ethan but I can buy for someone.

Detective Munser returned my call a couple weeks ago and said I could stop by downtown anytime and there would be a copy of the file with the locations to every tag related to Ethan. Today is the day to pick up the file on my lunch hour which came sooner due to my shopping expedition, perhaps in my mind if I didn't have the file in my possession I wouldn't have to move from this cocoon that I have created between reality and whatever state it is I have begun living. I inch downtown during the lunch rush, hoping to be back within an hour, just like normal, but in reality it doesn't matter, I am the director of the shelter's business incubator and can be gone the rest of the day or week for that matter and the place would run with me afar. Other people have ideas too, it can't be just me that lifts the dreams of others into reality. I am just addicted to the mechanics of the business and love to be involved in the behind the scenes program overviews, the success stories are my obsession, maybe more now than before, somehow I think in my mind that if I could have somehow, some way, any way saved Lorena that Ethan would be here now so I put my heart and experience into the peculiarities of a business raised out of a shelter, the buried plans of people that have hit bottom are quite enlightening to observe when their seed sprouts. It suddenly hits me that I may have passed some of Ethan's tags, this is how I got to where I am, not paying attention to the outside world. A trait I may have been born with but must change now to get through this unexpected, unfortunate, heart breaking time. I cannot stay in this state of mind for much longer, knowing I must change is even new to me, realizing the actions is my first step to difference. When I married Lorena, I thought that would be different, we were happy it appeared, was incredibly hard for her to change from her thug street ways into the mechanics of society as many see and live it. I wish I could talk to her now; she doesn't even know, she rarely calls. I wonder if she did call could I tell her?

I pivot my SUV into an unusual empty parking slot on Cherry Street less than a block away from my destination, it is extremely fortunate to have found a parking place within a half mile of my targeted location, I see that maneuvering around the city is done with ease at this time of day at least the parking part. As I exit my vehicle, not paying attention to my surroundings as usual a cold December gust of wind and leaves hits me fueled by nature, the movement of the city, and a white delivery truck that rushes by onto his next destination. The wind whips through the trees that are naked in this season of preparation, leaves resting on the pavement, I look down from the tree tops and right here, less than a block from the courthouse I see the very first E>, I stand a bit too long staring, as the herd of people careen on either edge of my being, I realize I am a man in a business suit wearing a trench coat flapping in the wind, positioned in the center of a sidewalk staring at graffiti that Ethan placed, just as it is stuck on the concrete wall it feels I am stuck on the sidewalk. It must look like I have taken a moment out maybe to never come back, then I realize people are used to unusual scenes in the downtown core and I am just an obstacle to walk around, them not knowing if I am dangerous or have just needed a moment to complete the task of reaching my destination. This is crazy in my head I can't even walk a block in the city like a normal person anymore, I continue with intention of walking the rest of the block that starts at a slight incline and enter the building from 5th Ave, I take notice that the building has brick, glass and metal, this is the first real conscience thoughts of taking note of my surroundings, solid matter.

I retrieve the file from the officer at the front desk, surprisingly it is over four inches thick. Somehow this was unexpected to me, for some reason I was picturing a manilla folder with a piece of paper or two not a mountain and this is only for the spray paint activity not Ethan's death but they are connected in a way I know this deep down in my spirit. I am hoping beyond anything else on this earth that this file is much larger, and the other investigation can be solved relatively fast so as not to drag our mind down road that didn't happen but to the truth. It is an uneasy feeling knowing that the person who killed my son is out there somewhere being a person, moving, talking, committing crimes, killing again possibly. I ask if Detective Munser is in, of course he is not, he would be out trying to pick up the zillion pieces of crimes that have happened before and after the heart wrenching one that has happened to Ethan. I have moved on a bit today shopping, seeing the first tag and picking up the file has helped, even just not eating my standard ham sandwich and apple at my desk has felt different, I shall stop for lunch on the way back to the office, a grilled cheese and fries with a soda is what I will have today, a different day, if I go back in today or the rest of the week, I have a file to attend to, one of my son, Ethan.

2021

Detective Munser

January 2021

THE CITY IS BEING STRIPPED OF THE LIGHTS AND CHRISTMAS ADORNMENT, 2021 rang in without a ripple, not even a new case for me, this is a blessing. I love the Christmas season; it seems like a time for families and cities to reset and it gives me time to peruse my files more in-depth, I don't have family, this is not something I talk about, they went on a vacation to Mexico over Christmas of 2004 and didn't return simply vanished, maybe that is why I like to spend the season alone and love when the lights come down. I pretend every year since that has happened, sixteen Christmas' ago that we all are spending the holiday together. I cook a full meal just like mom, it was me that had to clean out their house, their earthly possessions that laid in wait for them to return, moms, dads, the twins Joshua and Jill in their last year of college, I am the only J name left here, Jeffery. There were no more breaks, leads, not even a whisper on the cases of my family, Iris Mortelli and Ethan Wilson. I don't know how the car of a deceased woman could have been transferred numerous times, how could someone drop out of college and disappear. We still have not yet located the suspect in black who sold the VW to Joseph Collins. Everett Sunshine could have been an alias or someone who just doesn't work, have electricity or other utilities in their name, after a federal check there isn't even a driver's license under that name in the United States. The school said he paid for two semesters with cash and had the proper credentials from high school graduation, they said he graduated in Tacoma but there weren't any records at any high schools in all of Pierce or King Counties with someone named Everett Sunshine or with either name, we have even checked the court records for name changes, there were no social media accounts, this person was a ghost. Our concerns as solvers of crime are that he may be still out there doing the unknown or been involved in foul play himself for his part in possessing the VW.

Forensics has a lead on one partial fingerprint on the rear hood but it had been wiped down and a towel had been over the seat to prevent any hair or other body secrets, only a partial shoe print on two of the pedals. The fingerprint is from a Julian Hunter aka Five Pin out of Bowling Green, Ohio, this was as far as that got us for quite a while, even after the other detectives came back and worked the case.

Now trying to make the connection, after digging for a few days and transferring files with Ohio investigators we have learned that Julian belongs to a gang called Emerald Jetters out of Seattle but had returned to Ohio about the middle of 2017. His family stated he returned home and seemed depressed, so they just let him hang out because that is what family is for, not knowing he was laying low for a murder. After tracking down one of his fellow crime committers GEM, here in Seattle that was willing to spill the whole story, we were cooperative to listen in exchange for something we just weren't sure what yet.

GEM stated a group of Emerald Jetters had been at Alki for the day and the Cobalt Tribe had shown up, they weren't ready for trouble, didn't feel the need to create a scene, would get back on them later for their intrusion and really just wanted out of there since they had been cruising the beach all afternoon and early evening. The girls had replaced their bikinis for capris and they were done, after looking for quite a while they couldn't locate Five Pin so they left, and knew he had been wasted from drinking all day, maybe he was sleeping it off in an alley.

Pearl had shown up with the Cobalt Tribe, she may have arrived with them, but she wasn't loyal to anyone, not even herself, that girl made trouble around every corner. After getting ice cream right before closing she ran into her old friend Five Pin, they exchanged numbers and she went back to Axe and the Emerald Jetters like nothing had happened, she knew Axe wouldn't like her talking to Five Pin. About midnight, Pearl was back home, Five Pin called her and asked if she would like to go for a ride, they cruised around in the VW until about 2:00 am then he dropped her off at home, never asking about the new ride or Five Pin's inability to drive a four speed. I find it ironic that Pearl would be connected to two murders but we can't prove that yet, we locate her at school, bring her in, she is all made up with blue hair that sticks out the side of her head so far it looks like a permanent wind gust is on her, she has more makeup on than any drug store sells in one location, the pants are made of unknown material and she is wearing what barely passes for a shirt, I need to call in a female officer as a witness with Pearl looking like that. Who shows up at the police station all swirled up like her, she was pulled in after all and her appearance was not purposeful or for our pleasure? She states that she has no idea who Iris is, tells us the story of Five Pin calling her and the ride they took late at night but nothing of Alki beach or Iris. Said she was not involved in any murders or other crimes; her standard answer. She was not surrendering any more information. Also declared she had no idea where Five Pin went after he dropped her off, in addition asked us not to tell Axe about Five Pin and their ride. She did tell us one important clue about Five Pin that he had a wonky knee, so when he walked the right one almost twisted, that would possibly explain why there was a partial shoe print on the brake and gas pedal. I am sure there are other facts Pearl failed to tell us since she has a nervous habit of picking her lower lip when agitated and she was picking at her lip like she was chasing a flea during the entire interview, my police instincts tell me we will be visiting with this young lady again, hopefully soon.

We talked with Five Pins' cousin over video chat, he stated Five Pin showed up one night before summer in 2017, said he had ridden the train from Seattle, was riding on the breeze of his own wind and just wanted to come home to Bowling Green, Ohio, had seen enough of the west coast, no one thought it was strange how he came home, that was the way he had left, just one day up and gone. After floating around town and not doing much for over two years he gets a call from a someone named Pearl in December 2020. She shows up and he is all up for the city after hiding out in the basement of the tri-colored split level for over two years, they head into Toledo one night and come back with a load of cash, said the girl knew some stuff and had connections. They made another trip into the city a few nights later and Five Pin ended up dead, connected with something bad and a bullet or two. The police said they received a call from Pearl Swanson who was in town for the night visiting a friend for the holidays, she had been out for a walk to clear her head and heard shots fired, she had never been so scared, claimed she had not seen anything and was too frightened to come out from behind the boxwood hedge that was perfectly manicured, located in front of the gray two story Craftsman house with a snowman wearing sunglasses in the yard that she ducked in behind. She seemed like a nice girl, was dressed kind of sophisticated in a vest and skirt, like one you would wear to a private school, we took her information and let her go on her way. We would have never guessed she was connected to the robbery taking place just a block away, that was like the unsolved one in Seattle. One thing this Pearl had going for her is she was a convincing actress.

After bringing Pearl back in she agreed it was time for the whole story. She had been scared of being caught in the heist of medical supplies as they were scarce after the second wave of the COVID-19 pandemic, their plan for the heist didn't seem fool proof to her, there were too many loop holes and people knowing the movement of the load. She felt the load should change hands only once, pick up and drop off not truck to truck, that is what made this too risky for her but she was aware that since she knew the steps of the plan she would either have to play it out, leave or die, she wasn't willing to play or die. She was scared someone would turn them in or that they would get overtaken as The Cobalt Tribe was young and inexperienced with anything this large, she was reconsidering her poor decision to be with Axe and an inexperienced gang, that was why she asked Ethan to get her out of town precisely at that moment. After arriving at her aunt's house in

Kentucky, she found the slip of paper with Five Pin's number from a few years before in her old backpack, lucky for her to have another step to take another out in this game, she gave him a call, jumped a train and that is how she ended up in Ohio after barely seeing her aunt. The night she got there was bitter cold, he still had the gimpy knee but looked different, told her about the girl who owned the green VW, said he had to get it out of his mind, was glad she was there because she was connected to the story, what a way to be greeted upon her arrival. She figured that was miles ago, paid no attention to Five Pin's story since she had seen a few more sad cases in between their meeting at Alki and truthfully regretted coming to Ohio since the first thing she hears is that she is now an accessory to another murder, she had even been in the dead girl's car, she ponders on that thought filing it away but can't seem to forget that fact. Pearl knew how to make money now from following the plan the Cobalt Tribe had showed her, after making a few connections in Toledo for proper transportation for a load that big and place to unload for some cash they pulled off the plan once with perfection. The second time didn't go so well, Five Pin was dead, Iris was dead, Ethan was dead and possibly others all due to Pearl Swanson's actions, leavings, and dreams, although she didn't have a connection to Iris just an indirect fluke of events.

After our visit with Pearl and knowing the whole story or at least the parts Pearl knows and was willing to share I decide to break the news to Iris's parents then Daniel, in that order due to time zones or that was my logic anyway, not wanting to talk to either party. Daniel was the one here, the person facing Iris' death daily, the parents are across the country, what a nice family, I hate calling and bringing this up again, this will be the last phone call to the Mortelli household since the case is solved, my first call was during early morning coffee, this call will interrupt whatever rituals their evenings bring. Mr. Mortelli answers and is always grateful to hear from me, he says "hello, how may I help you Detective?" These calls make me feel guilty, like I shouldn't deliver any news but I am here on the line with him, tell him the story from start to finish, fill in the pieces that are missing to the best of my ability, answer his few questions, we still don't know Everett Sunshine but I am not sure that matters anymore, we have solved the actual crime while missing some internal pieces of the investigation that may never be solved. Mr. Mortelli seems deeply empathetic towards Five Pins family knowing they also lost a child. These are truly genuine people from right here in the heart of America, they let their daughter live her dream and are moving on the best they can. He asks one more question, wants to know if I have told Daniel and would I let him know they would not be contacting him anymore, "Please tell him thank you." I assured Mr. Morelli I would pass on the message and thanked him for his time, knowing this is the last call and memory we will have of each other, I think as I hang up, we are both men on this side of the soil, him a farmer me an investigator, both diggers of dirt. The death of these two young people gone from us sooner than needed, Iris the victim, Five Pin the murderer eventually a murdered victim, both lived in my city Seattle, both short term visitors, both dead, different reasons but the same result, gone. I leave the office knowing I must tell Daniel and relay the message from Mr. Mortelli, I will do that outside, where it is cold, and I can suffer a bit too. I drive over the West Seattle Freeway towards Alki Beach without thinking, pull behind Scoop it Frozen Creamery, I park next to where Iris' body was found, still alive, get out of my cruiser, sit on the curb and call Daniel. I tell him all I know but not where I am, I figured it was best to tell the story where the crime happened, maybe this will clear the air, help my head to wrap around this. My family's disappearance is why I attempt to solve all murders brought my way, people are people, we are all the same deep down, stripped of our banners that we proudly fly to show what we want the world to see, we are all feeling humans with connections present or severed, we are all broken in ways too hard to explain, we bear our wounds, scars and ailments, we all fall and get back up or try. Some of us move forward, others stuck in the stings from the past or terrified of the future. I keep a poetry book in my car for times like this. It helps in my music and rhythm of my being; this poem reminds me of the choices we all make daily.

Pumpkin People

We are all pumpkin people that is right
All of us are full of seeds we can choose to let grow
We have the option to make our future dim or bright
The seeds we keep will definitely show

Some of us have trouble letting go
Our bad habits like seeds we harbor within
Others figure it out and just know
Some of us don't know where to begin

We have all the cobwebs of our past
Scrape out the excess strings that bind
We need to open our minds and take off the cast
Leave the past and issues behind

Choose carefully the face you carve out
With wisdom carve your eyes and nose
What is in your heart will determine your route
You have the choice what to compose

©2004 **M. V. Meadows**

Detective Munser

April 2021

I ROLLUP ON THE SCENE OF A HEIST GONE WRONG, A YELLOW BOX TRUCK CARRY-ing electronic gear supposedly, the driver overtaken by a group of people fitting the description of any young set of people. These ones were wearing facemasks, like everyone else, hoodies, like everyone else, in their late teens or early twenties, like everyone else, yellow ear buds, not like everyone else and got away in a silver Nissan, parked around the corner with a female driving who stood next to the car picking her lip for fifteen or so minutes prior to speeding out of there with the suspects crammed inside like clowns as we see from the traffic cam feed. This scene has Pearl all over it, she is the mastermind of these charades, the instigator and always the getaway driver, never involved or close to the actual scene of the crime, the mind and escape.

According to the logbook located on the passenger side floorboard this truck was headed to Tempe, AZ. The driver a dark-haired man with prison tats all over, young to be exact, ex-con recently released from the prison system and already on the fly moving product inside of product. It is suspected this was set this up for the electronics heading out but what they didn't know was this truck contained 9mm's and 45's heading south, enough yellow ear buds to organize the west coast protests and pound upon pound of marijuana. It is not part of my job to inventory the product just to know the type and investigate later if needed.

They send me Tempe of all places, not somewhere that would suit my temperament or internal thermometer, it is only April and 87°, I am grateful this didn't happen three months from now, clouds and rain are my preference, how do they wear suits in this heat. Summer fills this Arizona city long before rolling onto any part of Washington. The grass is gone, city clustered next to mountains that are bare, trees pop-up all-over town but not towering like our evergreens, the place is so dry it looks like you could turn to dust and blend right in without anyone noticing.

I am 6'4", so bulky I don't bend, and they want me to pretzel into this micro set of wheels. I pull up in the minimalist rental car, the only one they had left. It is funny how our mind work, I know everyone does this sort of thinking at some time or another on their job. Look at all the different things people get paid to do, you drive by a construction site and there is a man in a whole with six others looking down, or one up a ladder and two holding it, people get good money for stuff like that.

Inside police headquarters that is nestled up into the Tempe Butte, I meet with Detective Allen, a man that is the exact opposite of me, nice enough and welcoming though. Short, thin as a string bean, tan beyond what should be natural and sporting bleached blond hair in a style I am sure has a name. Right out a magazine this guy came, I can even smell the pull-out perfume ads, maybe that is the bottle of cologne he applied prior to our meeting. Now onto the interrogation room we are using, he explains his office is being renovated, I am sure it is, at least it is cool in here.

We discuss the similarities of our case and the logbook with Tempe as the next stop. He stated there was a guy a while back they brought in with yellow earbuds, wasn't sure why this stuck in his head. He had turned informant, goes by the name Sanz Solley, he will try to locate him. Allen makes a call to another part of the department, while I sit propped in the chair that is designed to be uncomfortable surrounded by the small room with mirrored windows, waiting. He lets us out, asks if I have plans for lunch, I accept and ride in his city issued cruiser to a little drive up place

I had never seen before, just a piece up the road. Allen says it is his usual lunch time shack, Juice Mania, I am expecting to order a burger and fries and I get juice, I order something with strawberries to be safe. It may only take juice to keep this short guy going but I would like food, something to sink my teeth into, ketchup on the side please, that is not happening now.

After we get our order, Allen gets a call that Solley was located and would like to meet at the horseshoe pit at Kiwanis Park, he will be there at 12:45, that gives us a few minutes to get across town, I am thankful I am not in the micro machine. As we proceed into traffic the rain or should I say monsoon starts up, the ground so dry the water has nowhere to go but run to the low spots. When we pull into the horseshoe area a guy comes across the field wet, tiptoeing like that will keep him dry and he is the one who my whole case is built around and why I am here in this suddenly wet, normally dry land. Sometimes investigations can look not right to the natural eye, this Solley guy has intelligent information and may help us after all. Says there was a heist here last week, a riot was put around it for distraction, when the guy got hit in the head with the baseball bat so hard his hair stuck to it, that is when the truck got away. The two instigators of this ring also got away with the truck, all the weapons, electronics and pills, uppers, downers, levelers, and get too high pills he says. Doesn't know their name or affiliation, thinks these guys are working on their own, dangerous business to not have back up in a business like this.

After a day of hashing over notes from Seattle and Tempe Allen and I part ways agreeing to keep each other updated by email, we also agree he will be coming my way if we meet again. I fold back into the rental car, intending to return it, sleep off the rest of this hot day and catch the last flight out of the night back to my city. Seems my plans are altered no matter the location, I stand in line to return the car early and hear a police radio in the back office, listening closely as I am trained to do, I hear of a rental that was involved in a rollover accident, heading from Tempe to Phoenix on I-10 just west of Salt River. I step out of line and sit in a padded leather chair in the waiting room pretending to read a travel brochure, wishing I were anywhere but here. They said the driver was from Washington, passenger ejected also from Washington, both felons, neither talking and the large safe located next to the demolished, rolled vehicle, took an hour to get the search warrant for the safe which contained firearms, cash and pharmaceuticals that were stolen or purchased somewhere, the safe smelled like marijuana but didn't contain any, that would mean they had brought some in and were returning with the contents of the safe, trades . They each had a tattoo on their neck that said trouble without the vowels and were wearing yellow earbuds, their phones were blowing up with calls from a Chicago number. This was part of a nationwide ring, not just two guys gone solo, I entered the office and showed my badge, made the officer aware of my meeting and knowledge of Detective Allen. I tucked my gigantic body back into the micro machine that I thought for sure to never drive again, called Detective Allen to piece this together, hoping to still catch the late flight home and be out of this heat.

This turned into a twisted mess as the story unfolded, people were brought in questioned and released except the two from Washington who had rolled the rental, they were part of a national scheme to intercept com-modities that started during COVID-19. They set up young gangs across the nation in large cities to distract any law enforcement, funded them minimally, generally with stolen goods in exchange to use them in heists. This made these used kids feel powerful being in the know on a big deal like this, when in reality it appeared to be a one city operation, helping take supplies like we hear of on the news. They thought they were famous helping but in reality, they were pawns being used as a cover, tarp children I called them. The first things to acquire were masks, face shields, toilet paper, any medical supply, weapon, drug, really anything people think they can't do without, any commodity that isn't perishable. One guy said when this pandemic hit, he stockpiled coffee and weed, went home, sat down satisfied and realized he would need more than those two substances to sustain himself for an indefinite period of time, we all have our vices, monkeys on our backs.

I land at SeaTac with its circular garage, get hung up by the elevator and scan the plaque with an article about Barton Heavy Equipment and their contribution of building this garage, with a picture of Bob the groundskeep-er from the cemetery, I will have to ask him about that connection. Satisfied

I return home that night with the knowledge of my interview of the two guys detained in Tempe, one just married, who had been on the right track but couldn't resist an easy way out, still wore the neon reflective vest to act like he works, denial under the cover of the vest, the other someone who couldn't or wouldn't ever be able to conform to the way things happen in society not with his previous history, a stallion in his own right. I know but can't prove that Pearl had been connected and moved up in the ranks during her move from Kentucky to Ohio and now back to Seattle again but she will be the one I put surveillance on as soon as I roll into town in my police issued human sized cruiser.

A couple days later I notice Pearl has been hanging around with Ice and not Axe. Their senior year is wrapping up Ethan had plans, big plans according to Carl his father, but I am almost sure the others in that group don't have any plans. Ethan would have never been able to get away with his actions in a real gang, something didn't feel right then but this explains it further. They were and are just actors in a play, pawns to move around the board, all they have to do is drive, meet people, shut up and act like they are in the cheesy named gangs. They are supplied with drugs, weapons and anything else a teenager would want, being as there is Ohm It Warehouse helping the movement, knowingly or unknowingly, either way they are making a hefty profit too. After my search on the exact brand of yellow earbuds, I locate them wholesale at 12¢ a pair, selling thousands of pairs to this network of thieves for $7.00 a set wholesale has profited Ohm It Warehouse thousands in profit.

We bring in Axe, ask him what he knows about any of this here is Seattle or other cities. He says he doesn't know anything and has been distanced and distraught since Pearl dumped him, would have given his all for that girl and now she is off running, not sure who with. Admits that the Emerald Setters is defunct and never really was a certifiable gang, it just helped him with his position of entering high school, he is not even positive Ice was his friend but doesn't spill any info about the heists, act like he was involved, says they didn't do that kind of thing just heard about it.

The next suspect is Ice, he is rolling on people before we can get out the recorder or pen and paper for him to write a statement. He says he has big info but wants light justice for himself in exchange, we waited for his parents and attorney to arrive before our questioning so as not to jeopardize our investigation. He didn't want to go to trial, said he had been in jail mentally for his whole senior year and that was enough, no more long drawn out escapades, no more yesterday's spilling onto this day and the next; today was the day of confession, we just didn't know what he would confess, we were shocked at his words, thought he was just bringing us news and information of the network and products, legal and illegal, this was much different, more than anticipated.

Ice's aka Jasper Walters met with his attorney in his parent's presence for approximately an hour, a criminal attorney, one I recognized from too many court cases they opened the door and asked us to enter for a statement and any questions we may have. Ice proceeded to tell us he loved Pearl and always had, was jealous of Axe and he was the one who watched Pearl that night, the night of the heist and Ethan's murder. His part in it was handing over keys to the truck which he convinced them if they left it at 3rd and Jackson they could get out of town fast, he had this all meticulously planned, he had heard Pearl talk on the phone about going to Kentucky on the train by hiding outside her window nightly, he knew she was up to something, in his borrowed car parked not far from the train depot no one suspected him of following Pearl. Ice didn't know Ethan would take her, he didn't know where they would have talked, double crossers double crossing on his girl or she was the crosser, what he for sure didn't know and still doesn't is that Ethan didn't want anything to do with Pearl, he wanted her gone, as far from him as Kentucky. When Ice aka Jasper watched Ethan wave at the train, he was furious his girl was gone without her ever being his own or knowing he loved her, he knew that could have never happened anyway at least not here. His original plan was to follow her to Kentucky but then he saw Ethan and was planning on asking questions, but rage set in, he called his name once by mistake, it just came out of his mouth, something had to with the boil of anger seething up in his being. He shot Ethan for taking Pearl away, all the rage in that one bullet that has been a zero form of revenge since, it has weighed on his conscience minute by minute, he can't sleep, or do anything without the thoughts of Ethan and his body creeping in twisting in front of his eyes like vines, laying there, just fell over due to one bullet.

Axe was sad, Ethan was dead, and he was guilty. There was no way to catch him, no connection to the murder, he walked across the street after firing the weapon, changed clothes, threw the old ones out and watched someone pick them out of a garbage can, stuff them in a duffle bag happy to have clothing, he took the gun apart, put the pieces in his pocket, placed the biggest on the bumper of the truck, handed over the keys to the person who showed up with the code word "cardboard" and drove off like nothing unusual had happened, two crimes in one transaction. On his way back to drop the car, he threw the remaining pieces of the weapon out the window making sure no one was behind him the entire way, parked a block from home and went to his room to cry, he had never in his teenage years felt that he needed his parents to hold him like he did now, his worry has penetrated his mind every day that someone would find out, they had too murders don't just go unsolved. He started binge watching true crime shows to see where he went wrong, just waiting every second for that knock on the door asking for him, he knew when they arrived he would tell all, he wasn't good at keeping secrets as large as this, he would tell on himself immediately.

That was Ice aka Jasper Walter's crime, his proper upstanding parents stand at the edge of the table, looking like they will not continue the vertical stance much longer, shock and reality have taken over, I offer them the chairs that had been rigidly declined at the beginning of this interview, thinking their son was innocent and now having trouble digesting the raw facts that they had produced and had been living with a killer, calculating the length of time this fact was true. They accept the chairs and ask their son, "that is what you did, what can you do to help yourself?" A good question to ask at this point. I like the Walters family, they have taken responsibility and asked their son to help himself but stood by him all in the same moment, never missing a beat, starting this process of their new reality right where they are. The attorney asks if he wishes to proceed, Ice nods slightly with the harsh results and reality of his confession sinking in, this tall, lanky, young green eyed boy will not be going home today or anytime soon, he murdered a child, planned it to a tee but didn't plan it at all, he has loopholes to jump through and to trip himself up.

Ice proceeds with his story, head hanging, he stops and asks for water, a mint, gum anything, laying his hand flat on the metal tabletop like it is grounding him, I think he will pass out from the reality of letting loose his secret that didn't need to be told, he never would have been caught, he is aware of that now, getting a weight off his chest has buried him. All he knows about the group he gets his benefits from is Axe meets a guy in different locations, he has only followed once, they say I gotta go get some soda, it's all in code, they call this guy Soda Pop due to his pajama pants, Soda Pop meets Flame and they make whatever the system is of getting the goods out of town, being handed keys, a location, time and codeword. Someone before them must know when they arrive, Ice says this as it is his first thought of the matter. It is above where he ranks in this army of thieves, he only knows one small part, a part he should have never assumed, he should have walked away. We ask him to empty his pockets, he has change, an expensive phone, foil from candy previously eaten, $29.00 in cash, a wallet with a picture of Pearl and a new looking driver's license and a key to his house. We ask him to take off his belt, put this part of his life in a bag and hand it to his parents, ask Jasper to stand, put his hands behind his back, read him his rights, never suspecting this is how this would end with Ice, give him time to say his goodbye's, walk quietly to the fingerprint station, I nod with a heavy heart for his family and him, almost wishing he hadn't confessed, I turn this boy over to the system as I am called to do. Hoping the attorney has walked the Walter's out so I don't have to see them again today, knowing I will see them again looking older even if it is tomorrow or another month.

I receive a call from Detective Allen from Tempe, he will be escorting the two suspects to Seattle in exchange for information. Their crimes started in Seattle and they needed to be held here, the Tempe charges can be tacked on and ran consecutively. The suspects names are Bender George and Rizzo Loman, both met during their stay with the Department of Corrections in Washington, both wishing to add more charges to their already extensive rap sheets, felonies, weapons, drugs and connections to a ring of terror. These guys would be having a brief visit with us then handed back over to DOC for their extended stay, returning to their original holding pattern.

I meet with Detective Allen who has his set of facts from Arizona, I share my facts with him including the footage of the protest, and we turn the case and the two suspects over to the Feds, Detective Allen and I drive the roughly six blocks to attend the questioning, we were asked to be present in case there were more information needed of us. Most of the cases I work on are not multi-jurisdictional this was complicated.

Detective Allen and I had dinner on the waterfront and compared cases, not just this one but other oddities we encounter. I tell him of Vera and the strangeness of that, wishing someone had been there to catch her. Detective Allen will be heading back tomorrow, I am glad we met, it is a bit like two people discussing a common hobby, tips and tricks traded. Wishing each other well, shaking hands over this twisted common bond we know this will hopefully be the last time we meet, nod and part ways as he walks down the waterfront and I to my car.

It has been a long day, but I know I need to call Carl III to break the news that Ethan's killer has been caught, confessed and will be charged tomorrow, no trial just facts already written. It makes the death of a loved one become real again, brings the facts to the top when there has been an arrest, the funeral is over and the ones left here are trying to write a new chapter making life as normal as can be without their lost one and then I call. I can see them melt again, almost like if there were not news that would have been ok, the fact on their end is the same. I call Carl III, ask if he would like to talk on the phone or meet in person, I like to give them some options since there are other places in their life that options have been taken away. Carl III answers on the first ring, like it was a reflex, having no idea who is on the line, concentrating on another task, working himself into the wee hours to cover the empty spots in his life. He says he is at work and asks if I had time to stop by, gives me the address and says he would like Gloria to attend our meeting.

I pull up in front of the Woman's Shelter, parking a plenty this time of night, Carl III unlocks the front door, we proceed through the building to an office painted with a mural of downtown, Gloria is waiting behind a large wooden desk that I imagine many stories have passed over, she looks on edge, this was news of her grandson, the one she stepped in and raised as her own. They offer me a seat, I tell them the story of the what happened and why at the train depot, they are extremely broad minded caring people, I just told them about their Ethan's killer and they are asking me if the Walter family is okay. This is not what I had expected, I guess I hadn't thought about the reaction and never had any time prior to this but have not had one like this, some people cry, others are angry, some just sit and look at me like they want different information, while some yell that I took too long. They explained that the Walter family had lost a son too without an option, it just happened and neither family had a say so but were required to go on. I would have to say that this was the most unexpected bit of news given back to me. I leave thanking them for their time and again showing respect for their loss and kind ways, I think this case as twisted, warped, corrupt and wicked as it was has changed me, put me on a new level of seeing people, their tragedies and triumphs.

June

May 2021

I<small>T IS</small> M<small>AY</small> 25<small>TH JUST ENTERING THE FIFTY SECOND WEEK THAT</small> I <small>HAVE BEEN</small> through without Charles. I wonder what I will do with myself this upcoming summer. We had always celebrated Memorial Day, it was a special time for Charles and I since I had been raised military, we both knew what the lifestyle and sacrifice was for a family. For Charles prior to his personal military service his family had a tradition of traveling to Mille Lacs Lake, MN where his grandfather always met them to fish, Charles said it was like a holiday that gave a bonus to summer still almost a month away. There are still framed photos of Charles and his family in the little rowboat with one of them proudly holding up a fish recently caught. I always thought it was funny they would live next to one of the biggest lakes and travel to a smaller one for vacation. This is where Charles got his love of burned marshmallows, he would peel each layer then burn it again until it was gone, he always looked like a younger person when he was roasting and toasting as he called it. Of course this is not what Memorial Day is about, Charles and I both after our years here, there and everywhere celebrated every year, the ceremonies were similar but so moving as we paid our respects to those who are gone and have fought for our freedoms.

We missed the ceremony last year Charles was too ill to attend that is why I made the celebration in his room for him but this year to honor Charles and all the others buried near and far I decide to pay a visit to the cemetery. I love the entry with the lawn manicured and flags posted at both sides to drive through, there are graves here and there with different size flags flying from them, but the whole sections with a singular flag at each grave like where Charles is buried and someday I will be next to him. I am not here to think of that now, I am here to honor our military, each branch as its traditions and songs.

I stop to get a burger, potato salad, chips, 4 dozen cupcakes to share and don't forget my bowl of watermelon from home, I am off to have a picnic with Charles and suddenly am tired, just relieved to have made it through the steps of getting here but relieved that the pair of red, white and blue lawn chair which Charles insisted on purchasing are still in the trunk, we had to go to three stores to find a matching pair. I park, realizing I don't know what time it is or when the ceremony starts but sit quietly by Charles' grave in the shade of the large fir tree eating my lunch and placing watermelon at each corner of his headstone, I know it may be silly but we all have our traditions, I quietly watch the activity of the cemetery. Families come and go, some smile and wave others avoid eye contact, I talk to the groundskeeper, let him know what an excellent service he provides for a vast amount of people living and past, he accepts a cupcake, I give him a couple dozen to share around the cemetery with others he knows. He thanks me, stands and staring off into the distance, towards the mausoleum and nods as he walks away with his assortment of tools. It must be time for the ceremony I hear the roar of the Harley Davidson's that always calms my flutters, ah there the bikers are with their flags so proudly flying as the wide bikes rumble into place, at the podium is a speaker but I am too far away to hear what he says, he has a military hat and civilian suit, he talks a bit then the band plays, I love patriotic and military music, it brings me back to many times, always with family or Charles. Maybe it is a comfort because all the songs are familiar, the US Flag is waving in rhythm to The Star-Spangled Banner like it knows the words and has heard them before and how to dance to that deep-felt song. I hear *America the Beautiful* and words of the ceremony blown by the wind over the lawn and graves in broken segments to my old ears, words like brevity, nobility, twelve conflicts, world, peace. I leave my chair and slowly walk toward the podium to hear with increased clarity what is being projected just as the speaker says, "no matter what the cemetery, this is where everyone is connected. May it be recent or many years past we are connected." The trumpeter lifts his instrument as the sun reflects off the finger buttons and bell in a glare so bright, I know America is great as are and were the people who make it that way, military and civilian. I study the crowd, there are individuals from every branch of the military in their dress uniforms, blues, greens, whites, metals and ribbons, some stand erect others with canes and walkers or in wheelchairs. There are people who you have no idea how they are connected, maybe they aren't they are just connected to The United States of America.

As I slowly inch my way back to my lawn chair in my white netted new running shoes, not realizing I have walked so far to the ceremony. I notice a young man, an older one and a lady in her prime all eating cupcakes, knowing I was right to bring them, suddenly happy Bob was able to distribute the treats, we are all celebrating Memorial Day and our lost loved one. I feel disoriented with the sun starting to set and can't see my chair anywhere, it seems the cemetery is a different place from unfamiliar angles that I had not been prior to this, I am tired and want to get to my car but am worried about the chair, Charles would be upset the chair was gone, at least I still have one. I see the hood of my Shoreline Blue Pearl Toyota another thing Charles insisted on since we loved the water, we named her Blue, the car is just up the slope of grass, I really don't remember walking that far. As I approached Blue, at the driver's door I see my chair propped up next to the bumper, there was a hand scribbled note.

Mrs Fridley,

I hope you don't mind my helping keep your chair safe. If this was any trouble at all feel free to call or next time you pay us a visit, please tell me. Bob

On the way back to the car I had thoughts of being at home so much with the pandemic and how getting out today had affected me with all the commotion. You don't seem to realize how not being around people for an extended period can change you until you enter a setting with people, like suddenly at a play. I was so grateful for Bob, put the chair with its mate in the trunk, got into Blue with relief and drove home having a fresh insight of the day, it was a tremendous comfort to me just being outside, around people but not too close, we all had an invisible connection somehow to lives recent, past or people we never knew, the country, the music entered our ears, the atmosphere was of reverence, there was beauty in the people and nature, the colors of it all connected to the red, white and blue. The birds flew so gracefully overhead, listening I am sure to the ceremony and wondering why so many people were in their park. I think I have gotten to release a burden today and shall leave it behind. One of my favorite poems is called The Phone Call, I always wondered what the story was behind that title. I know now what it means to me, to unravel a life you have lived and move on with gratitude.

The Phone Call

It may be a softening of heart
Deep emotions break through
Tender moments to impart
At that very moment love you knew
It may be daily we change drastically
No matter what we are given we must convert
Move ahead enthusiastically
Whether the world gives us gold or dirt
Be at peace with yourself and your abilities
Keep your heart, eyes and ears open so chance will not pass you by
Always chasing the open doors of possibilities
Where you have been you cannot go back so spread your wings and fly

©2004 **M. V. Meadows**

I pull Blue into the garage of my wonderful modern home, a home I am comfortable with, after all the various types of homes Charles and I have had this one is the only one we knew we wouldn't have to leave. When I decided to go out today and attend the service I pictured myself coming home full of mixed emotions, mostly sad this day is quite the opposite I would never have thought in a million years that I would feel this grateful to be home and see Sandy stretching as cats do, from my perspective in the house as she opens her mouth silently meowing in the window, for me to come in and tell her all about my day, she will love the story about the birds and chair.

Made in the USA
Middletown, DE
03 September 2020